In Touch

Hans-Jörg Rheinberger

In Touch

Encounters between Art and Research

DIAPHANES

Contents

7 Preface

PRAGMATA

17 Tracing the Index: Paul Vanouse
29 Seriality and Cycles: Thomas Struth
41 The Bottle, for Example: Gaston Bachelard Looks at Albert Flocon's *Castles in Spain*
55 Grace at the Boundary of Knowledge: For Sandra Boeschenstein
63 Experiments, Traces, Data Streams: Hannes Rickli
73 Emerging out of the Procedure: Hanni Schierscher
85 Questions Arising from Matter: Katrin von Lehmann

ENCOUNTERS

93 On Hybrids. In Dialogue with Andreas Greiner
113 "You Can't Order Scientific Results Like Pizza." A Conversation Conducted by Susanne Witzgall with Jan St. Werner and Hans-Jörg Rheinberger
129 Microbial Performances. An Interview with Lucie Strecker and Jens Hauser
149 Contingency, Notation, Reflection. Exchange with Alex Arteaga

EXPERIMENTAL APERÇUS

169 Laboratory Worlds
175 Experimenting and Writing
189 On Seeing

197 Can the Sciences and the Arts Learn from Each Other?
203 Research and Design
215 Experimental Performativity
219 Acousmatic Experiences

THINGS
233 The Spiral and its Aura
251 Imag(in)ing the Wind Channel
259 Approaching the Sponge

271 Bibliography

Preface

This book is about an uneasy relationship. It reports on encounters that have challenged me, over the past long decade, to think of and deal with different facets of the connection between the sciences and the arts. When I entered academia in the mid-1960s, the university canon of disciplines still appeared to be intact, compact, and impenetrable. The buzzword of interdisciplinarity was only faintly delineating itself on the far horizon, mostly promoted by grassroot student initiatives. It was still the professors' habit to promote—and the pride of every serious mainstream student to become socialized into — one particular discipline, to the exclusion of any other. Not only the sciences appeared to be a foreign world to the humanities, within the humanities themselves it made all the difference whether you became a *real* philosopher or, say, a *mere* historian, and vice versa. Failing to understand anything of one another's discipline was not experienced as a shortcoming but rather as the signature and seal of one's own profession. And what held for the university's disciplines held even more for the gulf that separated the scholarly disciplines from the arts which, after all, had created their own academies in the preceding century and, in the course of time, appeared to have formed their own universe, completely separated from the sciences.

What should someone do whose interests in his schooldays had been broadly distributed between the life sciences, the wide spectrum of the humanities, and artistic ambitions in the form of writing? One had to make a choice, obviously. The art of poetry could not be studied, that much appeared clear to me. That was a matter of personally engaging with the existing literature and finding one's own way of expression. I opted for biochemistry, a brand-new study program at the University of Tübingen at that time. Thoroughly disappointed by its first year, after a hundred-and-eighty degree turn I found myself in philosophy. Not an easy choice, of course. However, if it had to be made, the intellectually most demanding discipline, as it seemed, would be just good enough. Things went their course. But what was to be done when the sciences remained knocking at the door? Pursuing different things in parallel was not an option. The right choice appeared to be to change camps once more and bring to an end what had been a failed attempt to begin with. And so, after six years in philosophy, I found myself back in biology. Molecular biology. A new branch of biology that stood in stark contrast to the traditional biological canon. I learned to do experiments. A new world opened up. To engage with nature at its joints, at the molecular level, by using comparatively mundane tools, was a revelation. The experience that existing knowledge could be challenged, that science had to be made, and that it had to be remade from time to time, even from day to day, left deep traces, traces that would accompany me for the long rest of my academic career. It would have an impact far beyond the laboratory bench.

Years passed, and with them, the feeling grew that I was missing my other self, the humanities. What should I do? After a long year of contemplation, I realized I had to change gears again, this time in the other direction. However, after a decade of laboratory life, philosophy *tout court* was no longer an option. The challenge was to find a way back into the humanities without losing ground, without losing contact with matter. Historical matter appeared to be the option: the history of the sciences as an epistemological laboratory, as it were. And once again the switch had to be radical. I became a historian of science, with all the forces at my disposal. Practicing the history of science as an epistemological challenge would become my occupation for the decades ahead. It was, after all, a synthesis. It was, however, a synthesis achieved by separation, the result of an uncompromising decision for philosophy, that most esoteric of all humanistic occupations and, in turn, for molecular biology, an experimental science *par excellence* at the time—a time when its conceptual bases were still in the making.

And what about the arts? My own forays into poetry had remained limited, at times completely receding into the background, at times flaring up again. The art of using words had, however, found its way into my writing exercises in the history and epistemology of science, and the history and epistemology of experimentation in particular. And it was precisely these writings that opened the door to a prolonged conversation with the burgeoning field of artistic research,[1] an opening that, to begin with, came somewhat as a surprise. I had neither expected nor anticipated that my particular way of approaching historical epistemology would find its echoes and resonances in artistic

1 A few examples of a vast amount of literature may suffice here: Thomas Trummer, *Artistic Research* (Köln: Walther König, 2014); Jens Badura, Selma Dubach and Anke Haarmann (eds.), *Künstlerische Forschung. Ein Handbuch* (Zurich and Berlin: Diaphanes, 2015); Doris Ingrisch, Marion Mangelsdorf and Gerd Dressel (eds.), *Wissenskulturen im Dialog. Experimentalräume zwischen Wissenschaft und Kunst* (Bielefeld: Transcript, 2017); Henk A. Borgdorff, Peter Peters and Trevor Pinch (eds.), *Dialogues between Artistic Research and Science and Technology Studies* (New York: Routledge, 2019); Priska Gisler, Guelfo Carbone and Philippe Sormani (eds.), *Practicing Art/Science: Experiments in an Emerging Field* (London: Routledge, 2020), Ruth Mateus-Berr and Richard Jochum, *Teaching Artistic Research: Conversations Across Cultures* (Berlin and Boston: DeGruyter, 2020).

circles. They were, however, on the way of experiencing their own work as a form of research activity, a prolonged process of experimentation. Contacts with artists resulted that were sometimes intense but remained limited, and sometimes extended over years, culminating in genuine collaborations. They challenged me to delve further into a relationship that had been absent from the horizon of my activities for a long time. Gradually I began to realize that the sciences and the arts could be fruitfully brought into contact with each other under the condition that one did not cling to the products of their respective activities, but to the conditions of their making. The chapters of this book testify to the effort of exploring the different facets of what can be addressed as the common ground which nourishes the sciences as well as the arts: They can be understood as ever new efforts to reveal aspects of their matters at hand that had so far escaped their practitioners' attention and that Gaston Bachelard once subsumed under the common denominator of an "imagination of matter."[2] Despite assuming widely different forms that at times may even appear to be incompatible with each other, it is this common ground that enables conversations which had long seemed completely out of reach. That we have only just started to explore this territory should not conceal the potential it offers for both the arts and the sciences. As the art historian George Kubler aptly says: It is all about recognizing, and taking advantage of, the "common traits of invention, change, and obsolescence" that bind the sciences and the arts together.[3]

2 Gaston Bachelard, *Water and Dreams. An Essay on the Imagination of Matter* (Dallas: Dallas Institute of Humanities and Culture, 1983).

3 George Kubler, *The Shape of Time. Remarks on the History of Things* (New Haven, CT and London: Yale University Press, 1962), 10.

The readers will realize that the writings of Gaston Bachelard have taken on the function of a kind of resonance chamber for the body of the texts that follow. This is not an accident. In parallel to the experiences about which they report, I had become interested—and became more and more engaged in—a thorough exploration of Gaston Bachelard's forays into the world of the arts during his Parisian years throughout the two decades after World War II.[4] Previously, he had been known to and appreciated by me as a philosopher of science attempting at and realizing a new synthesis between philosophy and history of science that eventually became known under the label of *historical epistemology*. Now, I realized that his interest in contemporary poetry and the arts was of no less importance for a thorough understanding of his attitude toward what he saw as the "new spirit" pervading the sciences,[5] the arts and the literatures of his time, so eloquently echoed in the words that Bertolt Brecht had the protagonist repeatedly uttering in his *Life of Galileo*: "*Denn die alte Zeit ist herum, und es ist eine neue Zeit.*"[6] Brecht's play was actually a mirror of his own engagement, as a writer, with the sciences, a writer who actually saw himself as a researcher, a scientific practitioner of his art. What both the playwright and the philosopher of science experienced in their day as a liberation was a feeling that cannot be exaggerated in

4 Hans-Jörg Rheinberger, *The Hand of the Engraver. Albert Flocon Meets Gaston Bachelard*, trans. Kate Sturge (Albany, NY: SUNY Press, 2018); Gaston Bachelard, *Imaginationen der Materie. Surrealismus und Nachkriegskunst*, intr., ed., and trans. Hans-Jörg Rheinberger (Berlin: Mattes & Seitz, 2026).

5 Gaston Bachelard, *The New Scientific Spirit.*, trans. Arthur Goldhammer (Boston: Beacon Press, 1984).

6 Bertolt Brecht, *Leben des Galilei. Schauspiel*. Werkausgabe Edition Suhrkamp, Band 3 (Frankfurt am Main: Suhrkamp, 1967), 1232–1233.

hindsight, namely that the squeezing of the sciences into the narrow confines of the Procrustes bed of received knowledge, and a mechanicist world view in particular, was definitely past its best. For both sides, the sciences and the arts, the solution was not to turn the back to one another, but rather to engage in a productive interaction.

*

The first part of the book reports on my encounters with the work of a number of contemporary artists. Some of these encounters took place in the context of exhibitions, others resulted from projects extending over longer time spans, still others from excursions into the recent history of art. They are not to be read as pieces in the tradition of art history, they are rather to be understood as a repeated tentative to sound out the forms in which research gestures realize themselves in the œuvre of an artist. The second part of the book is devoted to a series of conversations with artists and art curators, either in relation to book contributions or in the context of symposia and meetings. Hence the at times spontaneous digressions and a tentativeness of another kind, that of "the gradual construction of thoughts during speech."[7] In the third part, my reflections revolve, broadly speaking, around experimentation as the common ground on which the arts and the sciences can find ways and forms of exchanging thoughts about their respective activities. What is at stake here are a number of aspects under which experimental activities unfold themselves

7 Heinrich von Kleist, "On the gradual construction of thoughts during speech," trans. Michael Hamburger, *German Life and Letters* 5 (1951): 42–46.

in different contexts and can be taken account of accordingly. The fourth part, finally, focuses on a few exemplary objects that are of interest, in one way or another, to both the fields of the arts and of the sciences. They are meant as an incentive to direct the attention to a potentially much vaster field of comparisons that could open a new window of studying the intricacies which the relations between the sciences and the arts, both in history and in the present, can exhibit.

*

My heartfelt thanks go to all those artists, art curators and art enthusiasts, whose paths I had the invaluable opportunity to cross over all the years during which these reflections evolved and gradually took shape. Thanks are due to the Kulturstiftung Liechtenstein for its generous support. Not least, I would like to thank the International Research Center for Cultural Studies in Vienna and its Director Karin Harrasser for hosting me as a guest in the Summer Semester of 2024, during which I had the leisure to write down a first draft of this book. Karen Margolis carefully edited the English draft. I greatly acknowledge the continuous support of the library staff of the Max Planck Institute for the History of Science in Berlin. Finally, I thank Michael Heitz from Diaphanes for accepting the book for publication and his team for carefully accompanying it through the successive production steps.

PRAGMATA

Tracing the Index:
Paul Vanouse

Paul Vanouse is an artist deeply engaged with examining and at the same time deconstructing the media and means of representation, in particular nucleic acid sequencing, as they emerged in the life sciences in the age of molecular biology half a century ago. Ever since, they have become ubiquitous in all corners of biology, in medicine, forensics, anthropology, population policy, in tracing genealogies, and elsewhere. They have acquired iconic status and become the emblems of a whole era. Vanouse's installations provoke thoughts which I try to articulate here in some detail.[1]

I.

Molecular biology has been prolific in creating new digital and discrete preparation procedures which distinguish themselves significantly from the classical forms of analog and continuous preparations so well known from anatomy since the early modern period, and from 19th-century tissue and cellular micros-

1 Jens Hauser (ed.), *Paul Vanouse, Fingerprints ... Index—Abdruck—Spur/ Index—Imprint—Trace* (Berlin: Schering Foundation, 2011). The book was published on the occasion of an exhibition of Paul Vanouse at the Project Space of the Schering Foundation (28 January—26 March, 2011) and a parallel event in the context of the opening of the Transmediale, Haus der Kulturen der Welt, Berlin, February 2011. See also the website scheringstiftung.de, rubric "Rückschau."

copy.[2] These new discrete preparations based on molecular separation techniques have been accompanied by an equally new regime of visuality: the visualization of macromolecules and their building blocks. The representation of molecules using these new media is by no means restricted to the scanning tunneling microscope with its iconic images at atomic resolution.[3] It represents a whole world of indexical visualizations subsumed under the labels of chromatography and electrophoresis. The principle of these molecular separation techniques is straightforward. It consists in resolving a mixture of substances, macromolecules or their building blocks, into the constituents of these mixtures by exploiting physical and chemical differences between them, such as molecular weight, electric charge and hydrophilic or hydrophobic properties. Separations of this kind can be achieved in one or in two dimensions, depending on the devices used. After their separation, the constituents of the original mixture can be visualized in one of several ways: by taking advantage of their intrinsic physical or chemical characteristics, such as their ultraviolet-absorption capacity or fluorescence; by staining them with particular dyes; or by labeling them using radioactive isotopes, to name just a few of these techniques. Alongside the capacity of the chromatographic or electrophoretic separation technique, these additional procedures offer thus the possibility of further analytical distinctions—for instance, differential coloration.

2 See Hans-Jörg Rheinberger, *An Epistemology of the Concrete. Twentieth Century Histories of Life* (Durham: Duke University Press, 2010a), Chapter 12.
3 Jochen Hennig, *Bildpraxis. Visuelle Strategien in der frühen Nanotechnologie* (Bielefeld: Transcript, 2011).

They opened a new universe of representation based on tiny amounts of material not amenable to classical analytics.

2.

For his installations, Paul Vanouse makes use of standard laboratory devices for the separation of DNA (deoxyribonucleic acid) molecules of different length via gel electrophoresis. Principally, two variants of this technique are to be distinguished. Both of them separate according to molecular weight: Short chains move faster, long chains move more slowly. In the first variant, which Paul Vanouse stages in an installation referred to as the *Latent Figure Protocol* "Chicken and Egg" (Fig. 1), long chains of DNA that constitute the core of chromosomes (the hereditary material of organisms) are cut into pieces using what can be called molecular scissors, a particular class of mostly bacterial enzymes. They cut the DNA at defined, short sequence signatures. The distribution of these signatures over the chromosomes can vary from one individual to the next. When the fragments are run through a matrix substance such an agarose gel, they create a different banding pattern for each individual. The second variant, which the artist uses in his installation termed *Suspect Inversion Center,* as well as his production called *Relative Velocity Inscription Device,* is used for sequence analysis.[4] In short: Along a given strand of DNA (typically part of a gene), an enzyme synthesizes a new, complementary strand. Modified building blocks of DNA as an admixture lead to an occasional, statistically distributed

4 See also the artist's website paulvanouse.com under "artwork".

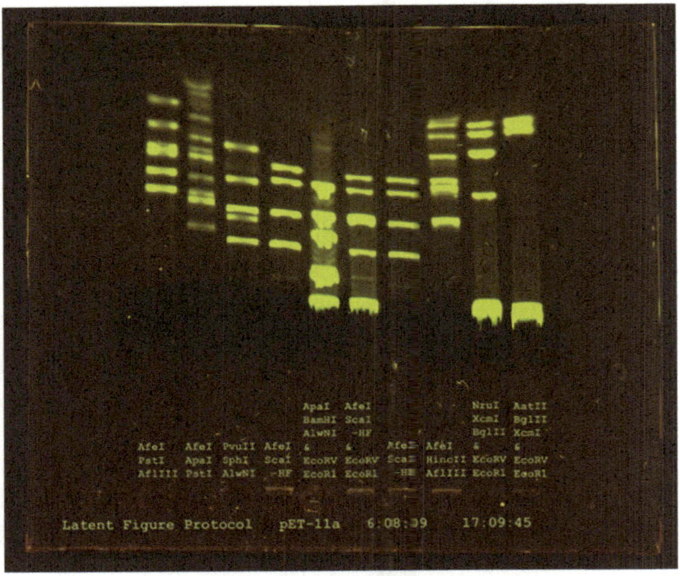

Fig 1: Paul Vanouse, *Chicken and Egg.*

chain termination at every position, so that a mixture of molecules is created in which each differs from the other by one building block. If resolved, for example, in a gel prepared from polyacrylamide, they form a ladder of bars when visualized by ultraviolet light.

3.

Powerful experimental techniques such as the ones described above—well suited to analyzing the sequence of deoxyribonucleic acids—are, in fact, instances of more general experimental strategies.[5] Two of them in particular come into play here. The first can be called a strategy of *dilatation*: What is too small to be seen and identified must be enlarged to become visible to our eyes. Microscopy is paradigmatic in this respect. But in contrast to this iconic option, we have to do here with indexical magnifications. Molecules are by far too small to be seen as individual entities by the naked eye. Dilatation or magnification strategies have to be used to create configurations that allow them to be distinguished from one another, if only in bulk. Chromatography and electrophoresis are instances of such an enlargement. The second is a strategy of *enhancement*: A given structure may well be in place and have the right size even to be seen the unaided eye but may not be discernible due to the lack of discriminative features. What is indiscernible must be enhanced. Coloration, or staining, is an all-pervasive form of enhancement in experimentation in the life sciences and elsewhere. Stiffening is another; freezing, that is, fixing in place, yet another. And of course, these modes of making something visible may be—and are—used in artistic contexts just as well as in scientific experimentation.

4.

Preparations, including preparations of DNA, radiate authenticity. To be authentic, in principle, means to be nothing other

5 For more details, see Hans-Jörg Rheinberger, "Making visible," in *The Exhibition as Product and Generator of Scholarship* (Berlin: Max Planck Institute for the History of Science, Preprint No. 399, 2010b), 9–23; Hans-Jörg Rheinberger, *Split and Splice. A Phenomenology of Experimentation* (Chicago: The University of Chicago Press, 2023), Chapter 3.

than oneself, or itself for that matter. Now, preparations, as the name tells us, are things worked on, things manipulated, things configured and reconfigured. To appear authentic, these procedures of working on, manipulation, configuration, and reconfiguration must, paradoxically, be rendered invisible in the final product. Preparations appear authentic inasmuch as the means and media used to create them, with all the vicissitudes involved, have been successfully made to disappear in the final product. We could even generalize this statement and claim that an authenticity principle holds, not only for preparations, but for the products of science at large, which include preparations as just one among many other types. We could also talk here about models and simulations. The outcome of an experiment counts as authentic, that is, as "true," if and only if the means used to achieve it can be said to be negligible or at least to not affect the essence of the thing in question. With DNA, authenticity of a particular kind comes into play. DNA has been identified as the material carrier of heredity in the living world, and it is generally believed that each and every individual's DNA differs, if only in minute details, from any other. Accordingly, DNA is believed to be an identity marker with a wide range of applications and uses, ranging from crime detection to familial as well as ethnic inclusion or exclusion. As the Harvard professor Walter Gilbert claimed, not that long ago, in the early days of the Human Genome Project (HGP): Time will come when a person will be able to hold up a CD containing their DNA sequence, point to it and say: "Here's a human being; it's me!"[6]

6 Walter Gilbert, "A vision of the grail," in *The Code of Codes*, ed. Daniel J. Kevles and Leroy Hood (Cambridge: Cambridge University Press, 1992), 83–97.

5.

One of Paul Vanouse's main concerns is to counteract such media short-circuits, to unmask the disappearance *of*, that sleight of hand performed *by* the media, using the very same procedures in a way that catches our attention and lets us be surprised. Vanouse's installations attempt to make the vicissitudes of the metonymic palpable to the viewer, vicissitudes—*quid pro quo, pars pro toto*—to which not only the consumers of the products of genomics, but also their producers tend to fall prey and to which the statement just quoted dazzlingly testifies. Thus, even scientists directly engaged in this work are inclined to blend out the epistemo-technical dimension of their work. When it comes to presenting their results, the plethora of research technologies and other resources necessary to engender the phenomena of their scientific interest tends to disappear behind the scene. We could almost say that they look through them, treating them as transparent and translucent and regarding them as allowing unadulterated and immediate access to the 'findings' themselves, these units in which the results of scientific activity come packed. In conversation with their peers, scientists presuppose that their colleagues are aware of what a technique can yield and what it cannot—and consequently, do not emphasize the "phenomenotechnical" dimension of their work;[7] in conversation with the public, scientists assume their audience is not interested in procedures

7 The term can be traced back to the epistemological work of Gaston Bachelard. See Gaston Bachelard, *Le Rationalisme appliqué* (Paris: Presses Universitaires de France, 1949), 3.

but in outcomes and, again, ignore this massive aspect of the scientific research process altogether.

6.

As mentioned, the discrete visualizations of DNA sequences produced by gel electrophoresis belong to the order of the indexical, according to the theory of signs proposed by Charles Sanders Peirce.[8] Characteristically, indexical signs stand in causal relationships to the things they represent: They are derived from their materiality. For example, smoke is taken as an index of fire; a human footprint as an index of a person who walked by. In a chromatogram of DNA, the spots, dots and bars visualized under ultraviolet light or, if radioactively labeled, made visible through exposure to photo-sensitive film, originate from and consist of bits and pieces of the stretch of DNA under consideration, and are thus also to be considered as indexical. Indexicality, however, does not by itself translate into authenticity, as we might be inclined to presume. On the contrary, an indexical sign is always precarious by nature, exactly on the grounds of its character as a trace—a precarity that the other forms of Peircean signs are lacking. Symbols, according to Peirce's semiotics, are purely conventional, and it lies thus in our hands to fix or change them. Icons bear a visually discernible similarity to the objects they depict, a similarity that can be checked and counterchecked. The index, by

8 Charles Sanders Peirce, "Logic as semiotic: The theory of signs," in *Charles Sanders Peirce, Philosophical Writings*, ed. Justus Buchler (New York: Dover Publication, 1955), 98–119.

contrast, is the incarnation of a trace, and it is in the nature of the trace that the thing it is a trace of is out of reach, for at least as long as it appears as a trace. So, we are left in uncertainty as to what is behind the trace. Indices are thus always and necessarily signs in tension, a fact that is well known, for example, from forensics, where DNA has come to play a major identificatory role despite the vicissitudes of its collection, allocation, amplification, and analysis. In one of Paul Vanouse's *Latent Figure Protocols*—is it natural, is it created; to which realm does it belong?—, the precarious nature of the indexicality of DNA patterns leaps to the eye, taking the paradoxical form of creating the icon of a symbol—with indices: DNA traces are reconfigured in such a way that the result is the iconic copyright symbol. The whole installation stands for the highly contentious practice of patenting bits and pieces of human, animal, or plant DNA as a result of molecular gene technology, undermining and rendering contentious the long-assumed distinction between non-patentable discoveries ('facts' of nature) and patentable inventions ('artful' creations).

7.

But just what is it that makes Vanouse's installations so intriguing? What is responsible for their attraction? We tend to be surprised when we see things we know from a context familiar to us being relocated in an unfamiliar one. The effect of the change of environment rests on the assumption that it leaves the relocated thing unchanged. And yet it looks unfamiliar. It arouses astonishment precisely for this reason. Procedures that create moments of such alienation are essential in poetry as well as in art. Indeed, the whole effect of Vanouse's installations rests on the assumption that the devices being presented are operated and work in exactly the same way they operate and work in a scientific laboratory. Of course, it makes a difference whether these technical procedures are used in an epistemic context in a research lab, or whether they are run in a technical context in a forensic or diagnostic laboratory. An oscillation between these contexts and the according conversion of epistemic things into technical objects—and vice versa—appears to be the hallmark of the modern sciences as we know them. There is actually nothing spectacular about this to-ing and fro-ing—not, however, if artistic use is made of these technical procedures. What happens then is paradoxical and catches our attention. Instead of leaving the spectator or participant with the impression that the techno-epistemic instrument in question is "abused" for purposes extrinsic to its regular, usual performance, one is left with the impression that it is being "surused."[9] This was one of the key procedures of surrealism, and it has not lost its efficacy to this day. One suddenly sees aspects of the procedural tools and their performance that seem to be hidden when embedded in their usual context. Rather than being seen as something added from outside, as a mere surplus, these intrinsic aspects of the device in question are now illuminated and become manifest in unprecedented ways. The procedure can be seen to resonate, in principle, with the modern scientific spirit itself. Gaston Bachelard, in his essay on "Surrationalism," characterized

9 Gaston Bachelard has played with the prefix "sur" on several occasions in his writings on contemporary art works. See Bachelard, *Imaginationen der Materie.*

scientific reasoning with explicit reference to the poetic surrealism of his time: "There will be established an *experimental reason* capable of surrationally organizing the real just as the *experimental dream* of Tristan Tzara surrealistically organizes the poetic liberty." And he concluded by demanding: "What is to be sacrificed? Is it our crude, pragmatic securities, or else the new, aleatoric and useless knowledge? No hesitation: one has to go into the direction where one thinks most intensely, where one experiments most artificially, where the ideas are least viscid, where reason loves to be endangered. *If, in an experiment, one does not risk one's reason, that experiment is not worth the trouble.*"[10] Bachelard meant this statement as a diagnosis of the most advanced physical and chemical sciences of his time and of experimental reasoning in the sciences more generally. And it is here, as we can see, that scientific research and artistic searching meet: risking one's reason, in the sense of throwing one's actual reasoning into question, exposing to scrutiny the forms of reason that are actually in use and are always in danger of becoming reified. Such is the message of Vanouse's *Fingerprints* ....[11]

8.

Paul Vanouse's work resonates with a broader artistic stream of work aiming to bring the sciences and the arts into productive

10 Gaston Bachelard, "Le surrationalisme," *Inquisitions. Organe du groupe d'études sur la phénoménologie humaine* 1 (1936): 1–6, on pp. 1–2 and 4–5. Translation by the present author. The reference in the text is to Tristan Tzara, *Grains et issues*, ed. Henri Béhar (Paris: Garnier-Flammarion, 1981).

11 Hauser, *Paul Vanouse, Fingerprints.*

tension. Over the past two decades or so, an increasing number of artists have recognized that the sciences, in their underworlds of infra-experimentality with their workshops for the generation of traces, the results of their instrument-mediated interaction with the world, and the conversion of these traces into a variety of data, offer working materials that can profitably be used as resources for artistic productions as well. Artistic performance, in one way or another, picks up materials that are being used or generated in laboratories and reconfigures them in novel forms and variants. Transposed in an aesthetic environment, these works and scenarios reveal something of the reflexive power of the alienation effect (*Verfremdungseffekt*) which was so forcefully exploited, for instance, in early twentieth-century epic theater. They offer ingenious and both scientifically and artistically effective ways to keep the media of knowledge production in suspense and to expose them in all their opacity. They present an effective antidote to the permanent and unconsidered tendency of the sciences to let their instruments and procedures disappear behind the thick curtain of "Materials & Methods" in their research publications.[12]

12 "Materials and Methods" is the heading of an obligatory section in a scientific research publication in which the methods and materials used for the work in question are listed and briefly described.

Seriality and Cycles: Thomas Struth

In his book, *Applied Rationalism*, Gaston Bachelard characterized the scientific view of the world with the following words: "In contact with an *experiment that brings to light a novelty*, one has to *renew one's thought* as well. [...] Scientific culture thus presents itself as a sequence of new experiments, of new experiences that have to be seen as so many *events of reason*."[1] Events of this kind are at the core of an experimental culture. What 'makes the difference' can only be experienced in the course of such sequential acts. "Sequences of experiments" have their parallel in the arts, frequently in the form of series, sometimes also—less luckily—called cycles. They are the instantiation of this experimental principle in the artistic realm: They revolve around an object or a topic in ever new attempts. It is in the nature of creative work that each new realization leaves something to be desired. It always points, endlessly, beyond a given state of the art. In this sense, it cannot come to rest.

One of the best-known German photographers of our present, Thomas Struth, usually produces sequences of pictures, such as "Unconscious Places" (urban architectures), "Landscapes" (empty of human beings), "Portraits," "Museum Pictures," "Paradise" (forests of the five continents). "Nature & Politics," an exhibition that took place in the fall of 2016 in Berlin's Gropius Bau, does not directly exhibit seriality in its

1 Bachelard, *Rationalisme appliqué*, 43. Emphasis in the original. Translation by the present author.

title.[2] The images, however, created between 2007 and 2015 in places throughout the world, all revolve around the confrontation between nature and technology, that paragon of reified politics so characteristic of the present state of the planet. Politics does not feature here as a narrative about actors, it glares at us as a depersonalized will to technology in eternally new and surprising constellations. And what is most disturbing: humans, the creators of these posthuman constellations, are conspicuously absent in almost all of the pictures.

An exhibition worthy of its name is like a landscape. As we move through it, it continually offers new, uncommon aspects. It is multi-perspectival and yet the different aspects are held together by a common topology. In the search for a unifying aesthetic principle for Struth's photographs, the term "landscape" itself appeared to offer a clue—landscape less in the sense of a classical genre of paintings than as the concept of a form of representation. Or in other words: landscape as a metaphor for a potentially endless complexity in detail. And indeed, the linguistic particle "scape" has been used to stand in for this intention. Accordingly, one can distinguish six different types of scapes, or metaphors of scapes in Thomas Struth's photographs: worldscapes, townscapes, technoscapes, labscapes or experimentscapes, fantasyscapes and seascapes. I will take them here as a guiding principle for navigating this unique exhibition, and will stop virtually at a few examples of each of these scapes.

2 Thomas Struth, *Nature & Politics*, texts by Tobia Bezzola, D. Graham Burnett and Dirk Baecker (London: Mack Books, 2016). Exhibition: Gropius Bau, Berlin, June 11 to September 18, 2016. The exhibition was previously shown at the Folkwang Museum in Essen and subsequently at the High Museum of Art in Atlanta and the Art Museum in St. Louis, United States.

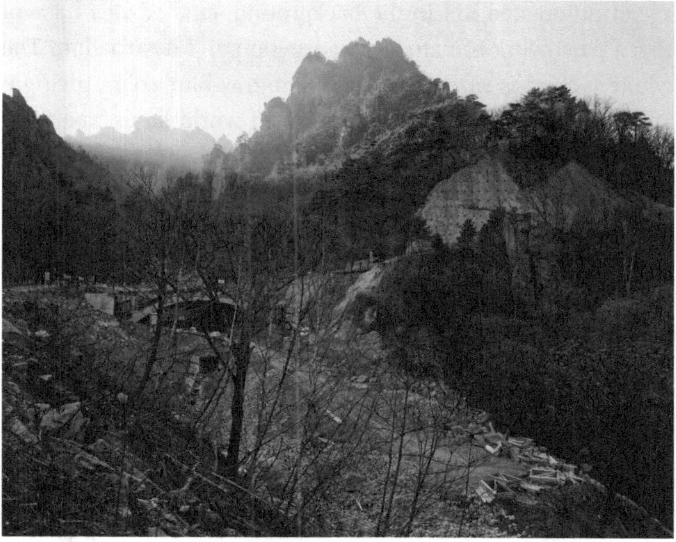

Fig. 2: Thomas Struth, *The Seven Brothers' Hills.*

Worldscapes

The catalog for "Nature & Politics" includes a photograph that explicitly points to characteristic features of the classical genre of landscape painting. Named after an area in the province of Gangwon-do in Korea, it bears the title "The Seven Brothers' Hills" (Fig. 2).[3] What we are looking at here is a worldscape of the twenty-first century: in this picture, nature and technology collide, if not clash, in a particularly harsh manner. A messy construction site in the foreground, a bridge under construction as well, a rock that has been dug into, and an ostensibly

3 Struth, *Nature & Politics*, 11.

as yet untouched hill in the background, clothed in a haze of fog: a patchwork of nature, construction and destruction. The whole picture is immersed in a light gray-blue color, giving it an appearance reminiscent of a Dutch world landscape from the sixteenth or early seventeenth century. But what a contrast! Whereas the early world landscapes exude cosmic harmony, the veil that Struth has laid over his picture does not soften the apocalyptic scene, it only sharpens the irreconcilable contrast. A stark impression.

Townscapes

Similarly, in Struth's townscapes construction and destruction are always closely related like the two sides of a coin. Ulsan, a growing South Korean metropolis on the shores of the Sea of Japan, inspired Struth to a whole series of photographs. In one of them, "Ulsan 1",[4] we see the Moloch as it prepares to engulf the last remaining green hills, to sandwich and devour them. It is an inverted technological lava stream. The irresistible force of its upward expansion appears to be inherent in the townscape itself with its skyscrapers. No human hands are to be seen, the flowing eruption of concrete has already extended its fingers into the sea and will continue doing so with the remaining green patches of uphill lands. It is principally in the nature of a metropolis that it has no boundary, no town walls that could ever confine its expansion. Struth succeeds in photographing what could be called a dynamic out of control.

4 Ibid., 128–129.

Technoscapes

With the technoscapes, we advance right into one of the centers of this exhibition. As in the townscapes, in the technoscapes people play, if at all, only the role of accidental impurities or non-functional interspersions—leftovers, we might say. Consider, for example, the photograph "Semi-Submersible Rig, DSME Shipyard, Geoje Island,"[5] taken in 2007. It is an oil platform of the Korean Daewoo Shipbuilding & Marine Engineering Company. On close inspection, two cyclists can be identified in the foreground to the left. They are busy with their bicycles and play no role at all in the picture. We could say that this is humanity in its corporeal, material form as a residual category; what is really and overwhelmingly present in this image is one of its gigantic technical realizations. Moreover, the image itself has dimensions such that it could not fit into any of the exhibition rooms. It had to be installed in the big patio of the art museum Gropius Bau, where its dimensions came to their own even more impressively.

Labscapes or Experimentscapes

Labscapes are another focus of the exhibition. Sometimes the labscapes are not easily distinguishable from the technoscapes but their dimensions are usually on a somewhat smaller scale, although by no means less complex. I will zoom in on them more closely and extensively—they give an appropriate impression of today's massive technical infrastructure of

5 Ibid., 27–28.

scientific research processes, the underworld of research technologies usually hidden from the spectator's eyes and located in laboratories, these spaces of knowledge generation *par excellence*. Here, complexity lies in the details, such as the intricately intertwined connecting cables of a measuring apparatus built from a myriad of different parts, each coming with their own materiality.

At first glance, many experimental setups shown on Struth's photographs look perfectly styled: blinking and blank devices, polished surfaces, cleared tables. Upon closer inspection, however, one discovers small "tinkered" elements or forgotten, non-functional relics of the working process everywhere. They add a touch of fragility to the whole arrangement in its splendor. Although they appear accidental, these interspersions are carefully staged. The resulting incongruity is a perfect *mise-en-scène* of what it means to perform an experiment, even under highly technologized conditions. Experimentation always comes with tinkered elements, with ad-hoc solutions.

With his camera eye, Thomas Struth has identified and staged the principle of technology-driven experimentation in continually new constellations. In an experiment, experimenters delegate their power of intervention to the interaction of a research technology with the phenomenon under scrutiny, which they have staged with all disposable knowledge at hand. The complex of technologies used in the experimental setup does not, as a rule, merely monitor or measure a phenomenon, it also co-produces it. This is why Gaston Bachelard has spoken about "technophenomena" in the context of the contemporary sciences.[6] From that perspective, the absence of subjects

6 Bachelard, *Rationalisme appliqué*, 13 sq.

in the image is a logical consequence; it lies in the nature of things experimental. The problem for the spectators, however, is that they can see the instruments, but not the *phenomenon* under scrutiny. They have to infer it. All that can be seen is the *research technology*. Struth has mercilessly put this dilemma into the picture. In contrast, when scientists talk about their craft, they move the phenomena center stage and render the research technology invisible.

"Stellarator Wendelstein 7-X Detail, Max Planck IPP, Greifswald"[7] and "Tokamak Asdex Upgrade Periphery, Max Planck IPP, Garching"[8] both portray parts of huge experimental setups for the exploration of nuclear fusion at the Max Planck Institute for Plasma Physics in its locations at Greifswald and at Garching near Munich in Germany. In these prototype plants, which are still in a stage of intense exploratory experimentation, hydrogen plasma heated up to millions of degrees Celsius, comparable to the heat in the sun, is generated. Under these conditions, two hydrogen nuclei fuse into a helium nucleus. None of the materials we know of would be able to tolerate such heat as a container. Therefore, it is mandatory that the plasma be kept enclosed by ultra-strong magnetic fields.

If one looks at these photographs closely enough, one will always be able to identify impurities in the clean picture, for instance, haphazard, messy plastic wrappings, a forgotten glove, a crack in the encasement of the Tokamak periphery—many signs of tinkering, perfunctoriness, and happenstance. And they are all signs of the fact that what we see on these

7 Struth, *Nature & Politics*, 54–55.
8 Ibid., 53.

images is just the outermost skin over a multilayered interior of the hypercomplex experimental arrangement.

Another picture in this series of laboratory landscapes is called "Measuring, Helmholtz-Zentrum, Berlin."[9] With the establishment of the Physikalisch-Technische Reichsanstalt in Berlin toward the end of the nineteenth century, whose first president was none other than Hermann von Helmholtz, Berlin became a world center of metrology. The Helmholtz Center Campus to which this photograph points is located on the periphery of Berlin, in Wannsee. That measuring is done here is obvious. But once again, in this photo what is really being measured remains in the dark. And here, too, we see signs of tinkering on parts of this immense measuring instrument: the provisional tinfoil jacket-casings that cover the connecting points of the apparatus, or a crumpled, forgotten piece of paper on the radiator.

Yet another category of images leads us into a labscape of a different nature: the operating room of a hospital. For instance, in "Figure II, Charité, Berlin,"[10] we see a highly technologized operation at the Charité, Berlin's main hospital. The patient, the object at stake, is almost completely covered and clamped inside the operating machinery: first invisibility. No operating personnel can be seen in the picture: second invisibility. What kind of operation is to be performed remains hidden as well: third invisibility. The image shows what cannot be seen. And here, too, an engine under the operating table, torn and worn from use, contrasts sharply with the rest of the perfectly clinical and aseptic image. There is a broader message to be drawn

9 Ibid., 118–119.
10 Ibid., 186–187.

from all these labscapes: Modern technology tends to blackbox what is going on inside. And yet, for those who care, the shining exterior carries visible accessories of its vulnerability.

There are, however, two exceptions in this series of labscapes that subvert this pattern, or stated otherwise: they present both of its extremes. Following Claude Lévi-Strauss, we could identify them with the contrast between the idealized figures of the engineer and the bricoleur.[11] One of the Tokamak interiors, "Tokamak Asdex Upgrade Interior 2, Max Planck IPP, Garching,"[12] is completely devoid of haphazard detail and any impurity. We see a perfect surface with no contamination—and nothing behind. And another of these images is dominated by a complete muddle without a recognizable order to indicate an experiment, and without a covering to conceal any of these flasks and devices. Not even the glass slide is closed. This photograph, "Chemistry Fume Cabinet, The University of Edinburgh, 2010," shows the fume hood of an ordinary chemistry laboratory at an ordinary Scottish university.[13]

I do not want to close this section without pointing to one last intriguing still. The only life-size figure that is to be seen in full in this sequence of labscapes is the bronze torso of an angel waiting to be analyzed in terms of its physical features. We could say that "AGLAE, C2RMF, Paris 2013,"[14] emphasizes the principle of the absence of human beings with its contrary in ore: not an experimenting subject, but a bronze subject turned into an object of investigation: literally an archangel. AGLAE

11 Claude Lévi Strauss, *Wild Thought*, trans. Jeffrey Mehlman and John Leavitt (Chicago: The University of Chicago Press, 2021), Chapter 1.

12 Struth, Nature & Politics, 50–51.

13 Ibid., 110–111.

14 Ibid., 165.

is a particle accelerator, 26 meters long and weighing 10 tons, driven by several mega-electron volts. It was installed at the Louvre in Paris in 1989 for the investigation of artworks and archaeological objects.

Fantasyscapes

The fifth type of landscape to be seen on Struth's photographs can be brought under the label of fantasyscapes. They do, however, not only exist in human imagination, but are scapes built in brick and stone. One example is "Mountain, Anaheim,"[15] an image of Disneyland in Anaheim, in Southern California's Orange County, displaying a rocky peak reminiscent of the Matterhorn in Zermatt, Switzerland. Here it is the contrast between cold snowy heights immediately adjacent to a blue water bay whose sandy shore has been replaced by mountain woods that puzzles the spectator. Yellow submarines in the foreground and a red magnetic levitation train behind the trees strengthen the impression of an environment whose elements are out of joint. The second fantasyscape, "Aquarium, Atlanta,"[16] shows the gigantic Georgia Aquarium in Georgia, Atlanta, the world's biggest marine aquarium, far from any seashore, containing 30,000 m^3 of salt water in which the great attraction is sharks up to five meters long. Again, the image stages a displacement: ocean-in-city we might call it. As far as the presence of human figures is concerned, this image is *the* big exception and, as such, the counterpoint to all the other

15 Ibid., 80–81,
16 Ibid., 142–143.

pictures in the exhibition. A crowd of people, mostly young children, sits and stands in front of the glass wall behind which fishes of all colors and size abound. In a way, it forms a bridge to another, earlier series of Struth's photographs: the Museum Pictures.

Seascape

This tour d'horizon would not be complete without the only seascape to be seen in this photo exhibition. "Seascape, Donghae City,"[17] marks its final point. In this image of the coast of the Japanese Sea near Donghae, nothing can be seen except water, foam and a few submerged rocks in the foreground under a cloudy sky. With this photograph, at the same time, we return to the beginning of the exhibition that started with the picture of the dead edge of an abandoned lane in St. Petersburg. In contrast to the Donghae seascape, in "Kovenskij Pereulok, St. Petersburg,"[18] aside from some weeds growing out of the cracks on the ground we see nothing but smeared walls. Here, not only humans, but all of nature has shrunk to a residual category.

These two images can be seen as bracketing the whole exhibition. And at the same time, they contrast sharply with the technoscapes between them: sheer nature on the one side, sheer masonry on the other side; breakers as a symbol of untamed natural forces, brick and mortar as a symbol of manmade construction. The experiment is located exactly in

17 Ibid., 198.
18 Ibid., 4–5.

between. It makes natural forces manifest, but it needs technical devices to do so. It unites both of these poles.

To sum up, a composition principle runs through these sequences of scapes. Contrast and opposition give them a shape that is not exhausted by mere additionality. It visualizes forces between the extremes.

The Bottle, for Example: Gaston Bachelard Looks at Albert Flocon's *Castles in Spain*.

The encounter between philosopher of science Gaston Bachelard and copper engraver Albert Flocon in postwar Paris in the late 1940s and throughout the 1950s has occupied and intrigued me for a long time, and it has and given rise to a number of publications.[1] Here, I will pick one example of their protracted interaction. It is the copper engraving that opens the collection of *Castles in Spain*, an artist's book to which Flocon contributed the images and Bachelard a shorter or longer contemplative reverie to each of these 'castles.'[2] It was published late in 1957 as the last collective work of the artist and the philosopher. I use the word "example" with purpose and for a particular reason. Ultimately, what is at stake is what an exemplary case revolves around: a dialectic of abstraction and concretion. An example is not an image of something, it is not a representation or a referral—rather, it is itself as something concrete, but a concreteness that at the same time points beyond itself. Let me mention in passing that this might also be a fitting definition of the experiment. An experiment is likewise always something concrete, but with a concreteness of a particular kind: it manifests as the embodiment of a principle. I will return to this point later on.

1 For more details, see, e.g., Rheinberger, *The Hand of the Engraver*.

2 Albert Flocon and Gaston Bachelard, *Châteaux en Espagne* (Paris: Le Cercle Grolier, 1957).

I will thus restrict myself to the description of a single image taken from the altogether fourteen large format *Castles in Spain*, including an equal number of separate reflexive notes. We can see the latter in turn as experiments in imagination, themselves castles in the air, but castles provoked by the peculiar materiality of the engravings. Bachelard also called them 'stories.'

Reflecting on the time the album was being compiled, Bachelard remarked: "How many stories did I tell myself in the course of that long winter during which, week after week, Albert Flocon brought me the loose sheets of this album!"[3] Flocon had engraved the copper plates over several years; he printed them himself on the hand-press of Georges Leblanc in Paris, and the completed slipcase could be delivered late in the fall of 1957. Here again, as in the case of their first collaboration, which had resulted in the album *Paysages*,[4] Bachelard stresses the creation of a resonance space in which the philosopher and the engraver did not communicate discursively but opened up to the impact created by the parallelism of text and image. In the end, Bachelard told his stories to himself, without any explanatory intention, and vice versa: "Indeed, Flocon never explained to me what he wanted to make. Between us, no discourse."[5]

For Bachelard, nevertheless, Flocon's engravings embodied a message. They were *examples* in the sense outlined above: standing for themselves but pointing beyond themselves.

3 Flocon/Bachelard, *Châteaux en Espagne*, 9. All translations by the present author.

4 Albert Flocon and Gaston Bachelard, *Paysages* (Rolle, VD: Eynard, 1950).

5 Flocon/Bachelard, *Châteaux en Espagne*, 10.

He states it immediately on the first page: "I love the engraving for its own sake, the autonomous engraving, the engraving that originally does not illustrate anything, and which I, in my philosophical musings, call the auto-eidetic engraving. It is, for me, the ideal of a story without words, compressed narration."[6] Flocon's engravings do not refer to an outside to which they would lend shape. Thus, they do not tell stories in the referential sense of reporting about an episode or an event. They are grounded in themselves, in the relation of their elements to each other—a relation rich enough to leave open options, food for thought. "All Flocon's 'castles' are shining,"[7] Bachelard states.

Flocon himself once confessed: "I always had a predilection for construction sites that show buildings in the making; I have built castles in Spain [...] all my life."[8] At stake here is the movement of gestation in its obstinacy, its capriciousness, its autopoietic reflexivity. Bachelard formulated the basic feature of the series as follows: "Flocon calls his collection *Châteaux en Espagne*. He is inviting us to measure the distance between what one sees and what one dreams, to cross what could be called the *space of projection*, to live in the *space-time of the project*. In this formulation, I, as the hopeless philosopher that I am, sum up Flocon's vision: Flocon is the engraver of the space-time of the pro-ject."[9] Projecting here means setting free, a movement in which gestation itself becomes thematic:

6 Ibid., 9.
7 Ibid., 13.
8 Albert Flocon, *Une Poétique de la vision. Du Bauhaus à la perspective curviligne/Eine Poetik des Sehens. Vom Bauhaus zur kurvenlinearen Perspektive* (Metz: École des Beaux Arts, 1992), 90. Translation by the present author.
9 Flocon/Bachelard, *Châteaux en Espagne*, 12.

"He [Flocon] loves catching the moment of construction, in which construction itself becomes the project."[10]

This long quotation carries an unmistakable echo of Bachelard's epistemological work on the dynamics of contemporary scientific research processes. The following passage can be found in Bachelard's *New Scientific Spirit*, a book that he understood as the manifesto of a non-Cartesian epistemology: "Above the *subject* and beyond the immediate *object*, modern science is based on the *project*. In scientific thought, the subject's meditation upon the object always takes the form of a project."[11] And he resumes: "A truly scientific phenomenology is therefore essentially a phenomenotechnique. Its purpose is to amplify what is revealed beyond appearance. It takes its instruction from construction."[12] In this sense, the project can also be seen as the foundational gesture of the modern experimental sciences. And as Sandra Pravica's vivid account shows,[13] the tentative, the searching outreach is at the same time the foundational gesture of Bachelard's philosophy of science.

It is this gesture that opens up a new space for the game of abstraction and concretion, a space that sheds light not only on both scientific *and* artistic production, but also on a philosophy that tries to do justice to their respective dynamics. The phenomenological is taken literally here. The point is not to search for hidden depths beyond or beneath the phenomena. The point is to grasp the forces at play *as* they appear. With

10 Ibid., 15.

11 Bachelard, *New Scientific Spirit*, 11–12

12 Ibid., 13.

13 Sandra Pravica, *Bachelards tentative Wissenschaftsphilosophie* (Vienna: Passagen Verlag, 2015).

respect to Flocon's engravings, Bachelard summarized: "The secret of the narrative richness of each of these plates consists in that our engraver is a master of simplicity. If one would have to search for a hidden value behind a plethora of contours and shadows, if one would have to dig in order to find, then one could take this as an explanation for the possibility of different and changing interpretations. And one could be proud to detect a hidden meaning."[14] But this is just *not* what is at stake here. The possibility space of these engravings is not organized vertically but rather horizontally: "Here, everything is simple, everything is obvious, everything is *engraved*. Flocon instinctively masters the wonderful plurality of the simple."[15]

It is now time to take a closer look at one of these castles in the air (Fig. 3). The index lists it as *La Bouteille*, and Bachelard refers to his remarks as the "*philosophical story of the bottle*."[16] Somewhat further on, he calls it a "cosmic bottle,"[17] and indeed, there is something solemn, if not sublime, about this vessel. To read it symbolically, however, would lead up the wrong track. Geometrically, the picture is governed by the severity of the vertical and the ease of the horizontal. Waves of an agitated sea curl before a low horizon. On the shore in the foreground, an upwardly rising structure cast in the contours of a bottle appears to suck up the sand that the sea deposits on the beach. In the foreground to the left of the image, this upward movement is taken up in a transposed and more abstract form. Another remnant of the sea, the shell of a mussel, serves as

14 Flocon/Bachelard, *Châteaux en Espagne*, 10–11.
15 Ibid., 11.
16 Ibid., 17. The plate is on p. 19.
17 Ibid., 18.

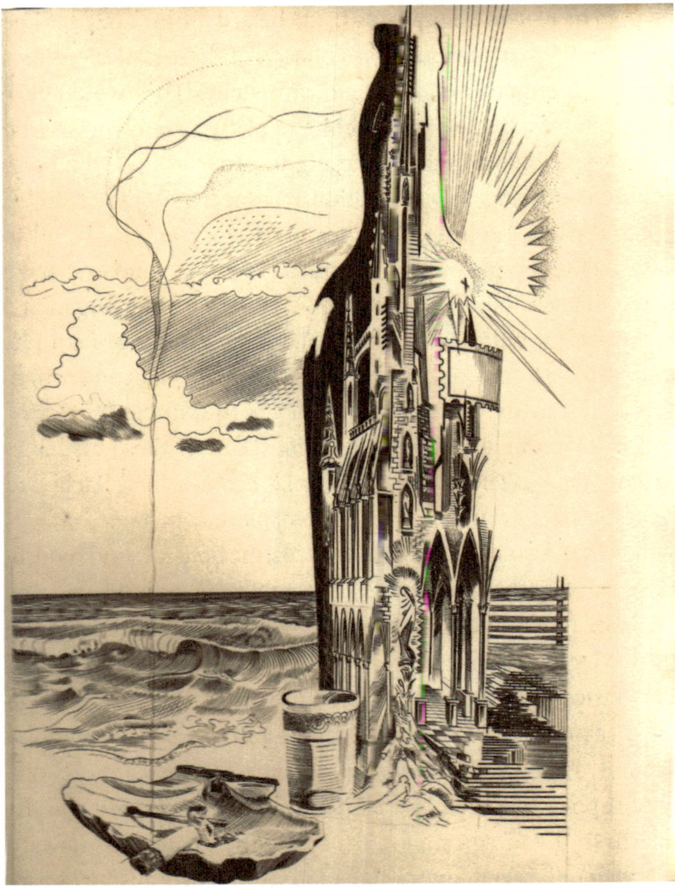

Fig. 3: Albert Flocon, *La Bouteille*.

an ashtray for an abandoned cigarette smoldering beside an extinct match and a stub. Its smoke winds vertically up in parallel to the bottle, mixes with the clouds, spreads out and disappears behind the bottleneck. The space between the bottle and the shell is occupied by a drinking glass. There is, however, no smoker and no drinker to be seen in the picture. The engraver has put himself in the picture with these utensils of pensiveness. In this manner, the castle appears to be eminently present as the product of his working table, and at the same time as transitory as the daintily rising cloud of smoke. Bachelard muses: "[...] engravings such as this one favorably evoke the polemic between the figurative and the non-figurative. Let me continue in my philosophical language: I would like to call such an engraving an abstract-concrete one. I connect it with all I love in the world, abstract thinking that guides concrete creation. With it, let me try to capture, as if in action, the unity of the abstract and the concrete, the embodiment of a thinking human being in a resilient nature, the synthesis of the non-figurative and the figurative."[18] And he further explains: "Flocon's plates do not copy anything; they do not accept the slavery of a figurative art. But not being content with a non-figurative art either, Flocon pictures all the unrealities that transcend the real."[19] The bottle appears as having been emptied by an absinthe drinker whose fantastic dream of a cathedral in the course of being erected has filled it at the same time. Or is it a message-in-a-bottle that that materializes itself after it was washed ashore? From whatever angle it is approached, the castle pointing in the air—or emerging from the depth of the sea—simultaneously displays its opposite. Whatever story we might imagine, it always refers back to itself.

18 Ibid., 13.
19 Ibid., 13.

This bottle is remarkable in several respects. To begin with, let us look at it from outside. The two halves of the bottle form a strong contrast that takes up the play of the vertical and the horizontal and even enforces it. It is the contrast between bright and dark, day and night, light and shadow. Surprisingly enough, the gloomy half is oriented toward the sea, the shining half toward land. Such unusual reversals occur again and again in this picture. Facing the observer, the bottle opens its interior and articulates itself as a towering gothic cathedral. Its central spire juts out of the bottleneck into the upper edge of the image. An army of roof workers appears to push it even further up, beyond the confines of the page. The choir is filled with a Madonna statue surrounded by rays of light, driven upward by a crowd of human figurines that comprise its pedestal. As soon as spectators concentrate their gaze on the cathedral delineating itself within the contours of the bottle, the latter appear as if "slit open," like a "provisional scaffold" on the verge of becoming superfluous as a temporary envelope and detaching itself from the building like a skin.[20] The tag of the bottle, too, seems to have become detached, and has lost its legibility in the gleaming light that the sun throws on the bottleneck and that, reflecting back on it, pours itself over the flask label.

"From the very first engraving—the bottle in front of the sea—," Bachelard contends, "one experiences these transactions between the function of the real and the unreal, transactions which constitute the life of the imagination. Once the artist has entered that zone of transaction, in which unreality troubles reality and the real ensnares the fantastic, it appears as if one could transfer the task of creating images to the objects

20 Ibid., 20.

themselves, and one is confident that the images, in the sense of reverie itself, take possession of and play about the objects."[21] This is a pointed and precise characterization of an important aspect of the work of Flocon. He rarely abandons the frame of the figurative, but he transfigures the objects in such a way that the power of the image comes into its own exactly through the surreal quality of the elements inviting us to touch them. What is at stake here is not representation, but the projection of a world, and while this is happening the process of projecting itself reflexively comes into the image as well. "Yes, indeed, engraving, and copper engraving in particular, is an extremely abstract technique," Flocon once stressed in a conversation with the French writer Gil Jouanard, asserting that there is nothing but abstraction left to the engraver: his craft consists in utmost parsimony.[22] Everything has to be built from a single gesture: the furrows the burin traces into the copper plate.

Flocon, in turn, once called Bachelard "the man of the abstract-concrete."[23] This description hits upon a decisive point in Bachelard's epistemological reflections. They stress the abstract, mathematical aspect of modern physics, but at the same time they link it with its very concrete phenomeno-technical apparatus. Thus, it comes as no surprise to find that Bachelard, in *Le Rationalisme appliqué*, one of his epistemological books written at the time of his encounter with Flocon, attests to the physical sciences of his time an "abstract-concrete

21 Ibid., 14.

22 Albert Flocon, "Main ouvrière et main rêveuse. Entretien avec Gil Jouanard," *Solaire* 10 (1983), special issue *Bachelard ou le droit de rêver*, 57–65, on p. 63. Translation by the present author.

23 Albert Flocon, "Le philosophe et le graveur," in *Bachelard* (Paris: Colloque de Cerisy, 1974), 271–278, on p. 271.

mentality," "realizing itself in a double action of abstraction and concretion."[24] Abstraction and concretion are to be taken as process categories that characterize the activity of a "*field of thought*" emerging from the "conjunction" of mathematics and experimentation: "No empty rationality thus, no incoherent empircicism—these two philosophical credos have found their close and precise synthesis of theory and experience in contemporary physics."[25]

Bachelard takes up his remarks quoted earlier on the relation between subject and object in the *New Scientific Spirit* of 1934, when he states: "It is no longer a question of confronting a solitary spirit with an indifferent universe. From now on, one has to act from within that center in which the knowing mind is determined by the object of its knowledge, and the former in turn, guides experimentation with even greater precision."[26] "Applied rationalism" and "instructed materialism" thus form the two inseparable sides of the same coin.[27] "We see that it is best to assure oneself of the rational characteristics of technical materialism and, vice versa, the real characteristics of applied rationalism, if we are to bring reason and the scientific object systematically into a dialectical relation."[28]

Reflection about the dynamics of the sciences must not shirk from this dialectic either. Accordingly, Bachelard sees his own philosophy of science as "a philosophy at work"—*une philosophie au travail*—, and he contrasts it with what he criticizes as the "philosophies of recapitulation"—*philosophies de résumé*—

24 Bachelard, *Rationalisme appliqué*, 1. Translation by the present author.
25 Ibid., 3.
26 Ibid., 4.
27 Ibid.
28 Ibid., 9.

of his predecessors and contemporaries.[29] He includes historians of science in this critique, reproaching them for shying away all too often from a reconstruction of certain obscure situations in the course of knowledge acquisition, that is, situations thus where the abstract and the concrete, concept and object have not yet reached a recursive coupling. In contrast, Bachelard claims to proceed in a process-oriented manner in his historical epistemology just as the sciences do in their own work, to which epistemology refers: "Epistemology has to be as mobile as science is."[30] If that means for the physicist that "each new experiment [...] exposes the method of experimentation to experience,"[31] it means for the epistemologist that "in order to understand, one has to participate in an emergence."[32] In other words, not a *prima philosophia*, not a "philosophy of the beginning," but a "philosophy of continuation."[33] One has to immerse oneself in this recursive process. No Cartesian rules reign here any longer. "In order to assure oneself of an object of scientific knowledge, one can no longer confide in the immediacy of an ego opposed to a non-ego. [...] The rationalistic *cogito* [...] must function like an emergence out of an existence that is, more or less, empirically confirmed."[34]

After this detour into epistemology, let us come back to our copper engraver, Albert Flocon. We can assume that Bachelard saw Flocon's work as an engraver involved in a phenomenotechnical process that resonates in a certain manner with

29 Ibid.
30 Ibid., 10.
31 Ibid.., 43.
32 Ibid., 11.
33 Ibid., 54.
34 Ibid., 50–51.

the process of acquiring scientific knowledge. Just as modern physics "is no longer a science of facts, but a technology of effects," a science that is no longer to be summoned as a "description of phenomena," but rather must be seen as a "production of phenomena,"[35] the work of the engraver is inscribed in a comparable space, the space of a "dialectic of nature and counter-nature,"[36] the figurative and the non-figurative, the real and the unreal, to come back to Bachelard's story of the bottle. What Bachelard there calls an "*intermediary time*" corresponds to this space.[37] Each of Flocon's castles in Spain invites us "to live in the space-time of the project."[38] Bachelard repeatedly returns to the aspect of intertemporality, a time decoupled from a beginning and an end, we might say. The possibility of a "contingency in contemplation" correlates to such a temporal oscillation.[39] "I do not tell myself today what I said to myself yesterday. Serious contemplation is capricious, it is pure caprice."[40] To change the register of *metier* once again: in the face of a complex reality, Bachelard sees the scientist in a comparable position as well. In the sciences, too, an object can provoke "several types of objectivation, several perspectives of specification; it can participate in different sets of problems."[41]

35 Gaston Bachelard, "Noumène et microphysique," in *Etudes*, ed. Georges Canguilhem (Paris: Librairie philosophique J. Vrin, 1970), 11–24, on p. 24. Translation by the present author.
36 Flocon/Bachelard, *Châteaux en Espagne*, 37.
37 Ibid., 13.
38 Ibid., 12.
39 Ibid., 9.
40 Ibid.
41 Bachelard, *Rationalisme appliqué*, 53.

"I loved pushing rationality to its boundaries," Flocon proclaimed, adding: "Beyond that boundary, enough mysteriousness remains."[42] The attitude of an experimenter could not be better expressed than with these words. Every really researching experimenter focuses the actually given knowledge in such a way that it becomes possible to take a step beyond it. Flocon practiced copper engraving as a form of ongoing experimentation. This is not to be understood in the simple sense of trying something out. Of course, he also played with printing techniques and transposed copper plates from their original use into new contexts.[43] But something different is at stake here: the fundamental dialectic of omission and the provocation of the unprecedented it renders possible: of concretizing by abstraction. The constrictions of the technique lead to the unheard-of and the unseen. Experimentation does not consume itself in the reproduction of something given, it unfolds a kind of immanent transcendence. In this sense, the structure of experimentation is that of a project. It is this tendency beyond itself, not in the sense of a mere generalization or in the sense of standing for something, not in the sense of merely spelling out an anticipation, but in the sense of reaching out for something through restriction, that constitutes the decisive aspect of its exemplary nature. The exemplary is distinguished by a peculiar kind of vicariance. It does not refer to an other; in pointing back on itself, it points beyond itself: it is a hypostasis.

Experimenting is the craft of the abstract-concrete. This is why Bachelard appreciated the copper engravings of Flocon as

42 Flocon, "Main ouvrière et main rêveuse," 64.

43 Compare, e.g., Albert Flocon, *Suites expérimentales, 1943–1983* (Vienna: Medusa/Bauhaus Archiv, 1983).

variations of a repeated effort to abstract from the concrete and, at the same time and in one and the same motion, to concretize the abstract. He therefore called Flocon's castles in Spain "abstract-concrete plates."[44] Just as Bachelard was interested in the real of the sciences—*le réel scientifique*[45]—and not in the representations it offers, in the same way as he was interested in the real of literature and not in the narratives it presents, he was interested in the real of the engraving, not in its options of representation, but in its auto-eidetic potential of iteration.

44 Flocon/Bachelard, *Châteaux en Espagne*, 26.
45 Bachelard, *New Scientific Spirit*, 6 (misleadingly translated there as "scientific reality").

Grace at the Boundary of Knowledge: For Sandra Boeschenstein

Recently I happened to open a copy of *The Raw and the Cooked* once again, the first volume of Claude Lévi-Strauss' monumental *Mythologiques*. Leafing through the "Ouverture" of a book whose index reads like a musical potpourri, the following lines caught my eye: "In a subject such as this, scientific knowledge advances haltingly and is stimulated by contention and doubt. Unlike metaphysics it does not insist on all or nothing [...] I shall be satisfied if it is credited with the modest achievement of having left a difficult problem in a rather less unsatisfactory state than it was before. Nor must we forget that in science there are no final truths. The scientific mind does not so much provide the right answers as ask the right questions."[1] These lines are written by an ethnologist, and one might be inclined to assume that they are specific to that discipline. In the natural sciences, however, the situation is not very different. In his reflections on the historical course of molecular genetics, the French molecular biologist François Jacob, a somewhat younger contemporary of Lévi-Strauss—who actually participated in a couple of memorable public conversations with the renowned field ethnologist[2]—spoke similarly

1 Claude Lévi-Strauss, *Introduction to a Science of Mythology I: The Raw and the Cooked*, trans. John and Doreen Weightman (New York: Harper & Row, 1969), 7.

2 François Jacob, Roman Jakobson, Claude Lévi-Strauss and Philippe l'Héritier (réalisation: Michel Treguer), "Vivre et parler," *Les Lettres françaises* 1221 & 1222 (1968), 1–7 & 4–5; "La logique du vivant: François Jacob rencontre Claude Lévi-Strauss," *Office national de radiodiffusion télévision française*. Docu-

of scientific research, calling it "night science": it "wanders blind," it "hesitates" and "stumbles" on uncharted paths in search of knowledge.[3]

From this starting point, let us try to access the issue of boundaries of knowledge that Sandra Boeschenstein thematized in her exhibition marking the fiftieth anniversary of the Center for Interdisciplinary Research at the University of Bielefeld.[4] The notion of "stumbling" could play a key role in this context. Actually, we only become aware of boundaries at all when we stumble. This means that to become aware of the current state of knowledge as a boundary, one has to stumble over it. The most authentic way to stumble is over one's own feet. In this case, one is dealing with a boundary produced by one's own presence. Transposing this situation into the realm of knowledge, we have to look for boundaries that are immanent to that knowledge, that are created in the course of knowledge production itself. Stumbling entails yet another connotation, however. It is the moment of blindness explicitly mentioned by Jacob when he speaks of "wandering blind." We "see," we become aware of the obstacle that made us stumble only after the event. Paradoxically speaking, uncertainty about the direction to take is necessary for successful advancement. Thus, the immanence of the boundaries of knowledge and the essential precariousness of the knowledge horizon do not

mentaire, Sciences et techniques, Arts et culture (réalisation: Roger Kahane), 1972.

3 François Jacob, *Of Flies, Mice, and Men*, trans. Giselle Weiss (Cambridge MA and London: Harvard University Press, 1998), 126.

4 Sandra Boeschenstein, *Die Grazie der Erkenntnisgrenze/Grace at the Boundary of Knowledge* (Bielefeld: Bielefeld University Press/Transcript Verlag, 2019).

close, but rather open the space of knowledge acquisition in unforeseen directions.

The French philosopher of science Gaston Bachelard gave a lucid account of this situation, which can actually be considered as the basic situation, the ground state of research. In his book, *The Formation of the Scientific Mind*, which he understood as a "psychoanalysis of objective knowledge," he developed the concept of what he called *obstacle épistémologique*, the "epistemological obstacle," and to which he devoted the first chapter of the book. It begins with the following words: "When we start looking for the psychological conditions in which scientific progress is made, we are soon convinced that the problem of scientific knowledge must be posed in terms of obstacles."[5] Bachelard's epistemological obstacle is not to be seen as an external barrier that one might assume to be associated with the complexity or even inaccessibility of certain phenomena up for analysis. It is, rather, firmly inscribed in the act of gaining knowledge itself, in the "appetite for objective knowledge," as Lévi-Strauss termed the quest for knowing in his book dedicated to *La Pensée sauvage*.[6] There are "obstacles to spiritualization that lie in the mind itself."[7] What does that mean? First of all, Bachelard argues, our taken-for-granted everyday knowledge is an obstacle to scientific knowledge. The latter is not a smooth continuation of the former, it involves a rupture. And second, as knowledge advances, the actually achieved state of knowledge itself is being transformed into an

5 Gaston Bachelard, *The Formation of the Scientific Mind. A Contribution to a Psychoanalysis of Objective Knowledge*, trans. Mary McAllester Jones (Manchester: Clinamen, 2002), 23.

6 Lévi-Strauss, *Wild Thought*, 3, 18.

7 Bachelard *Formation of the Scientific Mind*, 23.

obstacle that, time and again, has to be overcome. Overcoming or surmounting an obstacle never happens smoothly, it always takes the form of a break. Obstacle and break are the two sides of the coin by which Bachelard characterizes the eventful and punctuated nature of the acquisition of scientific knowledge. Obstacles are rooted in the very constitution of objective—or better perhaps: object-oriented—knowledge. And exactly because they are generated from within, external impulses are repeatedly required to overcome them. Scientific thought is in need of devices for outsmarting itself, and it acquires them in the very process of its own development. But neither they nor the epistemological obstacles are rooted in the phenomena themselves. Instead, these impulses are due to the means and the media with which we try to capture the phenomena. In the end, it is this form of exteriorization that enables us to overcome epistemological obstacles.

The natural sciences of the modern era have developed a device for situations of essential ignorance, that is, of ignorance about what we do not know, that offers options for acting and for maintaining action. This device is the *experiment* in its diverse forms. Scientific experimentation can be regarded as a process that allows one to surmount epistemological obstacles. Experiments are generators of events that cannot be anticipated. They are devised in such a way as to lead experimenters to clues that lie beyond what their current knowledge permits them to see and conceive. Experimenters are regularly confronted with options that cannot be derived from the horizon of their current knowledge and its boundaries. Experienced experimenters design their experiments in such a way that they can expect answers to their questions without, however, reducing their complexity to a degree that everything else is excluded. Although such experiments exist, we cannot call them research experiments any more. They belong, rather, to the order of demonstrations. We can also call them tests. Traditional epistemology has long been oriented towards demonstrative, not exploratory experiments and has been prevented from being able to deal with situations that give rise to epistemic novelty. An epistemology in the wake of Gaston Bachelard, however, has to orient itself towards research experiments. If, for once, we do not assume that there are boundaries to knowledge in principle—without succumbing to the illusion of absolute knowledge—then the question regarding boundaries is always tantamount to the question of how boundaries can be overcome, and the latter question is, in turn, tantamount to the question of how novelty comes into being. "New" in the emphatic sense of the word is what cannot be derived from what is given.

The process of gaining new knowledge via experimentation is often triggered by the fact that a research technology which was unexploited so far—whether because it was previously unavailable or merely neglected—is integrated into an already existing experimental design. To some extent this process can be compared to the biological cultivation technique of grafting.[8] Experimentation itself can be seen as a cultural technique—*Kulturtechnik*[9]—that is especially oriented toward the production of epistemic effects. Grafting can be characterized in two respects. First, the two entities that are being brought

8 See Rheinberger, *Split and Splice*, Chapter 4, and references therein.

9 Bernhard Siegert, „Kulturtechnik," in *Einführung in die Kulturwissenschaft*, ed. Harun Maye and Leander Scholz, (München: W. Fink (UTB), 2011), 95–118.

together are heteroclite in nature. And second, when joined, each of them preserves its own characteristics. Of course, joining like to unlike is not an obvious choice to begin with. But it is just this moment of counter-intuition that can turn out as a carrier of surprise. This holds not only for different research technologies that have to be made compatible with each other at their interface. It also applies to the ensemble of research technologies in their relation to the scientific objects toward which they are oriented, and about which one hopes to learn not only what had so far remained elusive, but what had not been visible on the horizon of knowledge at all. Surprising knowledge effects generally arise at these interfaces and from such connections.

In his book about *Water and Dreams*, Gaston Bachelard made use of the concept of "grafting" in his characterization of the emergence of new images of the traditional elements—fire, water, earth, air—in poetry and literature. In doing so, he sought to capture poetic imagination in the very act of writing itself—as an experimental activity, we have to add. Here, too, grafting means to add something new to what there is, something that cannot be derived from what there is. In its general form, it results in a displacement that surprises. And again, all while the graft adds something new, it also depends on the stock to realize its potential. Bachelard refuses to regard grafting as a "mere metaphor" here: to him, it is an original figure of poetic action, of "material imagination,"[10] which, just like epistemic imagination exteriorized in the experiment, has the structure of an event—it does not emerge from inside what there is, but is the result of a material confrontation that

10 Bachelard, *Imaginationen der Materie.*

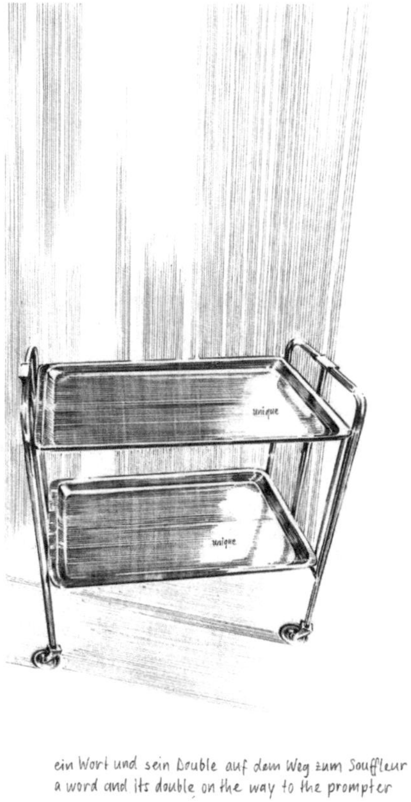

Fig. 4: Sandra Boeschenstein, *A Word and its Double on the Way to the Prompter.*

points beyond itself. "It is the grafting that provides material imagination with an exuberance of forms."[11] Exuberance is a fitting term for the kind of overflow we are dealing with here.

11 Bachelard, *Water and Dreams,* 10.

And while Bachelard, in the context of his poetology of the elements, focuses on poetic artwork, he adds in a generalizing, even categorical gesture: “By nature art is grafted.”[12] Artistic imagination is not nourished by a single, internal source, either. It, too, evolves from clashes of the heteroclite, from the displacement of materials, the conversion of approaches, of recontextualization. Perhaps from here, a window opens for thinking about both the arts and the sciences—both activities of their own, but both dedicated to things that cannot be anticipated, to dealing with the unprecedented.

The drawings and installations presented by Sandra Boeschenstein in her exhibition at the Center for Interdisciplinary Research in Bielefeld derive life and nourishment from unexpected juxtapositions (Fig. 4). Usually characterized by precise and sharp renderings of objects and their parts, obliquity comes into the picture when parts intuitively assumed to be central are missing, connections inverted, when gravity is lifted, water runs upward, interior appears as exterior. And the captions accompanying each installation and each drawing add yet another dimension of precision and sharpness turned against themselves. The viewer is left with the impression of moving in a space between captions and the captured where, despite all visual security, despite a kind of over-precision of the objects, an abyss can open up at any time where all that security disappears, forcing the spectator to question the traditional order of things. Sandra Boeschenstein's art consists in making the boundary of things visible and palpable, tongue-in-cheek, with grace. We can call her an experimenter of and with boundaries. She makes us stumble.

12 Ibid. Translation amended.

Experiments, Traces, Data Streams: Hannes Rickli

Back in 1992, I published a little book whose title read *Experiment, Differenz, Schrift*, a slim volume assembling my first forays into the world of experimental systems.[1] It happened to fall into the hands of the young Swiss artist Hannes Rickli. Inspired by the work of his brother, a biologist, on the movement of insects, he had constructed a rotating "tracking sphere"—*Spurenkugel* (Fig. 5). It was modeled on a globe that facilitated the measurement of movements of tiny insects, when they began crawling on its surface. Rickli had transformed it into a writing game of sorts based on light traces. When the sphere was placed in the center of a darkened exhibition room, visitors could interact with these light traces via light-barriers by way of their own movements in space.[2] The artist had contacted and invited me for a conversation on the occasion of his *Tracking Sphere* exhibition at Kunst-Werke Berlin.[3] Not knowing each other, we started to talk about experimentation, how it depended on the production of traces, and how, in an extended sense, one could look at this process as a graphematic activity, a kind of writing. Beckoning in the background of all that were Jacques Derrida's reflections on the generalization of writing

1 Hans-Jörg Rheinberger, *Experiment, Differenz, Schrift. Anmerkungen zur Geschichte epistemischer Dinge* (Marburg: Basilisken Presse, 1992).

2 Hannes Rickli, *Spurenkugel, ein Schreibspiel* (Berlin: Hochschule der Künste, 1996).

3 Exhibition, Kunst-Werke Berlin, October 14—November 19, 1995.

he had developed in his books *De la grammatologie* and *Ecriture et différence* in the late 1960s.[4]

It was the beginning of a protracted, if at times intermittent interaction. However, since our first encounter, we did not lose track of each other. In the summer 2000, I spent a guest semester at ETH's Collegium Helveticum in Zurich's old Federal Observatory, which had been built by Gottfried Semper for the astronomer Rudolf Wolf. On this occasion, Hannes Rickli, who taught at Zurich University of the Arts, and Jörg Huber, then head of its theory department, invited me over to a seminar with a bunch of students. It widened to a memorable mammoth session on the concept of "trace," one of the central categories of Derrida's *Grammatology*.

When Rickli launched his project, *Surplus. Videograms of Experimentation* in 2007, which was funded by the Swiss National Science Foundation,[5] a continuous exchange began to develop. On the initiative of the artist, it brought together, in various constellations, his co-workers, laboratory scientists, art historians and historians of the life sciences interested in scientific practice, as well as sociologists and philosophers of science. Rickli had already established contacts to a number of biological laboratories, among them to Hans Hofmann, a

4 Jacques Derrida, *Of Grammatology*, trans. Gayatri Chakravorty Spivak (Baltimore: Johns Hopkins University Press, 1976, revised edition 1997). The book had been translated by Hanns Zischler and myself into German as *Grammatologie* (Frankfurt am Main: Suhrkamp, 1974) in the early 1970s; Jacques Derrida, *Writing and Difference*, trans. Allan Bass (Chicago: The University of Chicago Press, 1978).

5 Research project funded by the Swiss National Science Foundation SNSF/DORE at the Institute for Contemporary Art Research of the Zurich University of the Arts, 2007-2009.

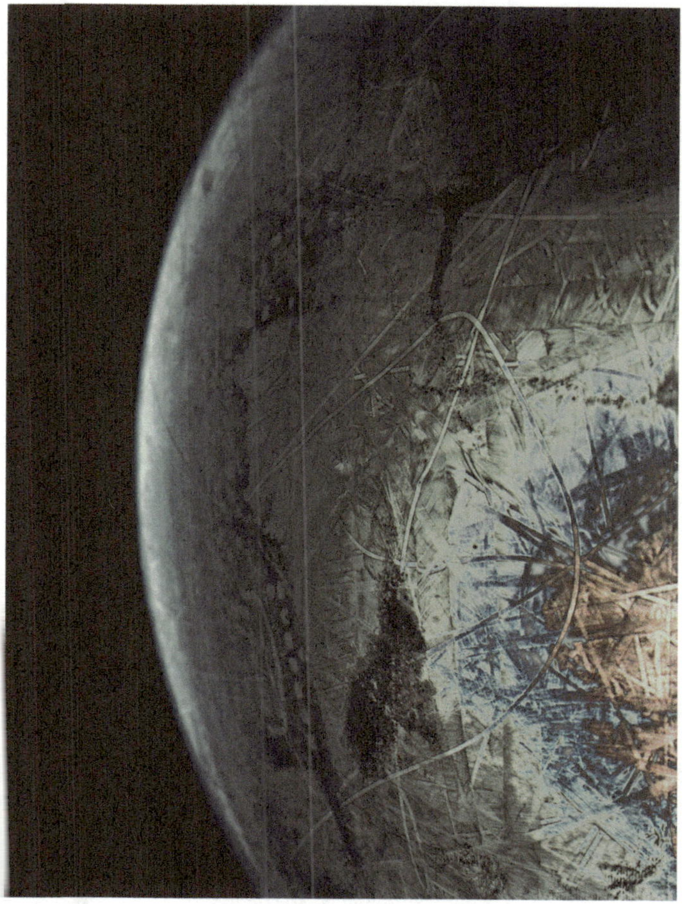

Fig. 5: Hannes Rickli, *Spurenkugel*.

geneticist working on the behavior of insects and cichlids, first at the University of Leipzig, and later at the University of Austin, Texas; to Steven Fry at the University of Zurich, who was investigating how the fruit fly *Drosophila melanogaster* controls its flight; and to Philipp Fischer from the University of Constance, who back then studied the acoustic communication behavior of burbots in Lake Constance, and later continued his studies on gurnards at the Alfred Wegener Institute on Helgoland and in Bremerhaven. The group met at regular intervals, usually once yearly for a couple of days at one of the participating research facilities.

At that time, Rickli had become more broadly interested in the manipulations that scientists developed in their laboratories in the course of interacting with the objects of their scientific interest, as well as the ways and means by which they recorded and stored their data streams. He followed them closely with his video camera and also used bits and pieces of the experimental data generated by the scientists while at work in their labs, as source materials for videograms. They not only traced the movements and sounds of the research objects themselves in their laboratory environment, but also the gestures of the researchers who endeavored to understand their animals' behavior.[6]

6 Hannes Rickli (ed.), *Videogramme. Die Bildwelten biologischer Experimentalsysteme als Kunst- und Theorieobjekt/Videograms. The Pictorial Worlds of Biological Experimentation as an Object of Art and Theory*. Schriftenreihe des Instituts für Gegenwartskünste, vol. 6 (Zürich: Scheidegger & Spiess, 2011). The texts were written by Michael Guggenheim, Vinzenz Hediger, Christoph Hoffmann, Nicola Müllerschön, Hannes Rickli and Yvonne Zimmermann. The publication was prefaced by Christoph Schenker. It accompanied the exhibition "Hannes Rickli: Videogramme" at Zurich's Helmhaus art space

Surplus (*Überschuss*) had become the keyword. The laboratories offered streams of data that the scientists filtered, cleaned and processed before condensing them into their scientific publications. The great majority of them, however, remained in data storages. What were remnants and rejects for the scientists became an ideal working material for the artist. What the scientists saw as redundancy, contamination, and outliers, in short, unavoidable noise, became an object of fascination for the artist: the data stream, the primary reification of the experimentally generated traces.

Up to that point, Rickli's attention had focused on the abundance, if not exuberance of the generation of traces in the graphematic space of experimentation, their representation as a stored data stream, and the parallelization of streams of images and streams of sound. Over the course of time, and as a result of his intense interaction with Philipp Fischer's efforts to construct an apparatus for following underwater life in the arctic region of Spitzbergen, as well as the vicissitudes involved in running the instrument at the bottom of the sea, his interest began to shift once again. More and more, he became aware of—and fascinated by—the traces the media of registration and representation themselves contributed to the recording process, and with which they unavoidably interfered. Stated otherwise, his interest shifted from the surplus centered in and around the epistemic object to one emerging from the analog and digital machinery necessary to get access at it. The new project, again funded by the Swiss National Research Foundation, was accordingly called *Computer Signals. Art and Biology*

September 6—October 25, 2009.

in the Age of their Digital Experimentation.[7] Now, the materiality of the digital shifted into the foreground and increasingly began to determine the artist's explorations. A first expression of this interest was the combined video and sound installation titled *Fischen lauschen* in the project space of the Schering Stiftung in Berlin Unter den Linden in 2013.[8] The exhibition combined video images and live transmissions from the underwater camera in Spitzbergen with sounds from hydrophones that the artist had placed inside and on the camera itself. They recorded the external and internal soundscape in and around the measuring apparatus at the bottom of the Arctic Sea.

Computer Signals continued into a second project phase (2017–2021). Together with a doctoral student, Valentina Vuksic, Rickli began to explore the multi-layered soundscape of the extended infrastructure of Hans Hofmann's behavioral genetics laboratory at the University of Texas in Austin. A sound panorama leading all the way from the basement of the University's supercomputer and its gigantic cooling system into the oilfields of the university, the primary source of its energy, exposed the infrastructure needed to keep the electronic facilities of the laboratory running. Without these energy-guzzling digital machines, activities such as, for instance, the genome-based behavioral research questions pursued there by Hans Hofmann would simply be inconceivable today. In the spring of 2020, the exhibition *Afrikanischer Buntbarsch #3, Sound-*

7 Research project funded by the Swiss National Science Foundation SNSF at the Institute for Contemporary Art Research of the Zurich University of the Arts, 2012–2015.

8 Exhibition „Fischen lauschen. Beginn einer Datenübertragung aus der Arktischen See." Schering Stiftung, Project Space, Unter den Linden 32–34, 10117 Berlin, January 25—March 23, 2013.

scape Texas in Zurich's Kunstraum Walcheturm conveyed an impression of the analog and digital sound-worlds that surround today's scientific research facilities.[9] An installation such as this captures visitors' eyes and ears, evoking the image of an underworld: that of the huge infrastructure of today's sciences, which usually escapes our perception. Its neglect decisively shapes the public image of the sciences with their digital media today.

In the context of the exhibition, a meeting was held on *Datennaturen/Natures of Data* to mark the publication of a book bearing the same title.[10] Discussions about the nature of data had come up again and again in the group's regular meetings accompanying Hannes Rickli's projects. At the beginning of September 2016, the group met for a two-day retreat on the Rigi Kulm, high above Lake Lucerne, and intensively discussed questions surrounding the nature of scientific data and their uses. This time, the conversation was recorded, transcribed and reworked, slowly evolving into a compact book manuscript that could be presented in print in the course of the exhibition.

I think that my own epistemological reflections about the concept of data, their place and function in scientific research have been shaped and sharpened to a considerable degree by these conversations. The chapters I devoted to the concepts of trace, data, and models in my recent book could not have

9 Exhibition at Kunstraum Walcheturm, Kanonengasse 20, 8004 Zürich, February 13—March 11, 2020.

10 Philipp Fischer, Gabriele Gramelsberger, Christoph Hoffmann, Hans Hofmann, Hans-Jörg Rheinberger and Hannes Rickli, *Datennaturen. Ein Gespräch zwischen Biologie, Kunst, Wissenschaftstheorie und –geschichte/Natures of Data. A Discussion between Biology, History and Philosophy of Science and Art* (Zurich and Berlin: Diaphanes, 2020).

been written without this background.[11] Let me summarize my thoughts about data in a nutshell at the end of this tour through an artistic research process that developed and extended over a period of no less than twenty-five years. To begin with, we have to distinguish between two spaces in which empirical research processes unfold. The first of these spaces can be called the experimental, or graphematic, space. It is defined by the constellation of a scientific object and the research technologies with which it is brought to interact. The interaction results in traces of sorts, indices of the phenomena under consideration. Since they are generally volatile in nature, researchers who want to work with these traces will have to stabilize them, to make them durable in one form or another. This second process presupposes a transition, or better, a transposition from the space of the experiment to the space of representation, and with that, from traces to data in the data space. Data are thus not the primary products of scientific activity; rather, they are the result of a transformation. It is a transformation of an ambiguous nature. On the one hand, the originary traces resulting from the experimental interaction are reified and thus stripped of part of their possible signification. On the other hand, the transposition into the data space opens a new field of working with these data which involves adding them up, subtracting them, juxtaposing them, ordering them according to a multitude of different ordering principles, and many more operations that characterize work in the data space. One of the most important operations in this space is the condensation of data into models. Models in turn imply questions that can be fed

11 Rheinberger, *Split and Splice*, in particular Chapters 1–3.

back into the process of experimentation and, accordingly, lead to the creation of further traces and data.

As we can see, a data space of sorts has accompanied empirical research from the very beginning, if only restricted to pencil and paper. It has, however, experienced an unprecedented expansion with the advent of the digital computer with its options of electronic data storage and processing on which almost all sciences depend today to a greater or lesser degree.

The massive development of suitable data repositories able to store, annotate, and process increasingly large amounts of data represents a technical challenge in terms of feeding data from different contexts into common repositories as well as creating suitable ontologies and toolkits for finding and retrieving the data sets relevant for a particular research question. Yet at the same time it is accompanied by the emergence of new epistemological provocations.[12] In addition, it is obvious that the massive expansion of electronic data opens up new possibilities for the establishment of virtual experimental environments, and thus for exploratory spaces in which *in silico* experiments and simulations can be designed and performed.[13] One example of such an experimental use of data bases presented by Hans Hofmann was discussed extensively in the conversation that led to the book described above.[14] If an epistemology oriented toward an understanding of scientific practice in general and experimentation in particular finds itself faced

12 Gabriele Gramelsberger, *From Science to Computational Sciences. Studies in the History of Computing and its Influence on Today's Sciences* (Chicago: The University of Chicago Press, 2015); Sabina Leonelli, *Data-Centric Biology. A Philosophical Study* (Chicago: The University of Chicago Press, 2016).

13 Franck Varenne, *From Models to Simulations* (London: Routledge, 2019).

14 Fischer et al., *Natures of Data*, Section "In silico."

with a challenge today, it is to achieve a better understanding of the nature and conditions of such digital experiments, and to relate them to analogous hard and soft, dry and wet experimentation that will no doubt continue to be a touchstone for in silico explorations. Today, however, the epistemological examination of the digital practices of the contemporary sciences is still far from achieving this goal.

Emerging out of the Procedure: Hanni Schierscher

Sans titre

It was in 2013, at an exhibition of Kunstverein Schichtwechsel under the roof of St. Florinsgasse 11 in Vaduz, Liechtenstein that I met Hanni Schierscher for the first time. A brochure published in connection with the exhibit combined Schierscher's paper works with one of my texts on experimentation.[1] The production team of the brochure had been of the opinion that the text and the images would match each other well. The images shown in the exhibition were titled "Without Title."

There was one hint, however. The word "Iris" was added in brackets after the title. The blue stains on paper were iridescent toward violet and brownish. They appeared to diffluence from the center to the periphery where they acquired sharper contours and density, as if frozen in their erratic microstructure. At first glance, they looked like pupils surrounded by an irregular iris.

Iris. The word leads us on another track. We imagine light winds blowing over early summer marshlands, spotted with blossoming *Iris sibirica*, forming a sea of pigments from white to yellow to the full scale of shades of blue. Each of the spots

1 Hanni Schierscher, *Without Title*—Hans-Jörg Rheinberger, *One Does Not Exactly Know What One Does Not Know. On the Art of Exploring the Unknown.* Publication Series "Positions & Discourses" (Schaan: Schichtwechsel/Liechtensteiner Kunstverein, 2012).

on the absorbent paper that Hanni Schierscher uses for their work repeats this up and down *en miniature*, condenses it, lets it dissolve. The moist paper has soaked up the pigments of the iris blossoms and redistributed them in another space, changing their contours beyond recognition and yet recalling them in their play of colors.

Let us not forget, amongst all that colorfulness, the part of the absorbent paper and its structure. The shapes of the colored spots are due to its micellar micro-composition and, consequently, differential humidification. None of the spots resembles the next. A new universe of distributions on a small scale arises, a pigmented microcosm that appears to push forward everywhere from the flat surface into three-dimensionality, from where it actually was derived. Once the beginning of the trace is set, it gains high-handedness. It takes over and becomes an actor in the creative process.

Rêves d'encre—Ink Dreams

From the middle of the 1920s, José Corticchiato from Vitry-sur-Seine, known as Corti, became notorious for his editions of the writings of dadaists and surrealists in Paris. His bookstore in the Latin Quarter at No. 11 rue de Médicis was legendary. He was an *homme des lettres* who spent his hours of leisure playing with ink, the liquid from which literature once emerged. In 1945, on the instigation of Gaston Bachelard, whom he had shown some of his images in the back office of his shop, he published a number of those "ink dreams" in his own publishing house. He called them "discovered images"—an indication of the auto-activity of the black essence. One of the short texts that accompanied the bundle of images was written by Bachelard himself. Corti had not only published his essay on *Lautréamont*,[2] but also his two reveries *L'Eau et les rêves* and *L'Air et les songes*.[3] Corti's ink images, which evoke echoes of bizarre wave formations, beach figurations, coral reefs and overgrown sea-beds, inspired Bachelard to his own "reverie on/of matter."[4] It begins as follows:

> "Because of its alchemical tincture, its color-giving life, the ink is able to create a universe, if only it finds its dreamer. The proof is found in this black album, in the moving contradiction between black and white. On twenty-four pages, José Corti renders back to the dreaming ink all their lost crystallizations. The chemist wanted to have it neutralized, the ink, dissolve it in its salts and sulfates, lightly bound, indifferent toward everything one writes with it. But if prior to any writing, prior to any effort of drawing an object, prior to any ambition to reveal itself as a sign, a great dreamer devotes himself to the intimate phantasmagories of a magical substance, if he listens to the confessions of the blot, then the ink begins to recite its poems, to register the forms of its long-lost crystals. For what has José Corti wanted to make? Only the ink can tell, for these *ink-dreams* are in fact the dreams *of* the ink. José Corti has rendered himself to the will of the black fluid; on the bottom of its will, he has sensed that nostalgia of iron and alum, which want to spread out, to fight

2 Gaston Bachelard, *Lautréamont* (Paris: Librairie José Corti, 1939).

3 Gaston Bachelard, *L'Eau et les rêves. Essai sur l'imagination de la matière* (Paris: Librairie José Corti, 1942); Gaston Bachelard, *L'Air et les songes. Essai sur l'imagination du movement* (Paris: Librairie José Corti, 1943).

4 Gaston Bachelard, "Une rêverie de la matière," in José Corti, *Rêves d'encre, vingt-cinq images présentées par Paul Eluard, René Char, Julien Gracq et Gaston Bachelard* (Paris: Librairie José Corti, 1945), n.p.

> against each other, to combine, invigorate themselves, pass themselves along, bump into each other, aim to recreate themselves."[5]

Hanni Schierscher, too, wants to trace the jostlings, the expansions, the convulsions and precipitations of ink and other dyes she applies to the large-format Japanese and India papers, allowing them to take their course, and finally bringing them to a halt. Not that she just lets things run free. Not at all. She sets precise initial conditions. The fibrillation of the paper, the mixture, viscosity, and liquidity of the pigments, the swelling state of the carrier, its inclination, the running times, everything is conditioned to contain the process. But then, once set, a plethora of interactions between paper and dye composition develops, between their respective local condensations and dilutions, and the whole game is no longer under the control of one's hand. A process is set in motion, and then one retreats and can't stop being astonished about where it leads to and what it suggests could be done next. Escalating and restricting movements become visible, horizons are formed, cumuli and veils interweave with each other, filaments undulate like algae in lightly moving water, ribbons and rims detach themselves and go wild, spots disappear, attractors suck up the surrounding substances.

In the course of these processes, patterns are created that no designer, no matter how perfect, no Laplacian ghost, no matter how competent, could ever have imagined. And yet, one does nothing else than to allow the attractions and repulsions of the pigment particles to act on one another, to leave them to

5 Bachelard, "Une rêverie de la matière," n.p. Translation by the present author.

the laws according to which they brace against each other and become entangled, spread out in fractal self-similarity and collapse again. Capillary ramifications arise, anastomoses along which precipitations and liquefactions happen.

From times immemorial, the *Arbor Dianae*, so beautifully described by Pierre Louis Moreau de Maupertuis in his *Vénus physique*,[6] had fascinated naturalists, since it so vividly illustrated the growth of crystals. Under appropriate conditions, one could even see the silver tree emerging from a solution of silver salt by adding a reductant. In Schierscher's creations, the attractions and repulsions of the pigments are complemented by the capillary forces of the medium: the papers she uses. At times, viewed from a somewhat greater distance, their large paper strips convey what appears to be contours similar to landscapes, sometimes silhouettes or bottom lines show up, or borders become crowded with threadlike, ramified filigree (Fig. 6).[7] In the event, not only the distributions of pigment, but also the fine structure and the imperfections of the paper achieve a visibility of their own. The paper, too, comes alive, acquiring breadth, height, and depth. The space of events that opens up here could not be expressed better than by Bachelard's words on viewing José Corti's ink dreams: "Out there is all the abundant wealth."[8] Or, as Maupertuis asserted when describing that "wondrous vegetation," the *Arbor Dianae*: human beings would have received their senses only to humil-

6 Pierre Louis Moreau de Maupertuis, *Vénus physique. Œuvres Vol. II* (Paderborn: Georg Olms Verlagsbuchhandlung, 1965).

7 Hanni Schierscher, *Innen und Außen*, ed. Axel Jablonski (Hohenems-Vaduz-München-Zürich: Bucher, 2020), 59.

8 Bachelard, "Une rêverie de la matière," n.p. Translation by the present author.

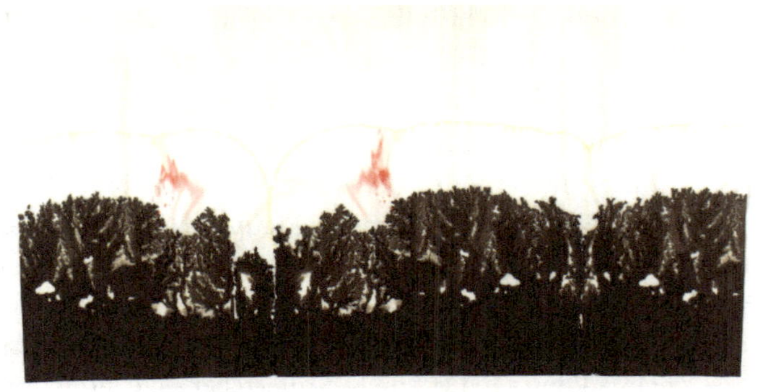

Abb. 6: Hanni Schierscher, *3C3A0905*.

iate their reason.[9] Just to note in passing, it is not by chance that Maupertuis placed the description of the silver tree at the very beginning of the chapter that deals with his conjectures about the formation of the fetus, that paragon of a miracle of acquiring shape in nature.

Chromatography—The Trail of Color

It is only since around the middle of the twentieth century that the molecular sciences, above all biochemistry, started making use of the differential capillary absorption capacity of paper in order to separate tiny quantities of larger and smaller molecules from each other. Its form-giving potential, however, in contrast to its analytical capacities, was discussed and explored already much earlier. One of its pioneers was Friedlieb Ferdinand

9 Maupertuis, *Vénus physique*, 86–87. Translation by the present author.

Runge, a chemist from Breslau, later Oranienburg, who specialized in the analysis of aniline dyes.[10] The principle of paper chromatography is comparatively simple: A few microliters of a mixture of molecules are spotted on strong, absorbent paper. Then the paper is put vertically into a tub filled with a solution in which the molecules can dissolve. Slowly, the liquid front is being lifted by the capillary forces of the paper. The molecules begin to move upward with it, becoming separated from each other according to their size—smaller ones move faster, larger ones move upward more slowly. In the case of pigments, they become visible as colored spots. Otherwise, they can be made visible by an appropriate color reaction after the process has been completed. Hence the name of the procedure: chromatography. The intensity of the coloration of the different spots can be taken as a measure for the quantity of respective components of the molecular mixture. With the help of chromatography, much smaller amounts of substances can be quantified than with the traditional analytical micro-determinations. To give just one example: around 1950, Erwin Chargaff and his co-workers at Columbia University in New York succeeded not only in separating the four different bases of deoxyribonucleic acid (DNA) from each other, but also in determining their respective quantities.[11] The resulting complementarity of two

10 Friedlieb Ferdinand Runge, *Zur Farben-Chemie: Musterbilder für Freunde des Schönen und zum Gebrauch für Zeichner, Maler, Verzierer und Zeugdrucker* (Berlin: Mittler, 1850); Friedlieb Ferdinand Runge, *Der Bildungstrieb der Stoffe* (Berlin: Matthes & Seitz, 2014). First published in 1855. The artist Josef Schwaiger recently devoted an artist's book to Runge's work: Josef Schwaiger, *Runge Revisited* (2018–2020).

11 Erwin Chargaff, "Chemical specificity of nucleic acids and mechanism of their enzymatic degradation," *Experientia* 6(6) (1950): 201–209.

purine/pyrimidine base pairs each became one of the keys for the subsequent detection of the double helix structure of DNA.

So far so good. I have, however, omitted an essential point without which the procedure could not be used as an analytic biochemical tool. And it is this point that distinguishes chromatography from the ink and color creations of Hanni Schierscher. If the procedure is to be used as an analytical one, everything depends on the regular shape and average size of the capillary tissue and cavities of the paper. The paper has to be homogenous with respect to these parameters. This, however, is never the case for handmade India or Japanese papers. On the contrary, the latter are even distinguished by the micro-irregularity inherent in their production. And it is this micro-irregularity that makes possible the interplay of colors and forms shown on Hanni Schierscher's large paper surfaces. Only in this way can the paper be transformed into a landscape. Landscapes are characterized by the fact that they are subject to determinable form-giving forces and the repetitions of fractal self-similarity that are empowered by these forces but, at the same time, are open to the vicissitudes and caprices of the aleatoric, the unprecedented. Only the cooperation of both principles results in the figurations which we perceive as unique, yet behind which we assume certain formative forces. For without the latter, we would only perceive a more or less chaotic muddle. As Julien Gracq remarked with respect to José Corti's ink dreams: "The inexhaustible source of chance is accompanied by a barely explicable sense of necessity."[12]

12 Julien Gracq, "Eclosion de la pierre," in José Corti, *Rêves d'encre*, vingt-cinq images présentées par Paul Eluard, René Char, Julien Gracq and Gaston Bachelard (Paris: Librairie José Corti, 1945), n.p. Translated by the present author.

Nature Printing—Once Again: Iris

Since the Early Modern era, naturalists, in particular botanists, but also artists, have experimented with nature printing.[13] In its simplest and original form, the procedure consists in pressing plants, or parts of them, such as flowers or leaves with marked veins, on absorbent paper. The resulting print ideally receives pigments of the respective plant parts and reproduces their contours and grain. It can be assumed that the beginnings of the technique go back to accidental observations accompanying the preparation of plants for Early Modern herbaria. In the course of the centuries, the technique underwent multiple modifications and, by way of transfer printing, also became available for larger numbers of copies. This is not, however, the place for narrating that history. It is useful here for a better understanding of our artist's activity. As far as nature printing is concerned, fleeting forms are contraindicated. The print aims at rendering the contours of the plant with utmost precision and sharpness. This is, in fact, the hallmark and key to the fascination of this form of print: the creation of a *sur-reality*. One should be able to perceive the contours with a sharpness that is not normally perceived when looking at a plant itself. Like a mirror image, its relevant parts should appear exactly at the place and in the dimensions that the prototype exhibits.

13 See, e.g., Johann Beckmann, *Beyträge zur Geschichte der Erfindungen*, Band 5, erstes Stück (Leipzig: Kummer, 1800), contains a chapter on nature printing; Armin Geus (ed.), *Natur im Druck. Eine Ausstellung zur Geschichte und Technik des Naturselbstdrucks*, with contributions by Armin Geus, Peter N. Heilmann and Stephan Oettermann (Marburg an der Lahn: Basilisken-Presse, 1995). Roderick Cave, *Impressions of Nature: A History of Nature Printing* (London: British Library Publishing, 2009).

The pigments of the original should be able to penetrate into the paper but not spread out. In this case the paper should be kept dry; its humidification should only result from the bits of sap that are released from the plant's cells when pressed.

In contrast, Hanni Schierscher's irises flow. Although they also result from a direct contact of the flowers with the paper, here, the contact sets different things in motion. The colors are allowed to mix, they can form gradients, they spread from their point of origin, irregularly and in all directions. Thus, what results is the exact opposite of a depiction. An autonomous process is set in motion, in which the pigmented materials, yet most of all the consistency of the paper, its imponderabilities, and the humidity regimen play the decisive role. Iridescence, movement itself becomes predominant. We are no longer referred to something else, to a nature out there that would have to be fixed and with which the result could be compared, even if figurations sometimes show up that lend themselves to comparison. In doing so, however, they demonstrate the precariousness of any such attempt. In these cases, too we are invited to follow nothing but the movements imprinted on the paper, to trace their intrinsic necessities, their caprices and, above all, to let ourselves be surprised by their micro-topic characteristics. For, as we know, there is nothing involved that could aid and abet mimesis. No camera is in play there and no eye. Nature's brush itself is in charge. Consequently, the paper surface itself becomes a space of experience and, paradoxically, it expands by focusing attention on the minute, the tiny detail. Such is the peculiar nature of these large, sweeping papers that refuse to be mounted. We could also say that they create their boundaries inwardly, and in order to be able to do so, one must let them flap in the wind.

Experimentation

The exploratory, searching experimentation of the scientist knows of an immersion in detail and an adhesion to the phenomena at stake that can be compared to that of the artist. Its operative motto is: "See what happens if …" One does not, however, merely experiment into the blue. There is a presupposition to such attempts at "seeing if" that at first glance might seem paradoxical—namely, an intimate familiarity with the material. Scientists who wish to productively experiment in the field in which they move and to enter uncharted territory have no choice but to immerse themselves in the details of the objects under investigation as well as the tools and procedures with which to approach them. Otherwise, they will not be able to respond to the signals emitted by the objects when brought into interaction with each other. Both factors, materials and procedures, come with their own challenges. But they cannot be separated from each other and taken individually. Apparatus and object reciprocate. The knowledge effects, the epistemic events that emerge from the experiment, result out of the interaction between procedure and material, material and procedure. They are generated at their interface, this source of friction they present to each other: the sparks they emit, their sheet lightning.

An experiment needs preparation. Experimenters check the results the previous experiment produced and track down inconsistencies. Is there something to be clarified? What kind of accent should be set? Experimenters calculate. They examine connections, mix reagents, prepare components afresh, tweak the arrangement. They may decide to vary one parameter here or add a control there. But when all these preliminaries are set, experimenters take a step back, abscond from the experiment, keep their distance and turn into spectators. Then, the fight of the elements against each other begins, the battle of the materials that have been positioned, the boundary conditions that have been set and in which they now have to move or to which they will remain indifferent. The process unfolds, leaving its traces which have to be trapped in order to remain available for the experimenters, since these traces are usually volatile. Intervening and retreating thus condition each other and alternate. And as an experimenter, one understands: once one has embarked on such a path of iteration, then one has made decisions with respect to one's range of operations for months, sometimes years, occasionally decades. One passes through a trajectory until a point is reached at which the range of variations appears to be exhausted and it is time for a new experimental setup.

With her papers, pigments and tissues, Hanni Schierscher as well engages in sounding out such spaces of experimentation. Naturally, that captivates the imagination of a former scientist. The works collected in the book for which this little essay was originally written, and one of which is shown in figure 6, revolve around that gesture of the experimental,[14] at times more dominated by the papers used, at times by the pigments. But they always listen in to the intimate life of the materials.

14 Schierscher, *Innen und Außen.*

Questions Arising from Matter: Katrin von Lehmann

> "Black flowers bloom in matter's darkness.
> They already possess a velvety touch,
> a formula for perfume."[1]

When, after years of studying biology, driven by the *big* questions of life and the living—such as: is there a general definition of life? What are the driving forces of evolution? What are species and how are they formed? What is a gene? How much genetics and how much environment are there in a human being?—one enters a lab and has to get familiar with the *small* questions, the microcosm of experimentation, Dante's *Inferno* with its inscription on the Gate of Hell readily comes to mind: "Abandon every hope, who enter here!"[2] In science shop talk, it is not unlikely that one will hear the laboratory director say: 'To start with, forget everything you've ever learned!' These are metaphors for a radical change of regime and direction. From now on, questions will no longer arise from current discourse, but from the matters under experiment and the approach chosen to tackle them. And the approach in turn is both enabled and limited by the respective options and constraints of the laboratory setting with its objects under investigation.

1 Bachelard, *Water and Dreams*, 2.

2 "Lasciate ogne speranza, voi ch'intrate!" Dante Alighieri, *Divine Comedy. Inferno, Purgatorio, Paradiso*, trans. Allen Mandelbaum, illustr. Barry Moser (Berkeley: University of California Press, 1980).

Claude Bernard, the great nineteenth-century French physiologist and one of the founders of experimental physiology, once described the laboratory as a "ghastly kitchen."[3] Yet once one has become accustomed to that "kitchen" through which one has to pass in order to attain knowledge about metabolic processes so far uncharted, the special appeal of an exploratory journey into the microcosm of experimentation begins to unfold. And it is this appeal that can keep an experimental researcher alert and dedicated to the phenomena under scrutiny for years, if not decades, smell and hazard notwithstanding. How can such a protracted process be described? To put it briefly: we can look at it as a game of repetition and difference, but one with epistemic, at times dramatic consequences. Leaving room for the contingency of the materials at hand is a sort of gamble. A material process is set in motion and, with time, may begin to develop a life of its own and lead in unforeseen directions. To put it paradoxically: the unexpected occurs in repetition. What might initially have caught attention and been qualified as an impurity can turn into a storm, capturing the entire process and steering it in new directions. It is crucial to realize that the development of a research trajectory is *at* hand, but not *in* our hand. Iteration is a proven method to access unchartered territory.

This is exactly what Katrin von Lehmann has been experiencing in her project "Empty Space of the Unknown/Nothing is Right Now," which she has been pursuing over many years.[4]

3 Claude Bernard, *Introduction to the Study of Experimental Medicine,* trans. Henry Copley Greene (New York: Dover Publications, 1957), 15; see also Anita Guerrini, "The ghastly kitchen," *History of Science* 54 (2016): 71–97.

4 The results of the project are presented in the volume: Katrin von Lehmann—*textura performativa* 5 (Berlin: Distanz Verlag, 2021).

Initially, as she remarks in conversation, she was inspired by a gesture that can be considered as fundamental not only to the natural sciences, but for research processes more widely, insofar as they are aimed at tracking down the unknown as well as the unseen: to be pursuing something that one is not able to delineate clearly at the outset. And yet the unexpected can only occur against the backdrop of a horizon of expectation, however precarious it may be. If taken by surprise, however, the entire process can be affected, even jeopardized—and the puzzle will have to start anew. Katrin von Lehmann imbues her drawing practices with a set of minimal rules, such as the number of pencils and their colors to be used, that they should be moved over the paper with right and left hand in alternation, and so on. These rules define a general framework, but give enough leeway for coincidences and chance encounters of the lines their pencils draw as they move across the paper and reveal unintended constellations. Everything depends on her readiness to perceive these moments and turn them into a point of departure for new moves. The outcome of this process is a series of large-format filigree drawings on paper, one of which is shown in the following figure (Fig. 7).[5]

What follows next is a second work phase marked by a different set of options for what can be done with a sheet full of colored pencil traces: it can be hung, glued, and mounted. But it can also be twisted in space and become a three-dimensional creation. The paper can be folded, layered, and stacked. It can be punched, pierced, and perforated. These processes can all be used to dive deeper into a drawing's unexhausted potentials. Here, a second level of contingency comes into play, which is

5 Lehmann, *textura performativa* 5, 102.

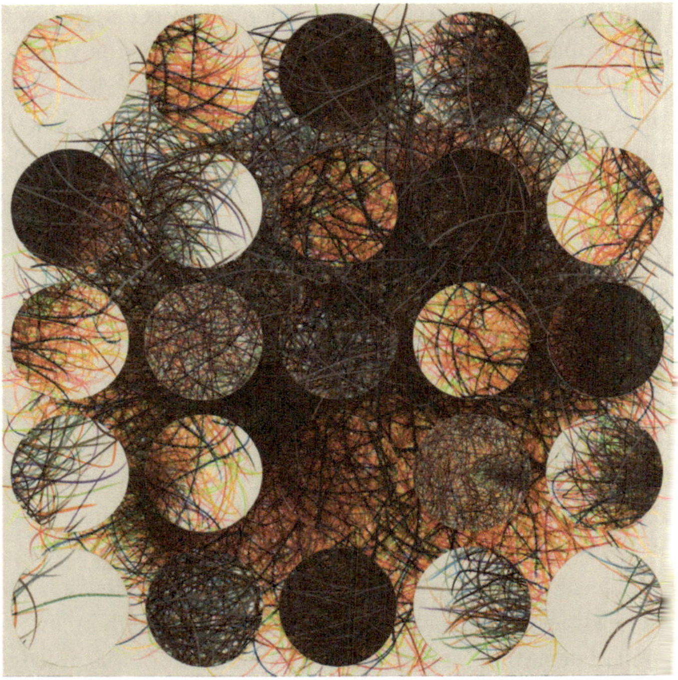

Katrin von Lehmann, *Proxy 8-07*.

independent from the preceding act of drawing and can once again lead to astonishing twists. These activities are configured by a further set of rules that overwrite the previous ones for drawing. The punched-out and left-over chads can be collected and gathered for display in receptacles to form additional new, iridescent figurations. Their combinations, too, obey forces that can be modulated, but not precisely directed, by shaking the containers.

Once set in motion, one can get lost in that game of chance and necessity. One can become immersed in the ramifications of the material. The paper works of Katrin von Lehmann are deeply tainted by such immersion. The moves that result from such a process can rightly be compared to an experiment. The skill consists in configuring experimentation as an ongoing trajectory in which the possibility of handing over control to the material becomes a creative force. Branches sprout, unexpected events inflect the direction in which they move. The experimenter listens to the work in progress and turns into an echo chamber by picking up and amplifying what might first have appeared as almost imperceptible, even completely impossible altogether, without exposure to the aleatoric forces of a protracted itinerary.

What can be said about scientific experimentation finds its equivalent in Katrin von Lehmann's artistic treatment of her papers. If, for instance, she punches holes in her drawings, she may reach a critical threshold beyond which the paper begins to bend and to take on three-dimensional outlines. The artist does not impose any preconceived idea on the paper. She merely responds to the tensions that occur in the material from the process of punching. She reacts with circumspection to the unexpected.

And can we not say the same for the writing of poetry? As Gaston Bachelard once put it: "It is the pen which dreams!"[6] And on another occasion, he added with respect to the writer: "What he had intended to say is so quickly replaced by what he discovers himself writing that he feels clearly that the written

6 Gaston Bachelard, *The Poetics of Reverie. Childhood, Language, and the Cosmos*, trans. Daniel Russell (Boston: Beacon Press, 1969), 17.

language is creating its own universe."[7] There are no better words to describe a creative process in poetry, the arts, and the sciences alike in and on their respective materials, if each with their own requirements.

7 Gaston Bachelard, *Air and Dreams. An Essay on the Imagination of Movement*, trans. Edith R. Farrell and Fredrick Farrell (Dallas: The Dallas Institute of Humanities and Culture, 1983), 250.

ENCOUNTERS

On Hybrids
In Dialogue with Andreas Greiner[1]

Andreas Greiner: I met you in the summer of 2014, when we both gave presentations in the old Veterinary Anatomical Theater at the Humboldt University in Berlin. It was our first opportunity to talk about Science and Knowledge in Art, the topic of the meeting.[2] A year later, we met again during a symposium hosted by the Schering Stiftung on the occasion of an exhibition in their experimental space Unter den Linden.[3]

Hans-Jörg Rheinberger: Of course, I recall our memorable encounter in the spectacular Veterinary Anatomical Theater. And the conference on "Evolution in Man's Hands" was part of an exhibition by the artists Revital Cohen and Tuur Van Balen. If I remember correctly, I presented a concluding commentary on the whole day of the symposium. By the way: Did you see the exhibition?

Andreas Greiner: Yes.

1 The dialogue was recorded in the fall of 2015 and first published in Andreas Greiner, *Anatomy of a Fairy Tale,* ed. Stefan Vicedom (Wien: Verlag für moderne Kunst, 2016), 124–149.
2 Symposium "Interferenzen IV—Kunst und Wissen," June 12, 2014.
3 "Evolution in Menschenhand," Berlin-Brandenburg Academy of Science, March 13, 2015. The symposium accompanied the exhibition of Revital Cohen & Tuur Van Balen: "assemble|standard|minimal." The exhibition took place in the Project Space of the Schering Stiftung, Unter den Linden 32-34, 10117 Berlin, January 23—May 3, 2015.

Hans-Jörg Rheinberger: What did you think about it?

Andreas Greiner: I mostly recall the living exhibits: the albino goldfish without reproductive glands that could only survive for one generation. The London-based artists Revital Cohen & Tuur Van Balen had commissioned the fish from a Japanese research lab, referencing the 1000-year-old tradition of goldfish breeding in that country. The fish themselves are biofacts — living creatures (co-)created by humans. Their genetic material has been manipulated, rendering them colorless and sterile. In a time of industrially produced, genetically modified foodstuffs, and facing a simultaneous diminishment of "naturally" formed life forms, I find it important to raise the issue of the responsibility and consequences of such genetic knowledge applications, as well as the possibilities—and impossibilities—that come with it.

Hans-Jörg Rheinberger: The aquarium stood next to a reproduction machine: a 'model' reminding that these fish were 'produced' artificially.[4]

Andreas Greiner: I presume, a model crafted by the artists, not a machine for laboratory use. Like the fish themselves, it highlights the dissolving dichotomy between nature and technology. And the beginning of an era in which humans not only produce life on an industrial scale, but also shape it. There are plump chickens that develop so fast that they can be slaugh-

4 Nicole C. Karafyllis, "Das Wesen der Biofakte," in *Biofakte. Versuch über den Menschen zwischen Artefakt und Lebewesen*, ed. Nicole C. Karafyllis, 1–16 (Paderborn: Mentis Verlag, 2004).

tered already after a month or so. They are custom hybrids, perhaps with a genetically engineered background as well. If you cross these first-generation meat hybrids, their properties split once again. Genetic copy protection, so to speak.

Hans-Jörg Rheinberger: We are dealing here with a biological phenomenon that is referred to as heterosis effect.[5] If you cross two pure-bred strains of a species, their genetically determined traits are combined. A new genetic makeup is configured. Often — not always — these first-generation hybrids are particularly luxuriating individuals. However, if they, in turn, interbreed, their genetic makeup splits again in the offspring. Breeders and the companies behind them know how to exploit this phenomenon. Think of Monsanto's hybrid corn. Seeds must be purchased anew for each season. You cannot harvest the corn kernels from your own field and then use them again as seed.

Andreas Greiner: Considering the complexity of procedures like this one, it is astonishing that meat consumption is so cheap in our day and age. Absurdly, the situation has flipped in our saturated societies: Wealth once used to be measured by the size of your Sunday roast; today it is a meat-free lifestyle that places you among the hip elite. But those who cannot afford ethically sound organic meat or vegan food will continue to buy cheap chicken breasts from Lidl and Netto or grab a kebab. Sadly, we

5 Plant hybridists had become aware of this phenomenon already in the 18. century. Compare Joseph Gottlieb Kölreuter, *Vorläufige Nachricht von einiger das Geschlecht der Pflanzen betreffenden Versuchen und Beobachtungen nebst Fortsetzungen 1, 2 und 3 (1761–1766)*, ed. Wilhelm Pfeffer (Leipzig: Engelmann, 1893).

often forget that these products are actually animal stuff. We're unfortunately losing touch with the origin of our food.

Hans-Jörg Rheinberger: The way the exhibition was set up, I felt something was lacking. Both the epistemic and the ethical aspects remained in the background. I have seen big labs with scientists working on fish. Geneticists usually manipulate little zebra fish, which are quite translucent. I once visited a huge hall with hundreds, maybe even thousands, of small cubes filled with water and stapled up on one another. They were all replete with zebra fish mutants, some of which couldn't swim any longer as they usually did. They tumbled around because they had lost their sense of direction. What became of all those zebra fish? Scientific conclusions were reached with their help; thousands of fish mutants were 'produced,' some only half-alive, others which didn't develop beyond a certain stage. The albinos in the exhibition, in contrast, swam around quite happily ... They gave a completely different impression ...

Andreas Greiner: We could see it also the other way around. In contrast to the conditions in huge labs you just described, the fish in the exhibition were carefully tended by two assistants—as far as I heard. On the one hand, we have animals as an anonymous mass; on the other hand, we witness intensive care for a single creature. The white cube makes the fish unique by defining it as a living artwork, rather than a tool for acquiring scientific knowledge.

Hans-Jörg Rheinberger: You are right. It evokes a need for debate. Seen this way, the exhibition fulfilled its purpose.

The Art of Knowledge

Andreas Greiner: I spoke with Stefan Vicedom, the editor of the present publication,[6] about the true nature of the interactions between scientists and artists: do they mutually create added value for both sides? He answered that certain conceptual systems — such as Niklas Luhmann's systems theory — tend to preclude such interactions on principle.[7] What do you think?

Hans-Jörg Rheinberger: Luhmann's basic assumption is that our modern society is divided into subsystems that each obey their own internal logic. We have a legal system, an economic system, a fact-oriented scientific system, and we have the arts. In their developed forms, these systems more or less exclude each other. Surprisingly, we can perhaps look at Bruno Latour's *Enquête sur les modes d'existence* as a somewhat softened version of such a theory. Although he thinks less in structures and more in terms of performance and recruiting resources, he eloquently defends the view that each of these modes, science, art, religion, economy, politics, law, fiction, and so on, have their own truth—perhaps better: authenticity—criteria, often perverted, but never 'outmoded,' as one could say.[8] At the beginning of the second half of the twentieth century there was a big debate about what became known as the 'two cultures divide' within academia, thus within the scientific realm itself.

6 Greiner, *Anatomy of a Fairy Tale.*

7 Niklas Luhmann, *Art as a Social System*, trans. Eva M. Knodt (Stanford: Stanford University Press, 2000).

8 Bruno Latour, *An Inquiry into Modes of Existence. An Anthropology of the Moderns*, trans. Catherine Porter (Cambridge MA: Harvard University Press, 2013).

On the one side, there are the humanities at large, on the other side, the natural and the technical sciences. They appeared to have grown so far apart from each other that representatives of the two camps were no longer able to talk meaningfully with each other and understand one another.[9]

Andreas Greiner: With regard to your own biography, this would mean that you no longer understand yourself! You have a research background in molecular biology, and today you are working in the field of the humanities as a historian of science.

Hans-Jörg Rheinberger: Exactly. And that's why I am skeptical about this kind of systems theory. Luhmann is a brilliant theoretical sociologist, no question. Boundaries exist, for sure, but they are permeable. Differentiation processes do occur — we encounter them daily in their form as social institutions, and discourses going on within them are not always immediately transparent to everyone; varying competencies have indeed evolved accordingly. In a recent debate in the field of Science and Technology Studies, two kinds of competencies were distinguished: Harry Collins and Robert Evans differentiate between what they call "interactional" and "contributory expertise."[10] If I have been trained and am working in one specific area, I will certainly be able to make myself acquainted with another area, so that I will be able to communicate with someone from that field. This means that first, I can "interact"

9 Charles Percy Snow, *The Two Cultures and the Scientific Revolution* (Cambridge, Cambridge University Press, 1959).

10 See Harry Collins and Robert Evans, *Rethinking Expertise* (Chicago: The University of Chicago Press, 2007).

with a person of that community, and second, that person will accept me as a conversation partner. This does not necessarily mean that I have the competence to become productively or creatively involved in that other field. In order to be able to do so, that is, to acquire "contributory expertise," I would need extended experience and the acquisition of practical competence, something you can achieve only by protracted participatory involvement.

The arts and the sciences may have grown apart to a considerable extent, at least institutionally, over the past centuries. But they have one thing in common: artists and scientists alike push forward into uncharted territory; their respective fields are geared towards bringing forth novelty. This is common ground enough for a kind of interaction and involvement on both sides that can even be rendered productive, not so much for taking over each other's work, respectively, but for being able to receive impulses and to learn from each other for one's own work.

Andreas Greiner: So, we have enough common ground to debate with and understand one another, but we don't have enough practical experience to swap roles at short notice. When we gave our talks at the Anatomical Theater, I was confronted with the notion of artistic knowledge for the first time. I have to admit that until then I had considered the question of knowledge a matter for science or philosophy. The idea of the artist as a producer of knowledge was thus new to me. An artist has, of course, a kind of personal archive of techniques, experiences and strategies acquired along his or her trajectory. But such a repository of individualized knowledge can hardly be seen as determined by rules or criteria. I imagine that scientific knowledge follows rules that distinguish themselves from those acquired by an individual artist.

Hans-Jörg Rheinberger: This image of scientific knowledge—rule-based, standardized, and impersonal—is one of the historical effects of art and science going their separate ways from the Early Modern period onward, although there have again and again been surprising overlaps and crossovers. Ultimately, a certain image of science emerged that now largely dominates the public debate, namely that scientific knowledge is given once and forever. This image of scientific knowledge is derived from the technical *products* into which it has become, at least partly, wired. However, if we look closer at how scientific knowledge is *acquired* in the course of research, a rather different image arises. We are used to deriving our image of the sciences from the way consolidated knowledge is presented more or less systematically in textbooks. And yet, not even textbooks are written forever, they have to be updated, they can become outmoded. My interest is not in the products and systematized scientific knowledge found in books. My interest is in the process of its production. I want to understand how it is acquired and what outlook we can gain from that perspective.

Andreas Greiner: Seen from that perspective, we can also say that what becomes visible as an artistic position, or an art movement, is in fact the result of an artistic research process. The role of novelty within the arts is probably due not least to the influence of art historiography on the artist. The accumulation of art-historic repositories and archives not only created an order of periods, styles and trends that acted as an incentive to leave repetition and replication behind in favor of looking out for alternatives. In contrast to the scientific textbook knowledge you mentioned, the canon of art historic knowledge is not determined by artistic practices alone but is also formed by art historians. The artist's research, on the other hand, is connected to his or her individual knowledge. Or so one could say, perhaps. However, I am not at all sure about the precise meanings of such a differentiation.

Hans-Jörg Rheinberger: I do not believe that the artistic realm is an exception in this respect. The self-image of scientists is also shaped by the cultural discourses about the sciences. What you call the individual knowledge of the artist is evidently knowledge that exists in a different 'aggregate state' in comparison to scientific textbook knowledge. But is it so completely different from the kind of embodied, mostly tacit knowledge that a laboratory scientist needs to acquire in order to be able to do her or his work successfully? Let us take knowledge as an umbrella term. Then we can distinguish between more theoretical, explicit, and more practical, implicit knowledge or better perhaps, reasoning, in a realm like that of the sciences. And we can distinguish between knowledges that exist and are being produced in other areas of cultural activity. There is poetic knowledge as well, and there is, of course, artistic knowledge. Let us take the example of medicine for a moment. Is medicine a science? Not necessarily, at least not if we see it as a curative activity focused on maintaining the health of a particular individual. This requires not only the routine application of scientific knowledge, often reified in medications and medical instruments; the vital, but tacit knowledge needed for dealing with the patient would leave a laboratory scientist looking completely lost. Or let us have a look at artisanal knowledge: here, unarticulated knowledge components might carry even more weight. I agree with you that non-articulated knowledge plays a large part in artistic work as well. By the way, artists are therefore sometimes surprised and, if somebody tells them what they are doing as seen by someone else's eyes, they acknowledge it … "I couldn't have said it in that way," you may hear then. But scientific research also is in need of a component of non-articulated knowledge. A laboratory scientist equally requires a type of material knowledge not gained from textbooks, knowledge that can only be conveyed by and become effective through plunging oneself into the work itself, and at times even getting lost in it. It may be, however, that to rely on someone else's knowledge in a collective, plays a greater role in most sciences than in most art forms, but certainly not in all, if we only think of cinema, for instance.

Andreas Greiner: It seems to me that collective work and trans-disciplinary collaboration is spreading ever more widely throughout the world of the arts today.

Hans-Jörg Rheinberger: But back to the laboratory bench and the atelier. I recently spoke with Michael Zimmermann, an art historian who was just in the process of writing a paper about Paul Cézanne and his way of still life painting.[11] Time and again, Cézanne painted still lifes with apples. Apples alone, a few apples, many apples, apples in company. He certainly went through hundreds of attempts — always with minimal

11 Michael F. Zimmermann, „Cézanne und die Zeit des Stilllebens," in *Allegorie. DFG-Symposion 2014*, ed. Ulla Haselstein (Berlin: DeGruyter, 2016), 303–332, 748–756.

alterations —, thereby exploring topological arrangements, color, haptic appeal, material radiance, and more. It remained a permanent challenge for him. Cézanne was certainly not interested in the final apple. The apple was an experimental object for him. That's how I see it.

Andreas Greiner: Transposed to science, this would mean that scientists are not interested in discovering the ultimate apple; they are focused on exploring its different aspects, and the ideas associated with trying to characterize them. We could also say: They are interested in an ongoing process. The fact that scientific knowledge can change may well disappoint tacit expectations. There is an attitude to expect definitive answers from the sciences that can explain and maybe even solve existing problems overnight. I sometimes get the impression that science is currently becoming a kind of substitute for religion. Whenever it comes to bigger, more ponderous questions, the sciences are expected to help.

Hans-Jörg Rheinberger: We have an appropriate term for that attitude in German for which there is no equivalent in English: *Wissenschaftsgläubigkeit*. And indeed, it is a legacy of the age-old battle between religion and science that had turned, by the end of the nineteenth century, in favor of the sciences. And in a way, the sciences managed to take over the image of infallibility, an image that many scientists themselves have often found pleasing and reassuring.

I, for my part, am not particularly happy with seeing the sciences as an answering machine, but rather as a means of generating questions. With every step and every answer, even if it should prove to be long-lasting—and there are long-lasting answers, for sure—new questions emerge. If a problem were solved definitely, if a task were completed and could be filed away without the emergence of a further incentive, that science would have come to an end. A science stays alive as long as every step brings new questions that are in turn in need of new decisions: What to do next? Which path to take? Every scientist, in the course of her or his trajectory, is confronted with such—smaller or bigger—decisions again and again.

Andreas Greiner: You referred to experimental systems as spaces for the emergence of new knowledge, and you shifted attention to the ongoing process of the production of knowledge and with that, into a practical space. In conducting such a system, knowledge does not come to rest in a resulting definitive model and the conclusions that can be drawn from it. The usefulness of the model consists in giving rise to new questions that can be addressed experimentally.

Hans-Jörg Rheinberger: In that sense, an experimental system can be seen a bit like an exteriorized question-generating machine. An experimental setup, of course, embodies knowledge. Knowledge is present in it in materialized form, not least in the form of measuring and processing instruments. A research instrument is, in fact, a reservoir of knowledge. That can go so far that the researcher may be able to operate it but is actually unable to fully explain it in its details. And yet it works.

Andreas Greiner: When the machine breaks, a technician is called!

Hans-Jörg Rheinberger: Knowledge has many different 'aggregate states' within a space for knowledge production. It is present in the experimental setup, which is assumed to be up to date. It is present in the instruments used, and it is present in the models that result from the experimental activity.

Andreas Greiner: Exciting. Might we find comparable systems in art?

Hans-Jörg Rheinberger: That would interest me too, but my experience with the arts is limited. That's why I would like to hear the artist speak on this question. I made the acquaintance of a copper engraver in Berlin, Heribert Bücking, who has been exploring his set-up and its options for decades.[12] It appears to be inexhaustible.

Andreas Greiner: I find it difficult to generalize. Perhaps one could say that the experimental system of a contemporary artist is roughly divided into a public sphere and a non-public sphere. The public sphere includes various types of exhibitions and the interplay between their art and society. The non-public sphere is everything else that belongs to the life of an artist, their so-called studio practice as well as their private life. The instruments of the experimental system of an artist are equally multi-layered. The most widely used are probably image-editing programs on the computer and the internet. After that, it

12 Heribert Bücking, *Kupferstiche und Zeichnungen 1994–1996* (Berlin: Studio Bildende Kunst Lichtenberg/Werkstattgalerie Bücking, 1996); Heribert Bücking, *Der lange Augenblick. Zeichnungen und Kupferstiche* (Berlin: Selbstverlag, 2011); Heribert Bücking, *Auf Bildsuche. Zeichnungen, Kupferstiche, Collagen, 1980–2020* (Berlin: Katalogdruck Berlin, 2020).

becomes hard to generalize: camera, tools, brushes, paints, a power drill, a welder, a piano, a micro-controller ... It depends. Most artists today think in terms of the exhibition space, which means that exhibition architecture and context play an important role. Others might work with the same equipment as biologists: laminar flow cabinets, incubators, autoclaves, Petri dishes. Or take Tino Sehgal, who works with actors and dancers.[13] The list is endless. Interestingly, since the 1960s a growing number of artists have been contracting external companies to produce their work. In Berlin there are a number of services tailored exclusively toward artists' needs, with large production budgets. For a long time, the artist who expressed their innermost worlds through artisanal skills was held up as the incarnation of an artist: a genius. However, the second half of the last century has seen this traditional technical knowhow splinter off into specializations. The requirements of the 'artist genius' have changed.

Dinosaurs

Andreas Greiner: On a different note, one of the most exciting things I've recently learned about is the history of extinction by which I mean the circumstance that for a long time, people had no idea that certain species could become extinct. George Cuvier was among the first to argue that dinosaur and mammoth bones discovered in increasing numbers didn't match an

13 Julian Heynen (ed.), *La Biennale di Venezia: Deutscher Pavillon/German Pavillon* (Thomas Scheibitz—Tino Sehgal) (Köln: Snoeck, 2005).

existing animal living in a far-off desert or forest, but that the dinosaurs and mammoths in question had indeed died out.

Hans-Jörg Rheinberger: Georges Cuvier was a proponent of what in his time was hotly debated under the label of catastrophe theory. He assumed that periodically, catastrophes shook the earth. Certain organisms became victim to these catastrophes and died out. This created new space and new life forms came into being.[14] Whether this was due to divine creation or whether other causes played a role was equally heavily debated.

Andreas Greiner: I find it interesting to see how Cuvier, with his *espèces perdues*—extinct species—or physicists with their big bang theory generated so-called 'knowledge.' In both cases it is hard to set up an adequate experiment and put the theory to test. We only have indices that point to the possibility of our assumptions resting on facts.

Hans-Jörg Rheinberger: Interestingly, both questions are historical in nature: the origin of the universe, the origin of species. And you cannot experiment on historical, unique events. But paleobiologists as well as physicists use a lot of experimental systems and procedures in order to capture, to analyze and to process what they take as indices of these events that have endured. And for sure, have physicists neither been able to recreate the big bang, nor have biologists succeeded, at least to this day, in creating life from inanimate matter. Actual life on earth still exclusively derives from earlier life.

14 Georges Cuvier, *Essay on the Theory of the Earth*, trans. Robert Kerr (New York: Kirk & Mercein, 1818).

Andreas Greiner: Some say we are currently in the midst of a radical planetary change. A part of this derivative life is bound to die out.

Hans-Jörg Rheinberger: The loss of biodiversity, which is currently advancing at a rapid pace, is frightening. The human species has brought about planetary changes as a result of which many companion species will disappear, with foreseeable consequences for the human species in turn. We are about to sever the basis of our own existence. Of course, the evolution of life on planet earth has seen other catastrophes that only a few organisms survived back then; for example, the so-called oxygen catastrophe that occurred when life forms began to evolve that produced oxygen as a result of the energy conversion of sunlight and consequently paved the way for life forms that depended on oxygen for their energy conversions.[15] But for most existing life back then, oxygen was a deadly poison.

Andreas Greiner: Could, what is currently happening in the world, be seen as a kind of experimental system? Due to the speed of this process of change, ecologists and other scientists — and when the changes become evident enough, everyone else — will gain a lot of new knowledge within only one or two generations.

Hans-Jörg Rheinberger: Sociologists today speak of *Realexperimente*—real experiments, or perhaps better, life size experi-

15 John Maynard Smith and Eörs Szathmáry, *The Major Transitions in Evolution* (San Francisco: W. H. Freeman, 1995).

ments—in such cases.[16] In principle, if you like, one might see evolution itself as a huge natural experimental system, just as Darwin saw experimental breeding as a prolongation of evolutionary change in natural procreation.

Andreas Greiner: To come back to our example of the goldfish at the beginning of our conversation, at Waseda University in Tokyo I came across an interesting scientific-artistic approach. It involves an experiment aimed at reverting these over-bred fish back to their original form, the carp, by performing successive reverse cross-breeding steps.[17] With this example, I would like to pose the question of responsibility: underlying the scientists' as well as the artists' practice is the fact of financial dependency; artworks as well as scientific work can and do result from economically and politically motivated commissions. As an example, let's take the development of a medication in the pharmaceutical industry, or the design of a monument for a politician, a government, or a rich oligarch. In your opinion, do science and art have an ethical obligation — if at all possible — to intervene in these developments? Can novelty that is necessary also stand for a step back — in a positive sense?

Hans-Jörg Rheinberger: Your question is multi-layered. It could mean: As a scientist or an artist, should I question the inten-

16 Matthias Groß, Holger Hoffmann-Riem and Wolfgang Krohn, *Realexperimente. Ökologische Gestaltungsprozesse in der Wissensgesellschaft* (Bielefeld: Transcript, 2015).

17 Tomoya Ishibashi is a member of Professor Hideo Iwasaki's metaPhorest research group. He works on The Goldfish Liberation Movement, a scientific project which is also presented in art exhibitions.

tions of the customer? Or: Should we decline such work? Or: Should we engage in other forms of collaborations, and maybe even resort to earlier, presumably less charged options? I believe we must differentiate. Regarding negotiations with potential patrons, it is, of course, utterly important to be aware of the consequences of the research outcomes they might expect as a result of a particular financial support. Yes, one has to be careful. Scientific as well as artistic independence, or freedom of research, is an extremely fragile good.

With respect to scientific work, two further, basic ethical aspects need to be distinguished. The first is that as a scientist you are responsible, you have to stand up for the integrity of a published result. That is a fundamental ethical principle, all the more in an age that is said to experience a replication crisis and an increasing amount of untrustworthy work bypassing serious peer reviewing. This does not mean at all that a published scientific finding has to be the ultimate truth. Your result can be superseded and still be understood as a relevant step in the process of knowledge acquisition. The second aspect is that as a scientist, making something public means opening yourself up for criticism. One cannot predict in advance in which direction criticism will sway. Sometimes criticism can tear you to pieces. That happens in science, but also in art, of course. But I nevertheless think the sciences and the arts are a little different with regard to how criticism is organized. In the art world critique has come to stand apart; fellow artists are only a marginal part of this domain. Art critics and the viewing and experiencing public are there to judge, not the artists themselves. In the field of science, the criticism comes predominantly from the scientific community itself, at least it has been so until now. When you criticize a scientific result, you can't just say that you don't like it. Rather, you have to make plausible that the wrong course has been taken and that you have been trying to do it better. An alternative must be offered to the scientific community. That is how criticism works in this case — ideally, at least.

Andreas Greiner: Yes, I have to agree. Ideally, knowledge thrives on critical feedback: on the one hand, immanently within a sub-system, and on the other as viewed from the outside. I suppose that is why it is important to look beyond one's own 'Luhmann-like' system and at the same time turn inward with a critical eye. Hans-Jörg Rheinberger, thank you very much for this conversation!

"You Can't Order Scientific Results Like a Pizza." A Conversation Conducted by Susanne Witzgall with Jan St. Werner and Hans-Jörg Rheinberger

Susanne Witzgall: Both of you seem to be invested in the creation of spaces of possibility that allow for the emergence of the new, of the unexpected. This is how you, Jan, referred to your installation *Molecular Hypnotics* (2014) at Cornerhouse in Manchester: as a "space of transition, of uncertainty."[1] Furthermore, your work *Transcendental Animal Numbers* (2013) has been compared to audio recordings of animals in the wild.[2] I also have the impression that in this piece — which consists of a video as well[3] — a kind of cosmic reconfiguration takes place, a reorganization of space and time, as if matter was continually disintegrating and attempting to reorder itself, although this order is never realized in the piece nor in the installation at Cornerhouse. Both works are in potential states of becoming. To what extent do you look for exactly these in-between states of becoming, where a conversation with the unknown could potentially take place?

1 Jan St. Werner, Lecture in the context of the panel "Experimenting Future", Symposium *Die Gegenwart der Zukunft* (December 2, 2014), Academy of Fine Arts Munich, audio recording, 54:47"–54:51" (Archive of the Academy of Fine Arts Munich).

2 See for example http://www.mouseonmars.com/news/new-transcendental-animal-numbers-cassette/ (no longer accessible).

3 See Jan St. Werner, *Transcendental Animal Numbers*, https://vimeo.com/80817468. Last accessed: April 9, 2025)

Jan St. Werner: As a listener or a viewer, I find the spaces that excite me to be the most interesting, actually. These are usually the moments when something is unclear or slightly dangerous, when the adrenaline rises, or when you might even need to defend yourself and some things make no sense. For me, these moments have proved to be the most interesting form of stimulation or wakefulness. The most interesting moments are those when I question the coherency that I nevertheless need to generate in order to be able to move on. The main question is: "How do I navigate a system so as not to bring these moments to a halt, to keep everything on a consistent level of oscillation, while at the same time not succumbing to a stimulation overload?" Joseph Vogl assembled several relevant examples of this in his book *Über das Zaudern (On Tarrying)*,[4] where he describes methodological hesitation, in which one can distinguish between a robust and an idiosyncratic theory. While the object of observation is clear in robust theory, idiosyncratic theory begins with undefined objects that are located in a nonspecifically defined field of research. He explains that this is not about describing a coherent object, but rather approaching the inner complexity of the observed object through the dissemination and fraying of knowledge. One moves within the 'organism of the subject under observation,' so to speak.

Susanne Witzgall: Hans-Jörg Rheinberger, in a number of your books and articles you have cited the passage in which American art historian George Kubler argues that every artist works in the dark and is therefore "guided only by the tunnels and

4 Joseph Vogl, *Über das Zaudern* (Zürich and Berlin: Diaphanes, 2007).

shafts of earlier work."[5] As you have stressed, this applies to the whole of material culture, not only to the arts, but also to the sciences and the humanities, provided they are in search of the new. This does not imply striving towards something, towards a particular artistic or scholarly vision or a kind of utopia, for example, but much more moving away from something given.[6] Could this be seen as a conscious move away from the known, a turn away from behavioral routines, for example?

Hans-Jörg Rheinberger: Yes, scientific practice, in particular experimentation, is always navigating this margin, moving on this borderline. Of course, this does not exclude elements of routine and ingrained habits, and even automatisms. They play a role in the game, but they are not an end in themselves. They are there to basically enable and facilitate those moments when a breakthrough is imminent, where one stumbles upon something that can be connected in a differential and recursive manner to these routines but cannot be anticipated. It's like walking on ice. You have a stockpile of well-rehearsed movements, but you need to question them in unforeseeable moments in order not to slip. There must be a certain virtuosity in handling, a certain mastery of the routines. But they are only the conditions under which unanticipated groundbreaking events become possible.

5 Rheinberger, *Toward a History of Epistemic Things*, 75; reference to Kubler, *Shape of Time*, 125.

6 See, for example, Hans-Jörg Rheinberger, "Episteme zwischen Wissenschaft und Kunst," in *Episteme des Theaters. Aktuelle Kontexte von Wissenschaft, Kunst und Öffentlichkeit*, ed. Milena Cairo, Moritz Hannemann, Ulrike Haß and Judith Schäfer (Bielefeld: Transcript, 2016), 17–27.

What I came to realize through my occupation with music and sound art in particular the work of Florian Dombois,[7] and what I came to question through it, is the fact that in the historical development of the sciences—and the humanities as well—attention has predominantly been focused on the visual for a long time, to the detriment of the other senses. Most of the familiar scholarly forms of presentation and representation appear as images, even when it comes to the most minimal two-dimensional curve. Interestingly, this holds also for a scientific discipline like acoustics, which is essentially built on a wave function. Ernst Chladni's sound figures come to mind.[8] One visualizes the sound when engaging in acoustics. Things become different when one immerses oneself in experimental music. Then one operates in an acoustic space, just as you, Jan St. Werner, have demonstrated in your compositions.[9] Yet the fundamental gestures in musical exploratory practice are comparable to those in experimental scientific contexts. One configures the materials with which one deals in such a way that they leave traces that subsequently give rise to further work.

Susanne Witzgall: Here we touch upon the aspect of materiality, which plays an important role in each of your respective fields. Hans-Jörg Rheinberger, like Karen Barad or Bruno Latour for example,[10] you stress the irreducible entanglement of appara-

7 https://floriandombois.net

8 Myles W. Jackson, *Harmonious Triads: Physicists, Musicians, and Instrument Markers in Nineteenth-Century Germany* (Cambridge MA: MIT Press, 2006).

9 Jan St. Werner, lecture in the Symposium *Die Gegenwart der Zukunft* at the Academy of Fine Arts in Munich on December 2, 2014. See also note 5.

10 See, e. g., Karen Barad, *Meeting the Universe Halfway* (Durham and Lon-

tus, i.e. technical conditions, and the research objects, the epistemic things that combine in an experimental system to bring forth what one later refers to as scientific results, as well as the concepts they embody.[11] And you, Jan, have shown how you deal with technical equipment, which technical devices play a role in your experimental arrangements in the studio, and how you interact with them. You also mentioned that for you, music is a kind of "matter or material that can become very porous again or very brittle, very elegant, like an element."[12] To what extent do the material autonomy of music or the material conditions of sound generation play a role in the search for something in the future, for the new? Do you consciously look for, or particularly try to incorporate this momentum of the material into your work?

Jan St. Werner: I have the impression that one can easily substitute the phrase *the new* with the notion of chance and that the new does not necessarily have to represent certain defined parameters, but that it often happens in in-between spaces: as a mistake or coincidence, in the form of the unanticipated, or as a surprise. One escapes in search for innovation with only one leg, of course, because the other is standing firmly on the ground of the concepts where one feels secure, which is determined by one's own preferences, personal partialities, conditioning, or simply the possibilities of one's own limited senso-

don: Duke University Press, 2007), 139, and Bruno Latour, "Do Scientific Objects Have a History? Pasteur and Whitehead in a Bath of Lactic Acid," *Common Knowledge* 5/1 (1996): 76–91.

11 Rheinberger, *Toward a History of Epistemic Things*, 28.

12 *Follow Jan St. Werner (Mouse on Mars)*, https://www.youtube.com/watch?v=cRMRbC51Bfo . Last accessed: April 9, 2025).

rium — because unlike the 350 shades of green that a native of the rain forest can distinguish, we can only distinguish between 15. To that extent, for each of us the new takes place only in limited spaces. For me, the new in and of itself is not a motivation to do something. I simply move in a field in which I have developed some degree of certainty that allows me to explore uncharted corners. When I think that no one has addressed a certain area yet, then I feel like I can also contribute something. To this extent, a connection to science does exist. This connection is necessarily located in the arts, because with each result you create an offer for others, wherever they are situated. You can open up possibilities in music — spaces of possibility — you can break taboos or combine things which maybe at first do not seem to be related in that way and immediately understood. It translates itself at a barely measurable speed.

The question of the materiality of music or sound is also a great myth, of course. On the one hand, it is only airwaves interacting with our eardrums. On the other hand, through our sense of hearing we construct a spectacular experience from them. No one has ever doubted a musician who talks about sound as material. Of course, one works with tools, instruments, mixing boards, effect processors, and speakers. One sees the membrane quivering, feels the bass in one's stomach, measures the changes in frequency with oscilloscopes and sends electricity through cables and patchbays. It all resembles a workshop in which a material is processed. But the only thing that carries music is air; particles of music do not exist. We've constructed a great mystery around the effect of music, which wants to be mundane and physically measurable, but that doesn't actually help when it's about explaining the effect of music. Music is an effective nothing, anarchy, nature, cosmos, memory, cotton candy. Essentially it exists only because of the dynamic conditions in one's mind.

Hans-Jörg Rheinberger: I guess I understand what you want to say: we are living in a time where discourses on embodiment and corporeality are going through an unprecedented, but often problematic renaissance. Yet, I dare to slightly disagree, physically at least. Have you ever heard sound in empty space? The air is full of material particles, of atoms and molecules that we breathe in and out every second, and without which no sound wave could make its way to our ears.

But I would like to zoom in on another point, the notion of chance with which you began your statement. Codified by American sociologists Robert Merton and Elinor Barber,[13] the term *serendipity* has been widely disseminated in academic discourse on scientific activity over the past decades. I presume that it quite precisely transports the connotations that you associate with the notion of chance. The point of the term is to draw attention to the fact that a reference to mere randomicity here would not point in the right direction. *The Three Princes of Serendip*[14] were surely interested and looking around curiously on their travels and not letting a dice decide what to do, but what they found always came as something they didn't expect—or better perhaps, would not even have been able to expect. To make things more concrete, let's take the example of

13 Robert K. Merton and Elinor Barber, *The Travels and Adventures of Serendipity: A Study in Sociological Semantics and the Sociology of Science* (Princeton: Princeton University Press, 2006).

14 The term is said to date back to a fairy tale by the Persian poet Amir Chusrau (1253—1325) and published in Italy by Michele Tramezzino of Venice in 1557.

a research technology without which the emergence of molecular biology in the 1950s would have been unthinkable, X-ray diffraction analysis. It is actually a physical technique. It works with very short waves, X-rays that are sent through crystalline or para-crystalline specimens and produce a visible diffraction pattern on an appropriate screen. By analyzing these patterns, one learns something about the molecular structure of the research object at hand. However, it is not that easy to crystallize living material. There is no protocol that one can follow to begin with. It is necessary to manipulate the macromolecular material within a range of options and treatments. This in turn induces alterations of the material that can also produce distorting changes. It is all a matter of empirical tinkering. Very unexpected things can emerge in this ongoing interplay between the research technology and the object one would like to explore more closely and know more about. The very constraints inherent in the use of a technology and the efforts to overcome them can lead to effects that one would never have thought of when merely sitting in contemplation at one's desk.

Jan St. Werner: This reminds me of Heinz von Foerster or Gotthard Günther's cybernetic ideas — one is always embedded in the system one studies, and directly influences it.[15] It is impossible to get a clean picture, because you are, in fact, part of the configuration yourself. This is what I meant in reference to a restricted field of view. Serendipity has something

15 See, e.g., Heinz von Foerster, *Sicht und Einsicht. Versuche zu einer operativen Erkenntnistheorie* (Wiesbaden: Springer, 1985); Gotthard Günther, *Das Bewusstsein der Maschinen. Eine Metaphysik der Kybernetik* (Krefeld and Baden-Baden: Agis-Verlag, 1963).

to do with roaming, with wandering in the desert and finding things, with taking time, and the knowledge that one needs time, because the distances are great. I have the feeling that I am actually sitting right in the middle, and everything I grasp around me leads directly to a result. Sometimes I even try consciously not to produce a result. I'm constantly connected to my computer or to apps on my iPhone. I can actually always produce something. Even when I read a book, I constantly create connections. I also see a problem with this and sometimes admire musicians when they take great pleasure in skillfully reproducing a piece of music that they might not even have composed themselves, in harmony with their instrument. This would never happen to me, but sometimes I enjoy the tranquility of just not producing something new.

Susanne Witzgall: The concept of *the new* is certainly not unproblematic, because it is so often associated with progress and innovation. Perhaps one should actually talk about the unexpected or the unknown, like you have done in your books, Hans-Jörg Rheinberger, following the nineteenth-century French physiologist Claude Bernard or the twentieth-century molecular biologist Mahlon Hoagland.[16]

I would like to come back to the balancing act we discussed before, between what is known on the one hand, and opening up to the unexpected on the other; between pre-existing knowledge and the limitations or regimentations this presents — certain forms of specialization in scholarly work might also limit one's perspective, for example — and the opening up of a space that allows something different to occur. To what

16 See, e.g., Rheinberger, *Toward a History of Episteemic Things*, 31.

extent do forms of transdisciplinarity, interdisciplinarity, or the transfer of methodologies play a role here? Can they succeed in deliberately bringing about such an opening in a scientific research process?

Hans-Jörg Rheinberger: Perhaps I can add one other brief observation regarding the notion of the new. I have always found the term *unprecedented* appropriate.[17] It avoids the trivial aspects associated with novelty and conveys the circumstance that one can only access it indirectly. You cannot simply head *straight towards* something that is unknown, you must allow for diversions—that can also come to naught — where the unprecedented finally may happen. The relationship between routine and surprise plays an important role in the course of these vagaries. There is no surprise without routine. They are mutually dependent. Even the way a researcher handles his or her equipment and experimental set-up, on the one hand requires an extreme familiarity with the matter, and on the other hand, there is a permanent necessity of stepping back and letting the familiar become strange. We are talking about minuscule details here, about a micro-space actually, the space of experimentation.

What, then, about broader scientific and scholarly contexts? Here as well, elements from various fields can be brought into contact that would not normally be put together, and in this way, similar effects can be produced. In that respect, one could say: "Okay, interdisciplinarity is a good thing," even though I myself never use that term. It has its origins in a time when it was still necessary to reject the superiority of disciplines that

17 Ibid., 31, 77.

were closed in on themselves. Today, we are living in another time and need another vocabulary accordingly.

Jan St. Werner: I had to think about the French filmmaker Jacques Tati's film *Playtime* (1967) just now, in which he walks through a Paris of the future. It has nothing to do with today's Paris; that only appears obliquely in reflections of particular doors, like the Eiffel Tower, for example. Tati experiences incredibly amazing things but has absolutely no plan. He abandons his original destination at the beginning of the film and wanders serendipitously through the rest. Tati reminds me of an early twentieth-century figure, the protagonist in *The Man Without Qualities*,[18] who lets the world project on himself as if on a screen, thereby reinterpreting it in turn. His activities — sometimes through very marginal interferences — lead to serious catastrophes, which never overpower him entirely, however. My colleague Andi Toma and I like the film of the same title a lot, because we see ourselves reflected in it. The studio or a setting of music-making is sometimes like a city or an artificial construct, like an architectural construction that one has built. One knows exactly where one has put something and why, but despite all precision, you always succeed in producing something different through every small shift.

Susanne Witzgall: My last question concerns the cultural conditions necessary for opening up possibilities in the arts and the sciences where the unexpected can occur. How can we create spaces of possibility in a larger social context that could allow

18 Robert Musil, *The Man without Qualities*, vols. 1 & 2, trans. Sophie Wilkins (New York: Vintage, 1996).

new perspectives for the future to open up? The British cultural critic Mark Fisher regards the current situation as bleak in this respect. According to him, and in contrast to all the neoliberal rhetoric about innovation from which we have tried to distance ourselves, the resources for producing the new are being taken away from artists. Fisher refers, in particular, to the situation in the United States. Here he registers a dramatic practical and ideological restriction of public services that once helped to set free both space and time for artists as well as academics, where they could work without the pressure of having to be immediately successful. Public service also became more and more market-oriented and, in this context, cultural production increasingly tended to reproduce what had already proven successful. Fisher sees musical culture as a barometer. He diagnoses a strong trend toward pastiche and repetition in the music industry, while the complete infrastructure of the distribution and consumption of music finds itself subjected to extreme changes.[19] How do you see this situation, Jan?

Jan St. Werner: This is definitely a complex subject. We had dinner with our agent yesterday, who remarked that we are witnessing a remarkable moment, because it has become hard even for the big names to get concerts. Right now, young bands manage to go far in a short period of time and have large audiences, sometimes even larger than a band that has worked for a long time on its career. The curators and those who do festival bookings often say: “Yes, we’d rather invite them, because they’re so hip at the moment.” This is

19 Mark Fisher, *Ghosts of My Life. Writing on Depression, Hauntology and Lost Futures* (Winchester VA: Zero Books, 2014), 11–16.

an intriguing phenomenon, of course, because the whole system as it developed has become insecure — including concert agencies and record companies. They might have worked for years to ensure that the system functions in a stable fashion. They might have built up an artist knowing that they have invested their time, money, and imagination in someone who would not suddenly disappear. Now everything moves extremely fast and unpredictably. But even if it may badly affect us personally, I find it quite exciting and don't go back to look for new things in places where I saw them appear before. It is possible, though, to work on conservative systems, in which nothing is new at first glance, in a way that lets productive moments emerge. The new is not only about rebellion and smashing old structures. The significantly new can emerge against the background of the old and the strictly defined. Paradoxically speaking, cultural pessimism, the negation of hype, a certain perseverance and stubbornness can also direct one's view on the up-and-coming. Thus, with respect to music or art, I always like reading the conservative culture section of the newspaper and take some of its socially conservative observations as inspiration. Of course, at the end of the day, critiques of this kind are ridiculous, because everything keeps moving and mixing, because proliferation and chaos are uncontrollable production machines. This process simply goes on, and one must contribute one's share to keep it interesting. Like a soccer game, it continues running and will not get any better if you stay on the sidelines and sulk.

Susanne Witzgall: What about the spaces of possibility in academic scholarship?

Hans-Jörg Rheinberger: We are witnessing the takeover of a new buzzword today. Interdisciplinarity, transdisciplinarity and the like have worn off a bit. Now the slogan promoted by the public funding system and echoing from everybody's mouths is *translation.* The pressure behind this is that the work going on in research laboratories be translated into marketable applications as quickly as possible. It is no longer the space between the disciplines—*inter-disciplinarity*—that is seen and promoted as a knowledge resource, it is the space between the research laboratory and the market that is addressed here, at times with the oxymoron of 'applied basic research.' In view of the fact that the biggest share of academic university research is publicly funded, questions like "OK, and what is the point of this?" are, of course, understandable. This is the mild version. The catch is that finally, it's all about making money with scientific results. History tells you, however, that the greatest achievements of our culture are a result of the fact that people who worked in the realms of the sciences and the arts were given time and were not permanently and directly confronted with questions of applicability. You simply must have the possibility of pursuing the intricate relations of your subject matter without being in the situation of having to present results the next day. I am convinced that this was, and will remain, fundamental for productive research. You can't order scholarly results like a pizza.

Kerstin Stakemeier: What could help us to avoid the negative side of a form of productivism where everything has to be productive and immediately exploitable? Where could limits be introduced in order not to fall prey to a condition of neo-liberal hysteria?

Hans-Jörg Rheinberger: Basically, the solution is terribly simple and old-fashioned because ultimately it goes back to the nineteenth-century idea of the university, often associated with the name of the brothers von Humboldt, as a space characterized by explorative learning and learning exploration. This simply means that where scholarly learning is practiced, and research carried out accordingly, a moment of alternative temporality and timing must be preserved, a temporal regime that derives from the requirements of the subject matters themselves, rather than from publication pressure or from predetermined or alleged extrinsic financial and economic necessities. I believe that a suspension of the pressure for immediate solutions is a prerequisite for any productive research in the long run. This is by no means to be understood as a license for idleness. Back in 2000, at the Collegium Helveticum in Zurich, I conducted a seminar together with its director Helga Nowotny, a sociologist. The topic was time management in research. We interviewed a good number of professors at the Swiss Federal Institute of Technology. All of them ran big labs. Not surprisingly, the general upshot was that all of them, on the one hand, bowed to the institutional publication pressure within what has become the narrow time frame of publicly funded 'projects.' But on the other hand, all of them also set aside enough money to pursue open-ended questions in a smaller or larger corner of their labs. And all of them set their hopes in the long-term outcomes from these niches.

Jan St. Werner: I would like to add something. I believe that one shouldn't let oneself be pressured for one's decision to become a scholar, a painter, or a musician. This does not imply that one has to be constantly productive. Actually, in my work, many things need many years. I work on something and can't get it out of my head. There's always a reoccurring problem that I want to resolve, and I don't manage to do it. This really can take years and then suddenly I jot down something in a week or two and can start production. It's like a play in the dark, where something is in gestation. Often you don't even know what you're doing when you do it. You're in a kind of microscopic state then. You get so close to the objects and their relations that you are no longer able to recognize them, and then you have to distance yourself in order to be able to see things in another form. For me, this microscopic work is the most important, what I get the most from. It is, of course, obvious that the additional work of giving all that a form and putting it into a larger context is also very important. I actually have many friends who gave up making music because they never managed to publish anything. One could ask, "Why do you have to make a record? Keep making music, this is what it's about." But it's not only about that. It's also about being able to deposit things, not into storage, but in a space where others can have access to and do something with them, interpret them, develop them further, take them apart, or maybe simply grind them up.

Microbial Performances
An Interview with Lucie Strecker and Jens Hauser

Jens Hauser: You have been passionately interested in the entanglements between philosophy of science, the experimental arts, and questions of representation. Your work with a focus on the history and epistemology of experimentation has inspired numerous artists as well. Against the grain of the 'two cultures' thesis that in the course of the twentieth century, the natural sciences and the humanities grew apart into fields of knowledge no longer understanding each other, you aim, from the point of view of a historian of science, to promote a new culture of mutual 'calling in and calling out.' What you have in mind is an epistemic universe no longer based on a dual system but rather on an irreducible plurality of ways of knowledge acquisition. Hence, you actively — and physically — contributed to the performative symposium "Applied Microperformativity" held at the Angewandte Innovation Lab (AIL) in Vienna in 2018.[1]

Your lecture on "Microperformativity and Experimentation" in Vienna was framed and thematically addressed by the art performance *Microbial Keywording,* which also repeatedly interrupted it and finally absorbed it, proverbially and biologically. On the one hand, your discourse became part of a symbolic–scenic performance; on the other hand, the phonemes

1 "Applied Microperformativity: Live Arts for a Radical Socio-Economic Turn." Curated by Lucie Strecker, Klaus Spiess and Jens Hauser. Angewandte Innovation Laboratory (AIL), December 10–19, 2018.

you articulated flowed into a microbiological process on a truly material level. When you pronounced the phonemes, the pH value in your oral flora was measured and, depending on its value, pheromones were released to micro-organisms, which in turn reacted to them on a level distinguished from the linguistic, ultimately 'sense' producing level. Speaking *about* biological processes acted as a stimulus *for* real microperformativity, that is, biological processes. How did you feel about this experimental performance situation?

Hans-Jörg Rheinberger: On the one hand, it fascinated me; on the other, I felt uneasy. I was talking about the laboratory as a context in which microperformative processes of such kind are used and manipulated in order to generate knowledge about the living beings involved and, in a sense, to make them speak — by creating plaques with different fringes and colors in a Petri dish, for instance, offering potentially meaningful signals to the experimenter who can pick them up, interpret them and finally translate them back into an ongoing research process. In the course of a prolonged experimental investigation, an "investigative pathway," to use an apt expression of Larry Holmes,[2] the procedure creates something like an infinite loop via the interaction between a human performer and her or his objects, the viruses, which infest bacteria, multiply and cause them to burst, which in turn generates visible spots. This is the kind of living feedback on the microperformative level I tried to describe in my lecture. In the context of the symposium, I gained the impression that this situation was, in a way, taken

2 Frederic L. Holmes, *Investigative Pathways: Patterns and Stages in the Careers of Experimental Scientists* (New Haven: Yale University Press, 2004).

up on a material yet strangely metaphorical, out-of-place level — with the same elements I characterized as acting in a laboratory context: microbes that only grow under certain conditions depending on the pH value and in need of their very specific micro-environments. So, I felt somehow torn between alienation and moments of recognition.

Lucie Strecker: Even if one might use terms such as 'sense' or 'metaphorical,' the claim of *Microbial Keywording* is nevertheless that the processes in question actually take place at the biological level itself and in real laboratory equipment; that Petri dishes are actually inoculated with the speakers' saliva, that the microbes' behavior and their molecular components change beyond the metaphorical.

Jens Hauser: Indeed, on the proverbial metabolic level.

Hans-Jörg Rheinberger: Terms such as 'metaphorical' have no absolute value; they always depend on the perspective. From the perspective of the scientific laboratory and the way microbes and Petri dishes are handled there, such an experimental art setting as we experienced and as you just described is initially seems metaphorical, despite its material character. Metaphors do not have to consist of words, they can have a material existence. But when I enter this alternative setting and become part of it, then its metaphoricity disappears for me, and I find myself in another context of action. It remains, however, of a different kind than a research laboratory setting, where you engage in an ongoing process of knowledge acquisition, maybe for years, about the things you handle; *Microbial Keywording* also creates insights, but of another character.

Instead of learning something about the microbes, you learn something about yourself, by way of the microbes—they have become tools for one's own experience.

Lucie Strecker: For me as a choreographer and artist who is staging a scientific–artistic symposium with Klaus Spiess and an interdisciplinary team, you, in turn, have become part of our experiment aimed at making the material itself — the theorist's utterances, actually — speak in a microbial form, that is, to transform it into a metabolic process. We have tried to bridge the gap between the realms of the abstract, the linguistic and the somatic. How did you experience the second part of the performance in a separate room, where a tube was put into your mouth and you then repeated the phonemes of your 'keyword' in an experiment?

Hans-Jörg Rheinberger: Now, in this laboratory-like setting, which made use of a microbiological cosmos, one was no longer just a spectator, but was involved and became entangled as an active part of the staging, in a performance without an audience. It triggered different associations and an estrangement of sorts in the participants. For me, the discomfort was also an important experience. With my laboratory background as a baggage, it turned into something like a decontextualization and recontextualization.

Lucie Strecker: In view of the possibilities of biotechnology today, the whole symposium attempted a change of perspective toward exploring how, within the performative arts and in choreography, the typical questions of staging a work are changing from "How do people act? How do they move? How do they speak?" to "How can anthropocenic approaches be expanded?" If one goes on to think about findings such as that gut bacteria can interact with cognitive or mental processes in the brain, one becomes aware of the power of the world of microbes to act — both as a friend and foe to humans.

Hans-Jörg Rheinberger: Yes, in all the activities of the Vienna symposium one was always somehow struck by the fact that so much microbial life is constantly present in everything we do and are. With our own microbiome, which has partly been made visible here, or in the performance of the *Last Supper,* which was staged like a communion, we live practically always and everywhere in a microbial, that is, in a microperformative interior and exterior environment which, however, we do not notice in our everyday experience.

Jens Hauser: In this sense, 'microperformativity' also implies becoming sensitized to other levels of spatiality as well as temporality than those accessible to the mesoscopic phenomenological realm of the human animal, which correspond to the very broad concept of performativity in art and theater studies, linguistics and anthropology. In your symposium contribution about microperformativity in biological experimentation in the test tube, you emphasize the importance of what you call 'compression' and 'dilatation': "What is too small to be directly investigated must be enlarged [...] What is too big must be downsized" [...] "What is too quick to be observed must be slowed down; and what is too slow to be recognized must be accelerated." My question is: Does the concept of performativity in general, and microperformativity in particular, make sense with regard to the experimental practices in the natural sciences? What does it add to understanding processes of knowledge acquisition, of experimentation and epistemic objects?

Hans-Jörg Rheinberger: The term 'performativity' was originally associated with human actions and activities on stage. The concept of performativity has been investigated for decades in interdisciplinary research collaborations, and was employed by Erika Fischer-Lichte,[3] among others, to describe action-theoretical aesthetic contexts more generally. Personally, I have always been interested in the actions you can observe on the micro-level of the objects you are experimenting with — what is it that they themselves are doing? With respect to experimentation, the concept of microperformativity then comes to designate the agency of things, epistemic things if you like. Of course, there are the activities of the experimenters who perform in their laboratories, push the Petri dishes back and forth, pour in a liquid here, suck something out there. But they do all that in order to get substances and organisms, or parts thereof, to interact with each other, creating a molecular environment and initiating processes in which such interactions can take place — and from which they can disengage themselves. Experimenters want to know how their microbes behave and not what they themselves have done to them. This is the conflict for any experimenter. Of course, they see themselves as people who arrange all this with skill, but everything is done in order to be able to withdraw from the game at the end, because what counts are not their own actions, but those

3 Erika Fischer-Lichte, *The Transformative Power of Performance. A New Aesthetics* (London and New York: Routledge, 2008).

of their bacteria, for instance. In the laboratory, two performative contexts collide — that's what is really exciting and interesting for me. On the one hand, there are the micro-processes, which as a rule are not accessible to our senses. On the other hand, they have to be amplified within experimental performative set-ups so that we can perceive them.

Lucie Strecker: You always emphasize the importance of the milieu as an artificially created environment and ask to what extent natural processes are still shown or 'mirrored' here, or whether the artificial environment alienates the objects of observation so that they react differently.

Hans-Jörg Rheinberger: To be able to have a close look at and to make work, in the *test tube*, a biological reaction that is supposed to take place in the *cell*, one has to destroy the cell. To learn about life in an in vitro or test-tube experiment one takes the cell apart and ideally, has to separate *one* reaction from all the other thousands of reactions that normally occur simultaneously in the cell. I assume that what I see there mirrors the intracellular process — whose natural environment is replaced by an artificial one in this context of experimental performance; a test tube environment is created as a substitute for the former. This is actually the essential tension from which the whole experiment lives. Following the biochemist and historian of science Herbert Friedmann, what was really new when test-tube cultures came into being toward the end of the nineteenth century, was the claim and demonstration that tissue extracts could provide and represent not just what have been called natural products, that is, *compounds* synthesized in tissues and organs, but natural *processes* as well.

Friedmann claims: "From now on, extract repeats or *mirrors* process."[4] What is thus at stake in the transition from a living system to a test-tube system is not just the transition from biology to chemistry or from physiological process to organic substance. What is at stake is something akin to a *reduplication* of life; life under other conditions. The milieu of the cell or the "*milieu intérieur*" of the organism, in the words of the nineteenth-century French physiologist Claude Bernard,[5] is being replaced by a milieu composed and concocted in the test tube. In this process of repeating or of mirroring life, however, a lot of things can go wrong, a fact that confronts experimenters daily with the possibility that what they see in the mirror is no longer 'nature.'

Microbiology became possible only through the creation of such artificial environments. And it is still the case today that only some microorganisms surrender to the brutalities of being cultivated in a technically created environment beyond their actual living conditions. For others, this does not work at all, so they are simply ignored — which does not mean, however, that they may not be very important and that we may perhaps only investigate the more unimportant ones, just a few small pathogens that thrive in the experimenter's hands — and on your 'stage.' Here lies a vast unexplored continent still waiting for the sciences.

4 Herbert C. Friedmann, "From Friedrich Wöhler's urine to Eduard Buchner's alcohol," in *New Beer in an Old Bottle. Eduard Buchner and the Growth of Biochemical Knowledge*, ed. Athel Cornish-Bowden (València: Universitat de València, 1997), 67–122, on p. 108.

5 Claude Bernard, *Lectures on the Phenomena of Life Common to Animals and Plants*, trans. Hebbel E. Hoff, Roger Guillemin and Lucienne Guillemin (Springfield, IL: Charles C. Thomas, 1974), Third Lecture.

Lucie Strecker: How do processes change when they are repeated in artificial milieus? Is there, perhaps, a comparable tension in performance practice between the body of work and the process it enables? For example, is it the dramatic text or choreographic notation that is essential, or the performance itself? How do these elements interact? Even if primarily related to human actions, the theater scholar Erika Fischer-Lichte emphasizes the fundamental transformative power inherent in the encounter between performers and perceivers.[6] The work of art then no longer resides in the text, but in the performance of the text. Parallel to this, one could argue that in anthropology it is not the *myth* that is written down and handed on which is most important, but the *ritual* as it is performed — that is, the action itself, the performance. All of this now focuses on the performance itself as a medium, rather than on the text that is being performed, and thus, thanks to this 'in-between,' it involves the spectator concretely as an essential element. This 'in-between' also seems to play a central role in your *Epistemology of the Concrete,*[7] where the focus is not on human action, but on the agency of non-human dimensions.

6 Erika Fischer-Lichte, *The Routledge Introduction to Theatre and Performance Studies* (London and New York: Routledge, 2014). In their Editors' preface, Minou Arjomand and Ramona Mosse underline the procedural and relational aspects in the subjective experience of performance by also elaborating on linguistic differences between German and English: "In contrast to the word *perform* the German *aufführen* is a more narrowly focused term that refers specifically to a live theatrical context and is distinct from *ausführen*, which describes the doing of a particular task; to *perform* subsumes the two and allows them to be aspects of a single concept."

7 Rheinberger, *Epistemology of the Concrete*, Chapter 11.

Hans-Jörg Rheinberger: Yes, of course, there is a recurring pattern: What comes first? Do we start from the practical context and move toward its symbolic horizon — or is the symbolic horizon always already there, and does it leave its mark on the concrete action? You pointed to theater performance and to the field work of the anthropologist, which of course are different in each case; but one also finds a comparable constellation in experimentation, epitomized by the metaphor of 'mirroring.' This tension underlies all of scientific experimentation. In the example I presented, the 'art' consists in creating extracellular milieus in order to provoke the desired visualizations, but here the experimenters want their micro-actors to do in the test tube what they would otherwise do in their proper milieu. The point is, however, that they do not have a direct access to the latter. Multiplying the experimental setups and comparing the outcomes with each other is the only way to go.

For example, the activities of viruses that infect bacteria can only be made visible by creating environments in which masses of dead bacteria form huge plaques that cover an enormous area compared to their own size. The effect would not be noticeable on an individual bacterium. Bacteriophages, which exploit the genetic apparatus of microbes to reproduce themselves, instrumentalize bacteria that farm themselves to death — a terrible process, but one which is presumed to take place invisibly in nature in every infection process. Its iterative events, however, remain invisible, unless they are captured in a specially constructed contraption which makes them visible as a plaque on a lawn of bacteria in a Petri dish.

Jens Hauser: This has further consequences for performance theory, when it is not about an aesthetic end product but about the microperformative process — in the perception of which aesthetic experience and visibility nevertheless play a role. However, the aesthetic dimension can also become a trap in this process, as Olaf Müller recently showed by the example of losing one's way in the history of physics — for example, when the seductive nature of the 'beautiful' leads to misinterpretations.[8]

Hans-Jörg Rheinberger: I have always had difficulties with this naive concept of the aesthetic, when there is talk about the 'beautiful' in the context of the history of the sciences: the elegant formula in mathematics, the striking image in chemistry, the golden section in biology—the simpler, the more beautiful. In contrast to associations such as these, what I have found in all the laboratory contexts I have experienced and analyzed in detail, is that precisely the opposite can be observed: it is not the simple and the elegant that is beautiful and pleasing, but instead that which is complex enough to be a challenge. We should separate the evening dinner-table talk of many a scientist from their morning discourse in the laboratory.

Jens Hauser: Here, your oft-cited figure of 'iteration' comes into play.[9] Transposed from philosophy and literature into the life sciences, the concept has taken on the meaning of a graphematic activity, an "epigraphy of matter" in the words of Gaston Bachelard,[10] the search for the unprecedented in the

8 Olaf Müller, *Zu schön, um falsch zu sein. Über die Ästhetik in der Naturwissenschaft* (Frankfurt am Main: Fischer, 2019).

9 Hans-Jörg Rheinberger, *Iterationen* (Berlin: Merve Verlag, 2005).

10 Bachelard, *New Scientific Spirit*, 168 (misleadingly translated here as "way of 'reading' matter").

process of scientific research. For molecular biology in particular, you have suggested that this cultural understanding goes hand in hand with the execution of a code one analyses in order to understand the basic metabolic activities of reproduction and development — "because the contemporary biologist also speaks of writing and *pro-gram* in relation to the most elementary processes of information within the living cell. And, finally, whether it has essential limits or not, the entire field covered by the cybernetic program will be the field of writing."

Hans-Jörg Rheinberger: This is actually a quotation from the first chapter of Jacques Derrida's *Of Grammatology*,[11] which I cite in *Iterationen*.

Jens Hauser: Exactly. So how important is the ongoing process of inscribing and overwriting, this performative iteration, in contrast to the preference for a final interpretation of an ontologically established fact — scientific activity as an interplay of writing and laying tracks, a game of differences?

Hans-Jörg Rheinberger: This brings us back to the concept of process, which overlaps here with that of microperformance: knowledge acquisition cannot be stopped; research cannot be brought to final rest. There is no point omega here — that is what makes scientific knowledge so fundamentally different from, e.g., theological knowledge. Scientific knowledge is not oriented towards an end state, it is always only defined by a certain dissatisfaction with its present state. The movement away from that state is unfinishable in its essence. For me, this is

11 Derrida, *Of Grammatology*, 9.

also the decisive aspect of performativity in the arts, perhaps performativity in general, at least of the iterative type.

Lucie Strecker: Another term from Jacques Derrida's toolbox that comes to mind is the *pharmakon* — which also inspired us in the *Microbial Keywording* performance. In his essay "Plato's pharmacy" Derrida poses the question of whether the written word is not poison for our capacity for memory.[12] Derrida deconstructs Plato's *Phaedros* and discovers a "pharmacological system" in Platonic writing that not only describes the ambivalence of every medicament, but also the essence and value of writing in general, as well as the identity logic of Western thought, with its pairs of opposites: remedy/poison, positive/negative, soul/body, mother/father, head/heart and so forth.

Hans-Jörg Rheinberger: Yes, in fact Derrida made some very pertinent points about the *pharmakon*. "Plato's pharmacy" is part of the early Derrida's reflections about the relation between the spoken and the written word and the revaluation of the latter against the background of millennia of occidental philosophy. But what exactly is the *pharmakon*? The *pharmakon* is one of these things that are hard to grasp, an in-between thing that keeps slipping away. It lies between a dose that has no effect at all, and the poison that torments us. Between these poles we find this not particularly large space in which performance can take place, in which things are allowed to express themselves and we are permitted to understand them. It is a relationship that is limited by boundaries on both sides.

12 Jacques Derrida, "Plato's pharmacy," in *Dissemination*, trans. Barbara Johnson (Chicago: The University of Chicago Press, 1981), 63–171.

Jens Hauser: So, to what extent is the performative paradigm useful for the natural sciences? The sociologist of science Andrew Pickering argues in favor of a performative instead of a representational idiom, as a "dance of agency"[13] that emphasizes the material aspects of scientific research by focusing on "knowing how" more than on "knowing that."[14] And already in 1986, Latour and Woolgar argued in *Laboratory Life* that "interpretations do not inform as much as they perform"[15] — which means that attention is increasingly focused on non-human actors, technical and biological apparatuses such as model organisms or bacteria. There seems to be a trend from interpretative literacy to performative corporeality, just as performance theory has developed from linguistics to anthropology and theater studies.

Hans-Jörg Rheinberger: That is one of the characteristics of science and technology studies in the tradition of historical epistemology. One attempts to get away from the question "What is there?" and rather to understand, "What is being done there?" So, it is basically an attempt to replace ontology by epistemology. But if it all ends there, it leads to the sort of arbitrariness that we know well from constructivism. There needs to be feedback to the ontic realm that keeps gaining on us. The quote from *Laboratory Life* can be interpreted in

13 Andrew Pickering, *The Mangle of Practice. Time, Agency, and Science* (Chicago: The University of Chicago Press, 1995), 21.
14 Dwight Conquergood, „Performance studies: Interventions and radical research," in *The Performance Study Reader*, ed. Henry Bial (London: Routledge, 2002), 311–322, on p. 312.
15 Bruno Latour and Steve Woolgar, *Laboratory Life. The Construction of Scientific Facts* (Princeton: Princeton University Press, ²1985), 285.

such a way that the traces left by the experimental process do not simply end in a conclusion. In order for these traces to remain virulent, they must assume a performative character themselves by tempting us to take the next material step in the experimental context. Seen in this light, it is clear that, on the one hand, script, "inscription" is again becoming action, whatever form it may take, and that, on the other hand, action can always assume something like a written form, so that it can be subjected to our interpretation. So, everything revolves around this to and fro between scripturality and materiality.

Jens Hauser: An important aspect of the performative, which you have described using the history of specimens and experimental systems, is that it can be used to reveal widespread media blindness. You emphasized the paradox of a preparation, which appears authentic to the viewer to the degree that the previous technical manipulation the object has been subjected to has been made to disappear, that is, the performative action is usually negated by the resulting object. However, as the philosopher Walter Seitter formulates it,[16] before there can be *Wahr-Nehmung*[17] there needs to be means of *Wahr-Gebung*,[18] but the latter—giving of truth — is often suppressed.

Hans-Jörg Rheinberger: One could say that the concept of the performative as a reflexive concept has the potential to counteract this kind of media blindness. Preparations, as the name

16 Walter Seitter, *Physik der Medien: Materialien—Apparate—Präsentierungen* (Weimar: VDG, 2002).

17 In German, perception literally translates as ‚true-taking.‘

18 In German, literally 'true-giving.'

tells us, are things worked on, configured and reconfigured. But to appear authentic, the procedures must, paradoxically, be rendered invisible, so that a preparation looks authentic if the media used to create it are effaced in the final product. There we meet again a dilemma similar to that of the experimenter, who on the one hand has to take all the necessary measures to arrange for, but on the other hand has to withdraw from the event as it takes place. Here as well, it is precisely this moment that creates media blindness: one subsequently lives in the illusion of seeing the things themselves, but what one sees is how one has done the job. I have always found it strange that it appears to be almost a necessity of life for scientists to hide the apparatus they use to make their objects visible. If you listen to a scientist, she or he never actually talks about the instruments he or she uses to tackle nature, but about the wonderful effects — which they have actually created — as the things themselves.

Jens Hauser: On the occasion of the exhibition and publication *Fingerprints,* about the biotechnological live installations by the artist Paul Vanouse,[19] you addressed the fact that such microperformative art reveals and demonstrates what is often hidden in a scientific article under the heading 'Materials and Methods.'

Hans-Jörg Rheinberger: 'Materials and methods' are mandatorily, but often rather briefly listed at the beginning of a research article — so it's easier to gloss over them. Paul Vanouse's genome-critical performative art goes against the grain of this

19 Compare "Tracing the index: Paul Vanouse," in the present volume.

general tendency on the part of scientists to hide the epistemic dimension of their work: the ever-changing means and media, the whole plethora of research technologies on which their activity rests. Vanouse looks *at* them, while scientists tend to look *through* them and treat them as transparent and translucent, to view them as allowing unadulterated and immediate access to 'nature' itself. Transposed into an artistic environment, Vanouse's biotechnological installations reveal something of the reflexive power of alienation (*Verfremdung*). This is an ingenious way — effective artistically as well as in science studies —of keeping the media of knowledge production in the game, in all their opacity, an antidote against the tendency of the sciences to make them disappear.

Actually, this reminds me of a telling situation I encountered when musing about a contribution to the *Iconoclash* exhibition curated by Bruno Latour and Peter Weibel at the ZKM Center for Art and Media in Karlsruhe in 2002.[20] Together with my colleague, the art historian Peter Geimer, we had a long in-depth discussion with Bruno Latour in Paris about the possibility of contributing a video to the exhibition. We approached a generally very open-minded scientist in Berlin to suggest collaborating on the video, which would show the resources needed and the efforts having to be invested into the technology of radioactive tracing in order to make it work. We wanted to document the visualization procedures and reveal the enormous technical input it entails — starting with the

20 Bruno Latour and Peter Weibel (eds.), *Iconoclash—Beyond the Image Wars in Science, Religion, and Art* (Cambridge: MIT Press, 2002). The exhibition carrying the same name took place at the ZKM Media Museum from May 4 to September 1st, 2002.

cyclotrons and atomic reactors by which the isotopes have to be produced before they are nicely packaged in small ampoules and sent to the molecular biology laboratory; we wanted to put the entire epistemology of this process into the picture. I was disappointed, but not surprised, that we were unable to convince this scientist of the interest of such an endeavor in view of the time and work that would have to go into it. Instead, he suggested producing a spot featuring the models that were the result of his experiments using the technology of radioactive tracing. Again, products — not means and media — would occupy center stage and, of course, the people promoting the establishment of these models. We spent a whole day in his lab and left in the evening without having achieved anything. The film was never made.

Lucie Strecker: In various branches of the performing arts, including choreography, we are currently seeing great international interest in questioning the human performers in their anthropocentric position as the main actors. The preoccupation with all these non-human agencies has long since taken hold here. Even top choreographers such as Mette Ingvartsen have sometimes banned human performers completely. Recently the Muffathall in Munich celebrated its twenty-fifth anniversary with a preview of the "performance of tomorrow" with the festival *"{un][split}: Micro performance & macro matters."*[21]

21 *"{un][split}: Micro performance & macro matters,"* August 31 to September 2, 2018, curated by Jens Hauser and Dietmar Lupfer, showed microperformative works by Julia Borovaya, Evelina Domnitch and Dmitry Gelfand, Yann Marussich, Katrin Petroschkat and Susanne Schmitt, Aniara Rodado and Jean-Marc Chomaz, Kuai Shen, Klaus Spiess and Lucie Strecker, Stelarc, Tina Tarpgaard and Paul Vanouse.

Jens Hauser: The exhibition was about the potential of the arts to create awareness of agencies that escape the visible and our mesoscopic bubble by expanding our habitual scales. Just as Kant once underlined the importance of other scales with the concept of both the dynamically and the mathematically sublime and in the encounter with the all-powerful, today what is no longer imaginable and experienceable perhaps becomes tangible when microperformative processes in art are confronted with their macroscopic effects. This seems all the more enticing to artists, since the representation of these scales often requires techno-scientific apparatus and media, from particle physics to climate research.

Lucie Strecker: Or from the biotechnological manipulation of microorganisms to questions of ecology.

Hans-Jörg Rheinberger: Even though our everyday performance takes place in a mesocosmos conditioned by the range and specificity of our senses, I hesitate to divide the scientific subfields themselves into micro, macro and meso — precisely because all the instruments that bring the smallest and the largest into our mesocosmos again and again break down such divisions. For example, instruments that allow us to learn something about the heavens work with micro-processes such as wavelengths far below any visibility. But it makes a lot of sense to take a close look at the relationships of agency between the micro-, meso- and macrocosmic dimensions. Such an analysis of the performativity of both non-human actors and the apparatuses is also welcome with regard to the much-cited term 'Anthropocene.' This term is not really a happy choice, it appears to me. It can rightfully be criticized, since it just fails to express what is actually happening here: a reversion of performance. The globe, the planet is striking back — and it is no longer primarily the people who are acting. Michel Serres described this reversion thirty years ago in his wonderful book *The Natural Contract,* a book that deserves much more attention than it is actually receiving.[22] Our environment has gained an independent ability to strike back, so to speak, exactly because of the way we have treated it—something we had not suspected. In the same way it was long believed that non-human things could be tamed by scientific and technological development, it is these things that are now making themselves felt. Of course, forces of nature were also there in a past replete with events so overpowering that they were interpreted as punishments of the gods. This kind of interpretation does no longer work well today. But on the other hand, theoretical offers such as those made by constructivism, as an extreme fantasy of omnipotence, have also failed. Today, the discussion about the power of action of things has become utterly urgent: 'agency is everywhere' — with massive consequences. It would not have needed the Covid pandemic to demonstrate it.

22 Michel Serres, *The Natural Contract*, trans. Elizabeth MacArthur and William Paulson (Ann Arbor: University of Michigan Press, 1995).

Contingency, Notation, Reflection

Exchange with Alex Arteaga on "Contingent Agencies"

Hans-Jörg Rheinberger: Over the course of two long panel discussions held during the concluding cross-disciplinary symposium of "Contingent Agencies," participants exchanged thoughts and discussed approaches related to the concepts and practices conceived, developed, and performed in the project.[1] What follows is an attempt at broadly reviewing and expanding on my spontaneous interventions into these discussions in dialogue with Alex Arteaga, one of the project leaders. I hope that this will evoke, if such is possible, something of the atmosphere and spirit that pervaded these afternoon and evening forums. Perhaps I should add that I saw it as my task in this cross-disciplinary symposium to maintain awareness of the perspective of the research process as it characterizes the sciences. Consequently, this will hold true for the remarks that follow as well. They will revolve around the notions of contingency, notation, and reflection, and the relations that I see existing between them in this context. They can also be read as a continuation of the deliberations on these

1 Nikolaus Gansterer and Alex Arteaga, Symposium, Vienna, September 19–25, 2022. Concluding event of the art-research project "Contingent Agencies," funded by the Austrian Science Fund's Program for Arts-based Research (PEEK). The results of the project are now available as a book: Alex Arteaga and Nikolaus Gansterer (eds.), *Contingent Agencies. Inquiring into the Emergence of Atmospheres* (Berlin: Hatje Cantz, 2025) and a website: https://contingentagencies.uni-ak.ac.at/.

topics gathered in my new book *Split and Splice. A Phenomenology of Experimentation.*[2]

Contingency

Hans-Jörg Rheinberger: Contingency is generally seen as being opposed to law-based or rule-directed and planned action, whether of the forces of nature or of human behavior. And law-based action is likewise generally seen as paradigmatically embodied by the work of the sciences. What follows is an attempt to deconstruct this image of scientific activity. As far as I can see, this traditional image is the greatest enemy and hindrance of a rapprochement between the sciences and the arts. Not least for this reason, I regard it as of utmost importance to draw an alternative picture of the role and facets of contingency in the scientific research process, that is, the core of what we call the sciences, the place where the pulsating life of the sciences is acted out. For too long a time, the image of the sciences has been dominated by what Ludwik Fleck once called their "official paper form," in contrast to their "living practice."[3] Experimentation is at the heart of the scientific research process. We can look, and rightly so, at experimentation as a practice invented by the sciences for the sake of charting unknown ground, for creating knowledge that cannot be anticipated. Generally, it is assumed that in an experiment

2 Rheinberger, *Split and Splice.*

3 Ludwik Fleck, "Die Krise der 'Wirklichkeit'," in *Ludwik Fleck: Erfahrung und Tatsache,* ed. Lothar Schäfer and Thomas Schnelle (Frankfurt am Main: Suhrkamp, 1983), 46–58, on p. 50.

anticipated knowledge in the form of a hypothesis is tested. But more often than not, what really happens is that a hypothesis is subverted by the experimental process, which points in unforeseen directions. What is really new, then, inevitably escapes our predictions. The experiment is a device that renders it possible to turn what may at first appear as an incident—or even an accident—into an event, or an impact into an outlook. The term 'event' is used here in its Derridean meaning: "The impossible is the condition of possibility of the event."[4] An event is an event exactly because it is impossible to foresee it happening. Contingency is something like the non-conceptual kernel of experimentation. It allows us to leave behind the mindset which encloses us at any point in time and within which we act. In order to be able to transgress it, an agency is needed that operates beyond this horizon. Researchers shape their experiments with all the ingenuity that is at their disposal at the time, but they do so in order to possibly gain something that they were not able to determine in advance. In his short text on "Surrationalism," Gaston Bachelard once captured this situation by claiming that what an experiment is all about is to "risk one's reason."[5] In addition to illuminating the above argumentation, the quotation transports a further message. In experimentation, contingency is not something to be feared or avoided; it is something to which researchers expose themselves in a spirit of adventure. The art of experimentation lies in the ability to distinguish between contingencies that arise

4 "Du mot à la vie: un dialogue entre Jacques Derrida et Hélène Cixous." Propos recueillis par Aliette Armel, *Magazine littéraire*, no 430, April 2004, 28.
5 Bachelard, "Surrationalisme," 4–5.

from the depth of the experimental setup and ones that are merely due to the foibles of circumstance.

Note that I am not talking here about contingencies in nature, such as the haphazard change in cloud formations, the randomness of quantum events, or chance occurrences in the process of biological evolution. I am talking neither about the vagaries of everyday life, nor of the contingencies of historical processes in general. I am talking about a particular cultural field of agency: the scientific research process. Experimentation is a peculiar cultural technique of knowledge acquisition. In its course, contingency is not encountered and experienced as something that befalls us from outside, but rather as something that emerges from inside out: it results from arranging things in such a way that knowledge effects can be engendered, that events can happen. Researchers are not subject to contingency, but rather the other way around: contingencies are subject to the researchers' work. They are embodied by and put into the service of the process of knowledge generation. We could, perhaps, describe it as the "taming of chance" for the purpose of extracting new knowledge from the process of experimentation, to borrow an expression that Ian Hacking used for a different yet not completely unrelated purpose.[6] Contingency is the driving force in the acquisition of empirically grounded knowledge about the world through experimentation.

Alex Arteaga: In "Contingent Agencies" we mobilized the concept of 'contingency' first of all in relation to its etymological

6 Ian Hacking, *The Taming of Chance* (Cambridge: Cambridge University Press, 1975).

roots (*contingere*: to touch). We qualified the agencies we situate in the focus of our research as 'contingent' because they actualize themselves in contact to one another. Could you refer to this relational aspect in the concept of contingency you are outlining here?

Hans-Jörg Rheinberger: My use of the term 'contingency' focuses on its meaning as an encounter in the sense of an event that comes as a surprise, another of the meanings of the Latin verb. It comprises touch or contact, but one that is essentially unintentional. I think that the usage of the term contingency in your project also stresses the surprising options that emerge from such unintentional encounters or contacts, from 'letting it happen.'

Alex Arteaga: Absolutely! The practices of notation that we proposed to develop in this project are first of all practices that allow practitioners to experience this 'letting it happen,' being the 'it' the process of unfolding of specific agencies entails, as a condition of specific atmospheres. The unpredictability caused by contingency in experimental settings can thus also be found in the dynamics of atmospheres. If you agree with this affirmation, could you speculate about further common features between experiment and atmosphere?

Hans-Jörg Rheinberger: It is not easy for me to answer this question. If you refer to the atmosphere in terms of the earth's envelope in which we move and breathe, contingency is, of course, everywhere. If you refer to the atmosphere in terms of a certain mood of a situation in which we happen to be, it is also everywhere. But just because of this ubiquity it tends to lose its sharpness, its singularity. Experimentation rests on focusing contingency, not dispersing it. Actually, experiments are not atmospheric, at least not in the colloquial sense of the word. But by zooming in they open up a new horizon of *possibles*.[7] Metaphorically speaking, we could perhaps say that they create an atmosphere of excitement in which novelty can play out.

Alex Arteaga: I definitely refer to the second meaning of the term 'atmosphere.' Although atmospheres are, as you say, 'everywhere,' they are always situation-specific, they have boundaries (although these boundaries are dynamic and vague). In this sense, every atmosphere is irreducibly singular and this singularity, in relation to the singularity of a particular agency, was the focus of Contingent Agencies.

Notation

Hans-Jörg Rheinberger: It appears appropriate to add a few words on notation here, and on how, in scientific research, notational activities relate to contingency.[8] In an experiment, research tools and matters of epistemic interest are arranged with respect to each other in such a way that an interface is created between them. The interface, in turn, generates a productive friction that emits sparks, which can meaningfully be interpreted as bits of information about the object of investigation—as long as one keeps in mind that they stem from the encounter with the research technology in use. These sparks,

7 In the sense of François Jacob's *Le Jeu des possibles* (Paris: Fayard, 1981)

8 For more on notation, see Rheinberger, *Split and Splice*, Chapter 5.

or traces, then need to be fixed in one way or another, in order to render them durable and available for closer inspection. This is an operation that, as unavoidable collateral damage, deprives them of some of their essential ambiguity but at the same time makes them amenable to a new 'game of the possible' on another playground.[9] With that, a novel space opens up, which facilitates operations that are excluded from the space of experimentation proper. Each of these two related spaces comes with its own materiality, which gives rise to a repertoire of manipulative options that is characteristic for each of them respectively. I have elaborated on these two spaces in more detail in *Split and Splice*.[10] They can be characterized as a space of graphematicity on the one hand and a space of representation, or data space on the other hand.[11] Each of them comes with its peculiar logic of proliferation but for both of them, contingency occupies a central place.

With the space of representation, we enter the realm of notation. It has also been described as the realm of "inscription," a notion favored by Bruno Latour in his early writings.[12] As you can imagine, with that, a new space of contingent agencies becomes available. It is a space in which trials can be conducted on paper or on a screen in a tentative and easily reversible fashion. They rely on and exploit the reduction to two dimensions

9 François Jacob, *The Possible and the Actual*, trans. Betty E. Spillmann (Seattle: Washington University Press, 1982).

10 Rheinberger, *Split and Splice*, in particular Chapters 1 and 2.

11 See also "'Forming and being informed.' Hans-Jörg Rheinberger in conversation with Michael Schwab," in *Experimental Systems. Future Knowledge in Artistic Research*, ed. Michael Schwab (Leuven: Leuven University Press, 2013), 198–219.

12 Latour and Woolgar, *Laboratory Life*.

that goes along with entering the space of representation. What is lost in spatial dimensions is gained in degrees of freedom to puzzle around, and to do so in a newly acquired time regime freed from the constraints of an experimental setup. Above all, however, what is gained are options for making things visible. Representation creates the possibility of visualizing relations that would otherwise remain implicit in the experimental setup and that could not be identified in the scattered traces it generates. You can name the possibilities that result from the fixation of traces: combination and recombination, juxtaposition and superimposition, addition and subtraction, diagrammatic arrangement and rearrangement, splitting and lumping, denomination and annotation, and many more.

A new degree of mobility is gained with respect to the space of experimental interactions. Just as easily, one can imagine that the results of such manipulative operations in the space of representation need to be fed back into the space of experimentation proper. Not everything that is possible and even plausible on paper makes sense with respect to the epistemic target under consideration. With that, a process of permanent iteration, of checks and balances, is set in motion that keeps the experimental machinery going, drives it forward and gives rise to ever new differentiations and modifications. Contingent agencies in different but related spaces start to interact with each other. Notation is thus nothing less than an essential ingredient of experimentation. It brings an iterative cohesion to the ongoing process.

Alex Arteaga: The way I conceived and practiced notation in the framework of Contingent Agencies has a structural similarity with the way you interpret this concept in the context of scientific experimentation. My point of departure also considers two 'related spaces.' In my case, the first is the space in which an atmosphere emerges out of the interaction of the agencies unfolding within one specific situation. In my approach, the presence of an atmosphere, the unfolding of agencies and the relationship between them are not objectual but 'operative.' I use this term in relation to the concept of "operative intentionality" (*fungierende Intentionlität*) as defined by Edmund Husserl and further developed by Maurice Merleau-Ponty.[13] Accordingly, atmospheres, agencies and their relations appear first and foremost as not (yet fully) constituted phenomenal objects but instead in an extremly vague, subtle and non-contoured way. In contrast to the components of the situation in which they emerge, they are not perceptually graspable but barely noticeable through an operative intentional act that I denominate provisionally 'sensing.' The practice of notation is based on the performance of sensing and its connection with other intentional acts (such as writing, diagramming, or the use of recording technology in sound, video and photography) that imply a certain mobilization of object intentionality. My idea is that these practices of notation unfold on the border between

13 Edmund Husserl, *Ideas Pertaining to a Pure Phenomenology and to a Phenomenological Philosophy. Second Book: Studies in the Phenomenology of Constitution*, trans. Richard Rojcewicz and André Schuwer (Dordrecht: Kluwer, 1989), 151–169; Edmund Husserl, *Formal and Transcendental Logic*, trans. Dorion Cairns (The Hague: Martinus Nijhoff, 1969), 157, 234–237; Edmund Husserl, *Cartesian Meditations: An Introduction to Phenomenology*, trans. Dorion Cairns (The Hague: Martinus Nijhoff, 1960), 77–80; Maurice Merleau-Ponty, "The philosopher and his shadow," in *Signs*, trans. Richard C. McCleary (Evanston, Ill.: Northwestern University Press, 1964), 159–81, 165; Maurice Merleau-Ponty, *Phenomenology of Perception*, trans. Donald A. Landes (New York: Routledge, 2012), lxxi, 407.

both types of intentionality, thus producing artifacts that are inevitably objectual and simultaneously *in resonance* with the connection between agencies and atmospheres, *in touch with which* they have been produced. Accordingly, these practices of notation do not notate what is in the focus of attention of the practitioner (the connection between one specific agency and one specific atmosphere) but they notate *with* it. They are in this sense contingent practices. The results, as in the case of the notation in the framework of scientific experiments as you describe them, also disclose a new space different from the one in which agencies and atmospheres unfold, and that allow for the realization of new operations which are intended to be different forms of reflection.

Instead of using the term 'representation,' due to the impossibility of representing non-objectual entities, I would rather consider the space disclosed by these practices of notation as a space of 'presentation' of objects contingent to (that is, realized in contact with) the practitioner's focus of attention. Would the term 'presentation' also work in your case?

Hans-Jörg Rheinberger: My own basic distinction with respect to the scientific research process is that of a space of graphematicity, that is, the space of the generation of traces in the experiment, and a space of re-presentation, or data space, in which notation, among other activities like modeling, can take place. The term, I understand, comes with a problematic baggage—it cannot easily be stripped of its meaning of depiction. But this is absolutely not what I am focusing on. I avoid the notion of presence—and hence, presentation, that is, present-making—because it is suggestive of an illusionary immediacy. Of course, the space of representation is a contingent space as well, because with its options of arrangement and rearrangement, juxtaposition and superimposition, enhancement and attenuation, it allows for the emergence of novel constellations. It appears to me, however, that in an artistic practice like your notational activities, these two spaces—the graphematic and the representational—possibly coincide, or even can collapse into a single space, so that the distinction probably makes little sense here, at least if we think of artistic notation where an artist and his or her pencil and the paper are in direct touch with one another. We cannot expect a one-to-one correspondence between scientific and artistic practices.

Alex Arteaga: My suggestion of using the term 'presentation,' without renouncing to the possibility of immediacy (which I consider to be a condition for aesthetic practices), rather intends to indicate the simple gesture of allowing an artifact to be perceived, and with that, to establish a certain connection with the non-perceivable presences to which the notation refers. Notwithstanding its unpretentiousness, notation should be seen to be endowed with a generative agency.

Hans-Jörg Rheinberger: As I have tried to make clear, tying notation to the space of re-presentation does not mean depriving it of its generative potential. On the contrary, it specifies that potential. But in the sciences, we are not concerned with creations *ex nihilo*. And that this, in contrast, could happen in the arts, is one of the ineradicable illusions of the profession. Gaston Bachelard, with his notion of "material imagination,"[14] reminded us how deeply our capacity for dreaming is rooted in

14 Bachelard, *Water and Dreams.*

the materiality of the elements that go into artistic production, be it drawing, painting, engraving, sculpting, singing, dancing, composing or poetic writing. It appears to me that the way you describe notation somehow testifies to this insight.

Alex Arteaga: I basically agree with the material basis of any form of creation. Nevertheless, it was also Bachelard who affirmed that "nothing prepares a poetic image..."[15]

Reflection

Hans-Jörg Rheinberger: At this point we can start talking about reflection. Reflexivity is usually taken to be both the anthropological hallmark of what it means to be human, and the hallmark of a mind beyond matter. Let us try to free ourselves for a moment from these abstractions. We can look at experimentation as a way to materially interact with the world in a reflexive manner and notation, in turn, as a way to materially interact with the experiment in a reflexive manner. The process of gaining knowledge is thus characterized by a two-fold reflexivity whose modes are inextricably intertwined with each other.

Alex Arteaga: I completely agree with this idea. I consider my practices of notation to be practices of "reflexive notation" exactly in the sense of a first reflection.

15 Bachelard, *The Poetics of Space*, trans. Etienne Gilson (New York: Orion Press, 1964), xxiv.

Hans-Jörg Rheinberger: Let us first look at the reflexive aspects of the experiment, that is, experimenters' interaction with bits and pieces of the world around them. There is a wonderful *bonmot* ascribed to the French surrealist poet and writer Paul Eluard which brilliantly captures the essence of this interaction. Since it is almost untranslatable, I shall quote it in French: *Il ne faut pas voir le monde tel que je suis.*[16] Experimenter and experiment have to engage in a fine-tuned interaction that at the same time involves an act of distancing. In an experiment, I do not want to learn something about myself, I want to learn something about the intricacies of the things that interest me. Essentially, this is achieved by an act of delegation. The essence of my interaction with the things in question consists in arranging them in such a way that they mutually interact in a manner that leaves traces. ideally, these traces 'reflect.' However, they do not reflect my own conscious action, but something of the relational states of the things under consideration.[17] We can characterize this situation with the notion of acting at a distance. Hans Blumenberg sees action at a distance as the grounding gesture of conceptualization *tout court.*[18] Conceptualization is nothing but another

16 An attempt at a translation may read as follows: "One must not see the world as I am." However, the ambiguity of the French "Il ne faut pas" as both being impersonal and personalized cannot be rendered in English without a grammatically weird disjunction. Gaston Bachelard used the phrase as a motto for his book *The Psychoanalysis of Fire*, trans. Alan C. M. Ross (Boston: Beacon Press, 1964).

17 For more on this, see Hans-Jörg Rheinberger, "Vom Subjekt des Wissens aus der Perspektive der Historischen Epistemologie," in *Selbstsein als Sich-Wissen? Zur Bedeutung der Wissensgeschichte für die Historisierbarkeit des Subjekts*, ed. Sandra Janßen and Thomas Alkemeyer (Tübingen: Mohr Siebeck, 2021) 25–36.

18 Hans Blumenberg, *Theorie der Unbegrifflichkeit*, ed. Anselm Haverkamp (Frankfurt am Main: Suhrkamp, 2007).

expression of reflection. An analysis of the experiment shows us how reflection, as conceptualization, is materially enacted in the process of knowledge acquisition.

Alex Arteaga: I consider the practices of notation I developed in this project as being phenomenological practices (or to be more precise: aesthetic-phenomenological practices). Accordingly, they cannot be based on any kind of distancing between the practitioner and its focus of attention. Distancing in this case can only be performed in relation to everything that needs to be bracketed to accomplish epoché. Furthermore, it is not possible in this case to perform an act of delegation, since it is through the experience of the notator that agencies and atmospheres can be sensed.

Hans-Jörg Rheinberger: We are on the track of an important differentiation here. Perhaps we should distinguish between two phenomenological traditions. Both of them can be traced back to Edmund Husserl's *Cartesian Meditations*, the result of two lectures delivered at the Sorbonne in Paris in 1929. One of them is epitomized by Maurice Merleau-Ponty, the other by Gaston Bachelard, Jean Cavaillès and Georges Canguilhem. Both share the point of departure, namely our interaction with the world and the practices it entails, but they look at it from a different perspective. One of them tries to think the interaction from the perspective of the phenomena, the other from the perspective of their perception, focusing on impact and intentionality, respectively.[19]

19 David Hyder, "Foucault, Cavaillès and Husserl on the historical epistemology of the sciences," *Perspectives on Science* 10 (2003): 107–129; Anton

But let us now move on to look at the activities of notating in the sciences from the perspective of reflexivity. Here, in the realm of representation, frozen traces (usually addressed as data) are handled, arranged, and rearranged in an always preliminary and tentative fashion. To use another expression that is untranslatable into English, this time a German one, we can describe the moves in the data space as *Probehandeln.*[20] It comes with its own material reflexivity. Just as in an experiment, not everything is possible here. Not every note matches with every other note in the realm of representation. The data space is refractory, it is a space of heightened tentativeness. Every notational move is tentative. We can say that here reflexivity equals tentativity. And what appears to match must then be fed back into the graphematic space of the experiment, where it has to stand the test. We now see that in the end we are dealing with a double reflexivity, or preliminarity, which connects the two realms, experimentation and notation, and contingency occupies a central place in both of them. Contingency, in the end, is another word for the fact that in both realms, and in their interaction, the outcome cannot be determined in advance.

Alex Arteaga: In your deliberations you treat reflexivity as an intrinsic aspect of experimentation and notation. Could you imagine understanding reflection as an autonomous field of

Vydra, "Gaston Bachelard and his reactions to phenomenology," *Continental Philosophy Review* 47 (2014): 45–58.

20 In the context of psychoanalysis, the term is sometimes, rather clumsily, rendered as 'behavior in rehearsal.' I prefer to keep the German expression here.

practice, that is, a field of practices of reflection distinguished from practices of experimenting and notating?

Hans-Jörg Rheinberger: I hesitate to regard reflection as an "autonomous field of practice." There is a long philosophical tradition that treats thinking—taken synonymously with reflection—as an activity *per se,* of and in itself, that is, pure reason. My impression is that we do not get far with such an assumption. I prefer to understand reflection starting from its originary meaning, that is, a light beam reflected by an impenetrable surface. When it comes to thinking, this means that there is always an interaction with matter at its core, a friction with, a resistance of matter.

Alex Arteaga: I fully agree again about the material foundation of any practice and therefore of any form of thinking. With the term "autonomy" I didn't point to a form of pure mental thinking. This would be deeply contradictory to my understanding of thinking as constitutively embodied and situated. What I meant is rather the possibility to completely differentiate the constituting dynamics of practices of reflection from any other practice.

But coming back to the question of 'distance': could distance, also as an aspect of autonomy, be understood as an intensification of the relationship with the investigated things?

Hans-Jörg Rheinberger: We are dealing with a dialectical relation here. In an experiment the objects of investigation, the epistemic things, are brought to interact with the investigative instruments. The experimenters have arranged for this interaction to occur. But at the moment of the interaction itself, they leave the scene. Hans Blumenberg, to whom I refer here, takes the animal trap as a prime anthropological example of such an interaction. The hunters create it with all their ingenuity, only to retreat and let the animal interact with the trap in their absence. This creates a reflexive loop. The outcome of the process is fed back into the arrangement's modification. This is the only way to come closer to things that escape our range of action.

Alex Arteaga: Let me stay for a moment with the idea of 'conceptualization.' To consider it as a synonym of 'reflection' excludes the very basic meaning of reflection: to give back what incides on another medium, as a mirror—inorganic matter. But organic matter is also able to do this, that is, to reflect simply but unfolding the immanent skills enabled by its inner form of organization. On this basis, would you admit the possibility of a non-conceptual reflection?

Hans-Jörg Rheinberger: Blumenberg calls his considerations a "theory of non-conceptuality." Again, it is the process that matters here, not a particular state of it. And again, Blumenberg uses the image of the trap to make his point. The device needs to be non-conceptual enough to be able to catch things that one is unable to anticipate precisely. And it has to be conceptual enough to serve what it is meant for. There is an essential indeterminacy involved here. Without it, concepts would not be able to function as investigative tools in a research process.

Alex Arteaga: In the closing panel of the symposium, you mentioned that notation and reflection require the manipulation of matter, enabled by or at least within or according to certain media—you referred to this briefly using the formulations "materially enacted" and "material reflexivity." Is there an immanent contingency in both fields, matter and media?

Hans-Jörg Rheinberger: There is contingency both in matter and in media. In fact, media are but another kind of matter. If we take matter as a synonym for the research object and media as a synonym for the investigative tools, we realize that there is no substantial property that could help us distinguish between both. It is the *position in the process* that defines them as either object or tool. In my terminology, epistemic things and technical things can change places. Epistemic things can become technical entities, and technical things can become epistemically challenging.

Alex Arteaga: Could you imagine the possibility of a specific and thus potentially different definition of notation and reflection, not in the realm of science but of art or aesthetics? Could this shift enable another kind of differentiation between reflection and conceptualization?

Hans-Jörg Rheinberger: As I remarked previously, there is no necessary one-to-one relation when it comes to the comparison of different creative activities. Each of them has—and lives by—its unique features and constellations. My remarks on the scientific research process are meant to be used as a possible differential *resource* for thinking *about* artistic processes, *not* as a characterization of them. I wouldn't really feel qualified for this latter task. This is why I am so interested in conversations like our's. It helps me to think further.

EXPERIMENTAL APERÇUS

Laboratory Worlds

The relations between laboratory and artistic research can be regarded from two rather different angles. The first concerns the occupation with and appropriation of materials and instruments that belong to the arsenal of a scientific laboratory as a resource for art work. The second concerns artistic work itself in terms of its laboratory and research characteristics, insofar as the term 'laboratory' can be taken as more or less synonymously with the research process as such and not just with the space in which it is carried out. I call the first angle exoteric, the second esoteric. More often than not, the two aspects are entangled.

Let me begin with the exoteric aspect. In the course of the past decades, a trend has intensified and gained additional momentum that can periodically be observed throughout the long history in the West of a separation between the sciences and the arts. In these periods, artists are seeking proximity to the sciences as spaces and reservoirs of—critical—inspiration for their own work. What appears new with respect to the actual situation is that scientific institutions, in particular scientific laboratories, are opening themselves to, sometimes inviting and hosting artists as residents for shorter or longer time periods and encouraging them to engage on the spot with the respective laboratory realities through conversation, observation, and participation. The artistic results of these exchanges are then usually presented semi-publicly or publicly as exhibitions in the laboratory spaces themselves.[1] On the one hand, these initiatives could be seen as a continuation by other means of a venerable tradition that once went under the name of 'art in architecture' and now spread from the exterior to the interior of scientific institutions, thereby acquiring a more performative character. On the other hand, there is something genuinely new about that recent trend. Both sides, the scientific and the artistic, no longer shy away from getting closer to one another, as far as their *practices* are concerned. The sciences are opening up to reveal the nitty-gritty of their daily work, and the artists are coming in close contact with the media and the materials of a particular laboratory as so many options of a creative appropriation.

Artists in the laboratory thereby have the choice between two takes. Their first option is to engage with the products of the work of a laboratory. As a rule, these won't be the abstract products, such as scientific articles or even mathematical formulae, but rather the palpable images that emerge from the application of analog or digital technologies of visual representation. In this domain, the scientists themselves, too, enjoy being confronted with the aesthetic aspects and effects of their research results—not least, they can be used to embellish the covers of their journals and textbooks. The title pages of journals such as *Science* and *Nature* abound in examples.

The second option for an artist is to engage with the technologies of data production and of visualization, that is, with the means and media through and with which the results of sc-

1 See, e.g., Mónica Bello and José-Carlos Mariátegui (eds.), *Quantum. In Search of the Invisible* (Barcelona: Centre de Cultura Contemporània de Barcelona, 2019). The corresponding exhibition was based on a collaboration with the European Organization for Nuclear Research (CERN) in Geneva.

entific work are being shaped. Usually this is the thornier path because it is in need of a more indirect, reflexive take on scientific data production and processing, an aspect of their work that scientists themselves usually leave aside when it comes to the public presentation of their results. Many recent examples could be quoted here, such as Paul Vanouse's engagement with the techniques of DNA sequencing,[2] the work of Evelina Domnitch and Dmitry Gelfand with physico-chemical procedures of producing dissipative structures,[3] or that of Hannes Rickli with the generation of traces and raw data, both visual and audio, in biological laboratories.[4]

In this field of confrontation between epistemology and aesthetics, however, the exchange processes frequently remain unilateral. It is mainly the artists who engage with the procedures and results of a particular research process and use them, in one form or another, for their work. The scientists from the respective laboratories frequently remain more or less passive spectators, exceptions notwithstanding.[5] We encounter here a phenomenon that is well known, if in a modified fashion, from the ethnomethodological laboratory studies in the realm of social studies of science and technology.[6] There, as well, the

2 See "Tracing the index: Paul Vanouse," in the present volume.

3 See, e.g., Evelina Domnitch and Dmitry Gelfand, *Opening Coccyx* (Milano: Die Schachtel Editions, 2005); see also Gunnar Schmidt, *Weiche Displays. Projektionen auf Rauch, Wolken und Nebel* (Berlin: Wagenbach, 2011).

4 See "Experiments, traces, data streams: Hannes Rickli," in the present volume.

5 Fischer et al., *Natures of Data*.

6 Michael Lynch, *Art and Artifact in Laboratory Science: A Study of Shop Work and Shop Talk in a Research Laboratory* (London: Routledge Kegan & Paul, 1985); Latour and Woolgar, *Laboratory Life*; Karin Knorr Cetina, *Epistemic Cultures. How the Sciences Make Knowledge* (Cambridge MA: Harvard University Press, 1999).

ethnologists entering a laboratory, although welcomed in the labs, are often regarded as a bit exotic by scientists, with exceptions here as well.[7]

Such artistic engagement with the realm of the epistemic can also be—and often is—connected to a critical stance toward the sciences, their technological presence and output as well as their social implications. When the scientists in question are willing to open themselves, however, to the artistic uses of their instruments and materials, a knowledge-critical surplus may result on their part. It may at least take the form of learning to see one's own procedures of knowledge acquisition in a new, somewhat distanced light.

'Esoteric' is my term for the second form of artistic engagement with scientific laboratory worlds. Maybe it should be added in passing that this is an analytical distinction; in the concrete work of artists, the exoteric and the esoteric aspect can go hand in hand. Here, and in parallel to the exploratory handling of materials under the auspices of knowledge generation, as it is characteristic for the scientific research process, we are concerned with exploring appropriate forms of handling materials from an aesthetic-epistemic perspective in the artistic realm. Four different moments, all of which are implied in artistic exploration, can be distinguished here and are in need of further delineation.

The first moment concerns the characteristic resistance connected to the respective materials being dealt with in scientific as well as artistic research. What it involves is, by handling the

7 An example is Nobel Prize winner Roger Guillemin, who received Bruno Latour and Steve Woolgar in his endocrinology laboratory at the Salk Institute for Biological Studies in La Jolla in the late 1970s.

materials, to squeeze effects out of them that are not obvious, and often seem not even to be plausible at first sight. One has to take certain precautionary measures and carry out certain performative actions in order to reveal the materials' peculiarities, which will only become visible as a result of these manipulations. What is needed here is a familiarity with these materials that can only be acquired in a protracted working process.

The second aspect may appropriately be summarized by the notion of immanent transcendence. Research processes—irrespective of whether they are of a scientific or of an artistic nature—have to be conducted so as to reveal things that were not experienced before in this particular way. Novelty in this sense cannot, however, be fully anticipated. It will happen in the working process itself, as a result of the procedural constellations to which the working materials will be exposed. Whereas in scientific research, novelty is predominantly epistemically connotated, in artistic research, knowledge of the materials goes hand in hand with aesthetic effects.

If one takes both of these moments together, a third characteristic results. Scientific as well as artistic research move in an exploratory fashion, that is, in an experimental context which typically extends over a longer period of time. The laboratory, or studio, or atelier, is its regular spatial confinement; it can, however, also take place in the form of work in the field or open air.[8] In the context of scientific research, the concept of experimental system has come into wider use with regard to

8 For an example from the artistic realm, compare Katharina Ammann and Priska Gisler (eds., vol. 1) as well as Florian Dombois, Priska Gisler, Schirin Kretschmann and Markus Schwander (eds., vol. 2), *Präparat Bergsturz* (Lucerne: Periferia, 2012 and 2013).

this aspect.[9] It stands for a certain relation between continuity concerning the material basis and changes in the perception of the material over time. Such a relationship can only be realized in the form of a trajectory, which then distinguishes it from other, more short-lived forms of artistic expression.

Last, but not least, research is an eminently discursive process. It is characterized not only by publicly exposing one's results, but also by making the procedures used available for discussion. And most importantly, research is a collective process. As a general rule, it is conceived and carried out by groups of people. When and where artistic research is understood as a kind of laboratory work, moments of the discursive and the collective will necessarily have to be thematized. In this respect, the forms of documentation and current public availability of the background processes of artistic research are still in a state of intense gestation, resulting in new forms of communication.[10]

9 See Rheinberger, *Toward a History of Epistemic Things.*

10 Compare, e.g., *Journal for Artistic Research* (JAR, since 2011); *Research Catalogue* (RC). An International Database for Artistic Research; compare also Michael Schwab (ed.), *Experimental Systems. Future Knowledge in Artistic Research* (Leuven: Orpheus Institute and Leuven University Press, 2013).

Experimenting and Writing

What follows is a short reflection on the processes of experimenting and writing as well as their relations to one another. It starts from the assumption that both literary writing as well as scientific experimentation share, as genuinely productive processes, a common basic structure. In the first part, I will expose the grounding features of experimentation in scientific research by interpreting a key passage by scientist and philosopher of science Michael Polanyi. I will then show, in the second part, that literary writing can be described and assessed from the same perspective, although each of them comes with its own material specifications.

Let us start with a remark that Heinrich von Kleist jotted down on the gradual construction of thought during speech: "For it is not we who know, but at first it is only a *certain state of mind* of ours that knows."[1] Kleist aimed at capturing that "certain state of mind" we have all experienced in one form or another. We have occupied ourselves intensely with some problem and carry it around within us, yet we have not yet got a clear perspective on it. We are not yet in a state to see it clearly in our mind's eye. Speaking is a means of lending shape to it, a shape that we might not have anticipated and that may surprise us ourselves. The kind of exteriorization that accompanies the flow of words is, at the same time, the condition for creating an event. In order to arrive at this point, however, speech must not be directed; one has to find a way to let it happen. It has to occur in passing—it happens literally *bei-läufig*.

1 Kleist, "On the gradual construction of thoughts during speech," 45.

Let us formulate the problem somewhat more generally: In order to enter uncharted territory, our minds have to rely on exteriorization.[2] Besides speaking, writing is another, even more powerful form of such an exteriorization, and one with peculiar characteristics—about which, more in a moment. First, however, let us make a short detour into the scientific laboratory.

Experimenting

With the experiment, the sciences have created a practice of exteriorization which helps over and again to succeed in letting oneself be surprised. The laboratory has become the privileged space in which epistemic events are made to happen and can materialize themselves. In experimentation, surprising results are comparable to exteriorized ideas. Experimentation is a "machine for making the future," as the molecular biologist and Nobel Prize winner François Jacob aptly wrote in his autobiography.[3] It has become my favorite metaphor. Research experiments continually break through the limited horizon of what we are able to anticipate in a given situation, which is as a rule, rather restricted. The epistemic appeal of the experiment consists in the fact that, from time to time, unprecedented things make their appearance that do not fit the given

2 Hans-Jörg Rheinberger, "Zeit zu schreiben," in *Vademecum der Inspirationsmittel*, ed. Christoph Markschies and Ernst Osterkamp (Göttingen: Wallstein, 2012), 126–127.

3 François Jacob, *The Statue Within. An Autobiography* (New York: Basic Books, 1988), 9.

frame and that can push the research process forward in completely unforeseen directions.

The Hungarian physical chemist and philosopher of science Michael Polanyi, who became widely known for his reflections on tacit, embodied knowledge,[4] once described the core of the matter as follows. It is a particularly succint version of a statement that Polanyi repeated in slightly different formulations in print as well—a hint of the importance he attributed to it.[5] It is a statement about what we could call the *research situation*, and it has as well acquired the status of a *locus classicus* for me: "This capacity of a thing to reveal itself in unexpected ways in the future, I attribute to the fact that the thing observed is an aspect of reality, possessing a significance that is not exhausted by our conception of any single aspect of it. To trust that a thing we know is real is, in this sense, to feel that it has the independence and power for manifesting itself in yet unthought of ways in the future."[6]

The quote implies, in a nutshell, a whole praxeology and poetology of research. It is worthwhile going into more detail with regard to a number of its aspects. This will also help to structure the later remarks on writing. First, it is noteworthy that from the start, the gaze is focused on the material conditions of the research process. To be sure, research implies the

4 Michael Polanyi, *The Tacit Dimension* (London: Routledge & Kegan Paul, 1966).

5 See, e.g., Michael Polanyi, "The unaccountable element in science," in *Knowing and Being: Essays by Michael Polanyi*, ed. Marjorie Grene (Chicago: University of Chicago Press, 1969), 119–120.

6 Quoted from a lecture in Marjorie Grene, *The Knower and the Known* (Washington, DC.: Center for Advanced Research in Phenomenology & University Press of America, 1984), 219.

mind of the researcher, but its results do not spring from the head of Zeus like a sudden epiphany. On the contrary, researchers' minds are always bound to a particular material situation. In the context of an experimental procedure that allows them to transform things into research objects, they encounter resistance. Things transformed into research objects can be described as epistemic. Without such transformation, there is no research process—it relies on these objects and the experimental setup they require. The scientific mind—*l'esprit scientifique,* in Gaston Bachelard's words[7] — presupposes this kind of exteriority against which it can rub and scrub itself. Without such a permanent challenge, it would not be able to do much more than to revolve around itself and, with luck, to gain something from its own fluctuations from time to time.

Second, Polanyi endows the things around which research revolves with agency, with the capacity for manifesting themselves "in yet unthought of ways in the future." They possess the potential to surprise the researcher, that is, to deceive by not matching his or her expectations, and to surpass one's capacity for foresight by their inherent revelatory richness. The question of who is the master in this game can no longer be answered in a simple fashion. To experiment means to organize the process of knowledge acquisition in such a way that the things are granted the—always—penultimate word, a word that cannot be spoken in advance. Thoughtful experimentation opens the door for 'unheard-of things.'

Third, the agency of things implies resistance, resilience against intervention. Their experimental malleability is restricted, we cannot do just what we want with them. There-

7 Bachelard, *New Scientific Spirit.*

fore, one cannot talk about empirical research as a constructive activity without further ado, neither in the sense of a technical nor of a social construction. On the other hand, experimenting does not simply amount to discovering in the sense of unveiling, that is, merely laying bare something that is already there but hidden from view. Experimenting revolves around manifestation. Manifestation is a wonderful word for designating a movement that lies in between: as the word suggests, the movement it describes is in need of the hands in order to be carried out; but the hands must feel out where the things lead them. They are hands that have to be in touch with their things.

Fourth, the epistemic valuation of things is transitory. They keep their epistemic character and interest only until their reference potential in a given context is exhausted. They function like a xenotext, as described by Brian Rotman in *Signifying Nothing*.[8] They do not redeem a defined promise; rather, they pose riddles. Their significance lies in the fact that they refer to further possible meanings. Likewise, it lies in the essence of epistemic things to point beyond themselves. Their promise is of a peculiar kind: the expectation they arouse surrounds things with an aura that has no sharp contours. It is precisely this indeterminacy that drives the researcher around the rims and edges of objects of concern without being able to predict what will show up behind them. In the end, the tension between being in reach of an interaction with the epistemic object and yet not being able to hold it firmly in one's hands refers back to the first point of this staccato-like characterization of the research situation. It also prepares the ground

8 Brian Rotman, *Signifying Nothing: The Semiotics of Zero* (New York: St Martin's Press, 1987).

for the basic second order category to which scientists usually refer—beautifully described by Ian Hacking in *Representing and Intervening*[9]—, the category of 'reality' that Polanyi, to return to the above quotation, attaches to the capacity of a thing to lead into the unthought-of. It is bound to the ever-precarious limbo between the known from which it propels away because it leaves something to be desired, and the unknown to which there is no immediate access. "Epistemological acts," to quote Gaston Bachelard, are thus necessary to surmount an "epistemological obstacle" in a given research situation. They lead to those "unexpected impulses" that determine the "course of scientific development."[10] Through their repetition they instigate an iterative process.

Not infrequently, such acts happen when the process of finding one's way through the epistemic maze of experimental traces *on paper* has begun. On paper, juxtapositions become possible that are foreclosed in the context of the material fabric of the experiment itself. Writing, the tentative ordering and assembling of data is thus an integral part of experimentation. It widens its possibilities, and it acts back on the experiment.[11]

9 Ian Hacking, *Representing and Intervening. Introductory Topics in the Philosophy of Natural Science* (Cambridge: Cambridge University Press, 1983), in particular the chapter "Break" in the middle of the book.

10 Bachelard, *Formation of the Scientific Mind*, Chapter 1; Gaston Bachelard, *L'Activité rationaliste de la physique contemporaine* (Paris: Presses Universitaires de France, 1951), 25.

11 Christoph Hoffmann, *Schreiben im Forschen. Verfahren, Szenen, Effekte* (Tubingen: Mohr Siebeck, 2018); Rheinberger, *Split and Splice*, Chapter 5.

Writing

With that, we turn to the process of writing. What about entering uncharted territory in the humanities? Unfortunately, the humanities do not have that special apparatus of exteriorized imagination, the experiment, at their disposal. However, the act of writing itself creates a comparable disposition of externalization, of exteriorized imagination. Let us try to differentiate the characterization of writing from this perspective. In doing so, we can build on the four aspects identified in Polanyi's description of working on epistemic things: materiality, agency, resilience, and iterativity.

First, the act of writing possesses a materiality of its own. Its rather trivial aspect derives from the fact that it requires a writing tool and an appropriate writing surface. Both have to be of such a shape and texture that they are compatible at the point where they come in contact with each other. The clay tablets of the Babylonians require a simple pointed shaft.[12] If necessary, a fingernail will do. The slate demands chalk or a slate pencil; paper a lead pencil or an ink feather; the screen a digital raster. With the typewriter, paper became surrounded by the complex equipment of the writing tool. In comparison to the pen, it brought with it a materiality of its own, which also required a different motility of the hand as compared to traditional handwriting. Friedrich Kittler,[13] in his incomparable fashion, demonstrated what the new distance to the paper entailed for the

12 Peter Damerow, Hans J. Nissen and Robert K. Eglund, *Archaic Bookkeeping. Early Writing and Techniques of Economic Administration in the Ancient Near East*, trans. Paul Larsen (Chicago: The University of Chicago Press, 1993).

13 Friedrich Kittler, *Gramophone, Film, Typewriter*, trans. Geoffrey Wintrop-Young and Michael Wutz (Stanford: Stanford University Press, 1999).

"logic of sense," to quote Gilles Deleuze.[14] Writing by hand is continuous; writing on the typewriter is discrete. At first, the computer took over this latter principle. Today, however, the material development of its display has made it possible to use a pen again. I will come back to this alternative when discussing the resilience inherent in writing.

Here, we can draw a first conclusion and state that the activity of writing, which draws on this arsenal of utensils, is subject to a twofold dimensional reduction. On the one hand, it forces ordinary action in three-dimensional space to transform itself into a movement in the two dimensions of a surface. It can only take place either horizontally or vertically. Consequently, the preparation of appropriate two-dimensional planes becomes a technological challenge. On the other hand, to cover these surfaces requires a further reduction of the range of gestures of the hand to a one-dimensional flow and, with that, to the strict linearity of an inexorable temporal succession. Thoughts must bow to linearity and become sequentialized through this bottleneck. The compulsion to linearity in temporal succession is shared by writing and speech. What distinguishes writing from speaking, however, is that the inscriptions of the former persist. Since they do not instantaneously fade away, they do not have to be received instantaneously, either. Once expressed, they can be passed on at a distance, both temporally and spatially. And their permanence allows for recursivity.[15] They open up a new space and a new time. This in turn gives rise to a new dimension of the epistemic: Let us call it

14 Gilles Deleuze, *The Logic of Sense*, trans. Mark Lester and Charles Stivale (New York: Columbia University Press, 1990).

15 Derrida, *Of Grammatology*.

the dimension of overwriting. Written iteration finds its basic form of expression in the palimpsest. Now, it becomes possible to change what is already there. It becomes possible to transcend what has been laid down. One can go beyond what exists. One can overwrite, displace, replace, and build on it.

Second, there is agency: it goes together with the aspect of preservation just described. The written word confronts us with its own materiality and, in doing so, it becomes a sparring partner of sorts. It can not only be reinforced, it can also cause doubt about what is written down. It can be perceived as insufficient, even 'odd' in a given context, or as lacking coherence, weight, or precision, either in its literary expression or in its cognitive content. It is ripe for reworking. Here again, the materiality of the writing surface comes into play. Entries on a clay tablet, once dried, can no longer be corrected. In contrast, a calculation carried out with chalk on a blackboard can be rectified at any time by wiping it away.[16] A word written on paper by a pencil can be erased. A sentence written in ink can be crossed out and replaced by another one. The clipping and pasting that had already become possible in principle with the advent of paper[17] has found its full unfolding only recently with electronic writing on a screen.

Now, what about the third property: resistance, resilience in the process of writing? As compared to other corporeal work,

16 On the role of chalk and blackboard in mathematics, see Michael Barany and Donald MacKenzie, "Chalk: Materials and concepts in mathematics research," in *Representation in Scientific Practice Revisited*, ed. Catelijne Coopmans, Janet Vertesi, Michael Lynch and Steve Woolgar (Cambridge MA: MIT Press, 2014), 107–130.

17 See, e.g., Anke te Heesen, *The Newspaper Clipping. A Modern Paper Object*, trans. Lori Lanz (Manchester: Manchester University Press, 2014).

writing 'flows from the hand' in a relatively swift manner. In order to keep the writing process going, writing tool and writing surface must interact with each other in such a way that the progress of the procedure over a longer span of time becomes possible without considerable physical effort. And yet, a peculiar phenomenon is to be observed in this context: it is a kind of reflexive inhibition. In his late poetologies, but already earlier in *L'Air et les songes*,[18] Gaston Bachelard has dealt in detail with the literary writing process and tried to capture it with poetic images.[19] There, we read of poets that they, too, "hear what they write at the same time as they are writing it, in the slow cadence of written language." This cadence lets them trust that "their pen would stop of its own accord if it encountered a hiatus, that it would refuse to write unnecessary alliterations."[20] Here, yet another aspect of writing becomes palpable. It hangs together with the writing tool. Just as the mechanics of the typewriter as a medium imply feedback at a distance with the written word, the pen allows for that proprioceptive feedback that makes itself felt as a resisting halt and condenses the resilience in the mediating tool between the person who writes and what is being written. Hence, "poetic images also have their matter."[21]

Without this material reference that manifests itself as resistance, there would be no poetry, only inner stammering. The real inside is the outside. Here, we have a meeting point with the sciences again, since the same holds for the latter. "In the

18 Bachelard, *Poetics of Reverie*; Bachelard, *Air and Dreams*.

19 For a more detailed description, compare Rheinberger, *The Hand of the Engraver*, Chapter on "Poetology."

20 Bachelard, *Air and Dreams*, 247–248.

21 Bachelard, *Water and Dreams*, 3.

depth of matter there grows an obscure vegetation; black flowers bloom in matter's darkness. They already possess a velvety touch, a formula for perfume."[22] And what holds for the writer also conveys itself to Bachelard the reader: "I am a dreamer of words, of written words. I think I am reading; a word stops me. I leave the page. The syllables of the word begin to move around. Stressed accents begin to invert."[23]

Let us now turn to the fourth characteristic: processuality, iterativity. It is Jacques Derrida who, time and again, has pointed to this aspect of writing. It is not only that the written text detaches itself from the author and, with that, begins to live a life of its own; it also invites building on it. In this context, Derrida repeatedly referred to images drawn from the arsenal of biological techniques of cultivation. He used the concept of 'grafting' to characterize the game with the heteroclite, the heteronomous and the heterogeneous, which he saw as the decisive mark of writing as a cultural technique: its intrinsic potential for permanent updating and recombination. "Writing means grafting," we read in *La Dissémination*.[24] Grafting means positing an other that does not organically emerge out of what precedes it, that is, it cannot be seen as its simple consequence, although it needs the precedent in order to articulate itself as an other.

In *Water and Dreams* Gaston Bachelard also made use of the concept of the graft in his characterization of poetic work on and with images of the elements—fire, water, earth, and air. In so doing, he aimed at stressing the peculiar movement pattern

22 Ibid., 2.
23 Bachelard, *Poetics of Reverie*, 17.
24 Derrida, "Dissemination," 355.

of poetic images in the process of writing. He, too, saw grafting as an appropriate image for adding something new to an already existing support, something that does not derive from the former in the sense of a mere shift of meaning. And yet, the graft itself depends on the support in order to be able to sprout. Quite explicitly, Bachelard does not want to understand the use of the word grafting here as a "mere metaphor," as he puts it. One could say he takes the metaphor literally. He does not want to understand it as a mere transference of sense, but rather as a figure of "material imagination." Structurally, it is comparable to an event: it does not accrue from within, it is rather the result of an extrinsic encounter with matter. "It is the graft that can truly provide the material imagination with an exuberance of forms, that can transmit the richness and density of matter to formal imagination." Exuberance is a fitting word for the kind of excess with which we are concerned here. And although Bachelard is specifically occupied with poetic artwork in this context, he categorically adds: "By nature, art is grafted."[25] The arts live from the encounter with the materials that enter into them. In the written work, pictorial matter and linguistic matter in the narrower sense of the word are interwoven; they engage with one another.

In writing—as in speaking—one does not simply express oneself, one brings that "certain state of mind" to manifest itself of which Kleist speaks in his essay mentioned above by feeding something from outside into it. In writing, thoughts slip in. It is a process of being subverted that hangs together with the material *dispositif* of writing. It is an experimental arrangement, a generative disposition in the sense of Pierre

25 Bachelard, *Water and Dreams*, quotes on pages 14–15.

Bourdieu and Loïc Wacquant,[26] a culture of "accession to an emergence" in the sense of Bachelard.[27] One can get entangled in it. And just as with the experiment, its outcome gives rise to further experimentation, writing up and writing out can proliferate, and poetic as well as knowledge effects can happen in the process of iteration. They depend on writing *as a process*; they happen only in its course and flow. Indeed, one does not write toward something, where the movement would come to rest and cease, one writes away from something; one launches oneself. This is the challenge and at the same time the appeal of writing, and it is comparable in its movement with the experiment—it stands on an equal footing with it.

26 Pierre Bourdieu, *The Logic of Practice*, trans. Richard Nice (Cambridge: Cambridge University Press, 1990); Pierre Bourdieu and Loïc Wacquant, *An Invitation to Reflexive Sociology* (Chicago: The University of Chicago Press, 1992); Loïc Wacquant and Aksu Akçaoglu, "Pratique et pouvoir symbolique chez Bourdieu vu de Berkeley," *Revue de l'Institut de Sociologie (ULB)* 86 (2016): 35–60.

27 Bachelard *Rationalisme appliqué*, 133.

On Seeing

The question of whether we can trust in what we see has occupied philosophy from its inceptions. This is, however, not the place for an extended foray into philosophy which would lead us into the ramifications of its history. I will leave it at a few basic insights that have resulted from a scientific and a philosophical debate that both had their origins in the 19th century. They refer, on the one hand, to the physiology of the senses culminating in the work of Hermann von Helmholtz.[1] On the other hand, they rely on an epistemological position that proceeds from the basic assumption that our knowledge, and our scientific knowledge in particular, including its categories, is subject to continuous historical change. We may call it, therefore, a historical epistemology, of which Ernst Mach's critical and historical account of mechanics can be taken as an early instantiation.[2]

Can we believe what we see? Perhaps we have to ask another question to begin with: What can we see at all? Generally speaking, philosophers of the eighteenth-century Enlightenment were convinced that we are able to perceive the world as

1 Hermann von Helmholtz, *Treatise on Physiological Optics*, 3 vols., trans. Optical Society of America, ed. James P. C. Southall (Menasha, WI: Banta Corporation, 1924–1925); Hermann von Helmholtz, *On the Sensations of Tone as a Physiological Basis for the Theory of Music*, trans. Alexander John Ellis (London: Longmans, Green & Co., 1895).

2 Ernst Mach, *The Science of Mechanics. A Critical and Historical Account of its Development*, trans. Thomas J. McCormack (Chicago: The Open Court Publishing Company, 1902).

it is, if only we keep our distance from superstition, trust our senses, exercise them accordingly and enhance them, if necessary, through the use of instruments. Both of these convictions, the possibility and necessity of educating our senses, and the assumption of an in-principle transparency of the instruments directed toward the observation of natural phenomena, became problematic at the beginning of the nineteenth century.[3] The instrument makers as well as the scientists working with their products had to take account of the inherent shortcomings of their apparatus. The physiologists occupying themselves with the human senses, in particular seeing and hearing, had to realize that the senses were equipped with 'specific nerve energies,' each of them unique for the respective sensory organ, as the famous nineteenth century physiologist Johannes Müller put it.[4] Whatever stimulus might be directed toward the eye, for example, be it light or pressure or electricity, the organ would always react with light-like responses. So, what do we see? We see the transformations that our sense receptors operate on the incoming stimuli—whether from outside or from the interior of the body—on their way to the brain.

In the late nineteenth century, the physician, physiologist and physicist Hermann von Helmholtz, the 'imperial chancellor of physics' in Germany, as he used to be called then, drew

3 Christoph Hoffmann, *Unter Beobachtung. Naturforschung in der Zeit der Sinnesapparate* (Göttingen: Wallstein, 2006).

4 Johannes Müller, *Zur vergleichenden Physiologie des Gesichtssinnes des Menschen und der Thiere nebst einem Versuch über die Bewegungen der Augen und über den menschlichen Blick* (Leipzig: C. Cnobloch, 1826); see also Johann Purkinje, *Beiträge zur Kenntnis des Sehens in subjectiver Hinsicht* (Prag: Franz Vetterl Edler von Wildenbrunn, 1819).

the consequences from these early investigations: we have to learn from scratch how to deal with our sensory impressions.[5] In order to transform them into perceptions that have relevance for our actions, permanent comparisons and adjustments are necessary. Helmholtz's distinction between sensation and perception is crucial here.[6] Our perception of the world is a continuous experiment in which we permanently check assumptions derived from the influx of sensations, and from which we permanently draw new conclusions and condense them into perceptual groupings—sometimes consciously, but most often unconsciously. In this way, we are gradually put in a position to find our way through space and time and to cope with our everyday life without stumbling at every corner. And each new and lasting experience requires a new habituation. Michael Heidelberger aptly qualified Helmholtz's position as "experimental interactionism."[7]

The sciences, in turn, do not make things easier for us. On the contrary, they force us to cope with yet another new experience. It was the French philosopher of science Gaston Bachelard who pointed out emphatically that scientific knowledge requires a rupture with our common knowledge, our habitual knowledge. We do not arrive at scientific knowledge by

5 Hermann von Helmholtz, „The facts of perception," in *Selected Writings*, trans. Russell Kahl (Middletown: Wesleyan University Press, 1971), 366—408.

6 Lydia Patton, "Helmholtz's physiological psychology," in *Philosophy of Mind in the Nineteenth Century*, ed. Sandra Lapointe (London: Routledge, 2018), 96–116.

7 Michael Heidelberger, "Force, law, and experiment: the evolution of Helmholtz's philosophy of science," in *Hermann von Helmholtz and the Foundations of Nineteenth-Century Science*, ed. David Cahan (The University of California Press, Berkeley CA, 1993), 461–497.

means of, but rather against our everyday convictions. Here, another form of experimentation comes into play, this time a consciously operated form that transcends sensory perception. The scientific experiment enables an interaction with the world around us that is directed toward objects of knowledge which are not immediately accessible to our senses. To rely here, for purposes of illustration, on images taken from everyday experience will at best be unrewarding, and at worst would reveal itself as an "epistemological obstacle." Bachelard gave telling historical examples of such obstacles. In the seventeenth and well into the eighteenth centuries, one used to imagine "diluted" or "rarefied" matter, such as the air surrounding us as a sponge which had pores and could be compressed, and which was able to absorb other particles of matter.[8] Unfortunately, this image turned out to obstruct an understanding of gaseous bodies rather than advancing it. No physical science could have been built on it.

There is no once-and-forever state of the art in the sciences. All scientific knowledge, once constituted, can sediment, as such be taken for granted and then potentially turn into an epistemological obstacle itself. The history of the sciences is full of ruptures with what appears to be evident, or what at a certain point in time is taken for granted and handled as something given and thus with what we 'believe we are seeing,' to take up the question we began with and upend it linguistically. Who would not immediately be reminded here of the transition linked with the names of Nicolaus Copernicus and Johannes Kepler, the shift from the geocentric to the heliocentric con-

8 Ibid., Chapter 4; see also "Approaching the Sponge," in the present volume.

ception of the world! For thousands of years, humanity saw the earth standing still and the sun circling around it. It took a certain dissatisfaction with the traditional models embodied in astrolabes, sharp new observations and keen assumptions to break with the old and establish a new view of our cosmos. On another note, the conclusions Galileo Galilei drew from his experiments on the free fall of bodies seem counter-intuitive at first sight: we are used to seeing light bodies falling slowly and heavy ones quickly. From that time on, they would all fall with the same velocity in a vacuum. We could continue with Isaac Newton's postulate of action at a distance: masses act on each other without touching each other. There are good reasons to label this era with the term 'scientific revolution.'[9] And at the beginning of the twentieth century, Albert Einstein's theory of relativity and quantum physics both confronted scientists with paradoxes that were plainly perceived as a break from appearance. How could a four-dimensional continuum of space-time be imagined? What should be done with what appeared to be a sheer contradiction, namely that it depended on the experimental arrangement whether an energy quantum showed itself as a particle or as a wave?[10]

The life sciences, too, have come up in their history with radical breaks in our habitual views and conceptions of living beings. That like begets like and that it had always been that way was a foregone conclusion well into the nineteenth cen-

9 Steven Shapin, *The Scientific Revolution* (Chicago: The University of Chicago Press, 1996).

10 Helge Kragh, *Quantum Generations. A History of Physics in the Twentieth Century* (Princeton: Princeton University Press, 1999); Christoph Lehner, Jürgen Renn and Matthias Schemmel, *Einstein and the Changing Worldviews of Physics* (Basel: Birkhäuser, 2011).

tury. It was only the beginning of imagining deep time, connected with the names of the geologist Charles Lyell and the natural historian Charles Darwin, periods that lie beyond our temporally restricted life experience as humans, which made it possible to envisage an evolution of organisms from common ancestors buried since time immemorial in the strata of earlier geological eras: a change that cannot be seen but only reconstructed from remaining traces and indices.[11] And the possibility of looking at biomolecules as carriers of information for their own reduplication as well as for the regulation of metabolic and developmental processes—this dimension of metabolism only became experimentally accessible with the molecular revolution around the middle of the twentieth century.[12]

I will stop here. These short remarks are titled "On Seeing." The title is meant as an indication of the fact that what we believe we are seeing is bound into a twofold, continuing experimental process: we cannot see it as something static; it is in constant motion. In other words, all our knowledge is experimentally constituted, cognitively as well as epistemically, seen from inside as well as from outside. On the one hand, our individual experience, our orientation in space and our handling of objects in this space is subject to permanent palpations and often minute adjustments that we do not even perceive. And on the other hand, what in our experience has revealed itself as being stable and lasting is again and again subverted by the

11 Steven Jay Gould, *Time's Arrow, Time's Cycle* (Cambridge MA: Harvard University Press, 1987).

12 Horace F. Judson, *The Eighth Day of Creation. The Makers of the Revolution in Biology* (New York: Simon & Schuster, 1979).

collective experience that we owe to the communal process of scientific knowledge acquisition. Time and again, scientific development teaches us otherwise, points behind our senses and decomposes the phenomena that we aim at capturing through them. And yet, we have to acknowledge the fact that we can match these corrections of knowledge, be they individual or collective, always and only with what we are 'seeing,' even if that vision, these pieces of evidence can only be provoked experimentally and must appear to us as being multiply mediated. Think of the highly filtered traces of a particle produced by the European particle accelerator in Geneva, or the color signals of the molecular product of a reporter gene which has been smuggled into a living cell. Without this spiral movement forced upon us by the processual character of knowledge acquisition, our vision, be it individual or collective, cognitive or social, would soon be trapped in a "harmony of illusions," to formulate it with a striking expression coined by the immunologist and epistemologist Ludwik Fleck.[13] Fleck described them as traps into which scientific thought collectives can be caught when yielding to the temptation to close upon themselves. The phenomenon is much more general, however. It occurs wherever communities of belief are formed. We call and experience the devastating consequences of these encapsulations today as social "bubbles."

13 Ludwik Fleck, *Genesis and Development of a Scientific Fact,* trans. Fred Bradley and Thaddeus J. Trenn (Chicago and London: The University of Chicago Press, 1979), Chapter 2, Section 3.

Can the Sciences and the Arts Learn from Each Other?

As a first spontaneous answer, we often hear: 'I don't think so.' We are inured and accustomed to perceiving the sciences and the arts as two separate realms whose inhabitants appear to live in different cultural worlds and occupy themselves with incompatible and incomparable things. But who tells us whether that vision is fallacious, and whether we are letting appearances deceive us? Generally, the sciences and the arts are judged according to their—indeed widely different—products. The sciences create knowledge that circulates as information and can bring social benefit in one technical realization or another. The arts create singular, unique or limited objects of varying duration that one can marvel at but that are, today at least, not destined for everyday consumption. The art historian George Kubler described this perspective once as follows: "Although a common gradient connects use and beauty, the two are irreducibly different: no tool can be fully explained as a work of art, nor vice versa."[1] Let us call it the perspective from the reified products.

This is, however, not the only perspective from which we can regard the sciences and the arts. If, just for once, we leave the realm in which the products of the sciences and the arts circulate, and direct our gaze at the realm in which these products are in the process of making, things suddenly begin to look a bit different. Here, in the world of becoming, of gestation, of emergence, where novelty awaits its breakthrough,

1 Kubler, *Shape of Time*, 11.

we can observe surprising structural similarities between the sciences and the arts. Here, other criteria prevail than in the sphere of distribution, be it the market place of art works or that of scientific information, including its technical artifacts. Both the sciences and the arts are navigating on the cusp that separates the known from the unknown, the heard from the unheard-of, the seen from the unseen, the present from the unprecedented. Both aim at creating things that did not yet exist in this particular form and, in order to achieve this aim, all the forces—small as well as big—are set in motion that are at their disposal. Here, both the sciences and the arts move in a space of the possible, a space of research, which deserves more detailed examination.

As a rule, spontaneity is seen to be located on the side of the arts and methodically strict approaches are generally aligned with the sciences. However, the *practices* of both of them combine what is exclusively ascribed to one side or the other. This is due to the fact that both arenas, the sciences and the arts, depend on engaging with the vagaries of their respective materials. In both realms, novelty is not a brainchild, but the result of an engagement with the material with which one works and whose properties one explores with the hope of discovering new facets.

In order to explore the resilience and power of things to manifest themselves from angles that were previously hidden from view, the modern natural sciences have developed a tool that has revealed itself as more powerful than any other procedure: the research experiment. The experiment is a search engine that remains unequalled to this day. But experimentation is to be found everywhere in the arts as well. However, i appears to be much less appreciated because, in a sense, tenta tive moves and tinkering do not match the image of a creative genius and tend therefore to be relegated to mere handicraft. But it is exactly here, I think, that both sides have the chance to learn from each other, the artists from the ingenious practices of the laboratory and the scientists from the no less ingenious practices of the atelier or studio. Literally, the laboratory is a space where one *labors* around knowledge; the atelier is a space where scrapings and chippings fall off; the studio is a space where one *studies* a phenomenon. What both sides have yet to learn is to create, seize upon, and multiply the opportunities for looking over each other's shoulders while at work, instead of merely talking over and about one another. Then they will realize that their respective searching activities, in the laboratory as well as the atelier, have more in common than prevailing wisdom is ready to accept.

Experimentation has many facets and can make use of many gadgets and more or less sophisticated devices, depending on the materials at hand and on which of their aspects the interest of the artist or the scientist is focused. Its practices can differ to a considerable degree accordingly. But there appears to be one peculiarity that is always and everywhere in play and that is shared across the worlds of the arts and the sciences. To engage in an experiment means being ready to let oneself be surprised by the materials with which one works and which one would like to explore, whether motivated by scientific or artistic intentions. In the course of these processes, effects that turn out to point in fruitful directions mostly emerge unexpectedly—that is, off the beaten track. In the end, one experiments not only to find answers to questions that one is already able to articulate clearly and distinctly, but to be confronted with questions that one might not even have dreamed of. This is the core of the modern term serendipity:[2] the unexpected and intriguing finding that reveals itself as powerful enough to overturn the habituated and the known. The philosopher and art historian Edgar Wind, who frequented the circles around Ernst Cassirer and Aby Warburg during the 1920s in Hamburg, was intimately acquainted not only with the arts of the renaissance, but also with the advanced sciences of his time. In his epistemological *chef d'œuvre* from the early 1930s, *The Experiment and Metaphysics*, he stressed that doing an experiment amounted to nothing less than being ready to throw into question the very procedures on which the experiment rested: "We [...] cannot escape the conclusion that the ultimate purpose of the experiment is to test its own presupposition."[3] I think that this is an apt description by which both scientists and artists might find their respective activities nicely summarized.

To return to the title of this short intervention: on the experimental grounds briefly exposed here, what remains is revising two deeply engrained self-images—that of the sciences as encapsulated in rigid methodological prescriptions *and* that of the arts as being the incarnation of freewheeling subjectivity. Let me summarize, by way of a conclusion, the message of

2 The term was coined in the realm of the sciences by the sociologist of science Robert Merton. See Robert K. Merton, *Social Theory and Social Structure* (New York: Free Press, 1957); Merton and Barber, *Travels and Adventures of Serendipity*.

3 Edgar Wind, *The Experiment and Metaphysics. Towards a Resolution of the Cosmological Antinomies*, trans. Cyril Edwards (Oxford: European Humanities Research Center, University of Oxford, 2001), 19; see also Edgar Wind, "Some points of contact between history and the natural sciences," in *Philosophy and History: Essays Presented to Ernst Cassirer*, ed. Raymond Klibansky and Herbert James (Oxford: Clarendon Press, 1936), 255–264.

a paper that Paul Feyerabend published in 1994, the year of his death, carrying the somewhat cryptic title "Art as a product of nature as a work of art."[4] First, Feyerabend claims, one must not regard the sciences and the arts from an ontological perspective, but rather view them from an epistemological angle, that is, one has to look at *what take* they choose on their objects and not what they are supposed *to be*. If one does so, second, possibilities of comparison as creative activities arise and invite to further reflection. Third, what needs to be put center stage is the engagement with the respective materials rather than to fix one's gaze on what are perceived as geniuses in both realms, however they might be disposed. We could also say, one should avoid to succumb to what Edgar Zilsel had castigated as *Geniereligion*.[5] As a consequence, fourth, it also becomes understandable that one will find an irreducible plurality of such takes, for in the end, they need to correspond to the respective materials. This does, however, not lead us into relativism, because the results of the sciences as well as those of the arts are not arbitrary products: they are wrested from these materials themselves in all their inexhaustible abundance.[6]

4 Paul K. Feyerabend, "Art as a product of nature as a product of art," *World Futures* 40/1 (1994): 87–100.

5 Edgar Zilsel, *Die Geniereligion. Ein kritischer Versuch über das moderne Persönlichkeitsideal mit einer historischen Begründung* (Frankfurt am Main: Suhrkamp, 1990).

6 Not by chance, Feyerabend's last book on which he was working until his death and that was published only posthumously carries the title *The Conquest of Abundance: A Tale of Abstraction versus the Richness of Being*, ed. Bert Terpstra (Chicago: The University of Chicago Press, 1999).

Research and Design

The notion of design is usually associated with ideas of streamlining, of giving a finishing touch, of wrapping, of conveying shape by anticipation of a particular application. Thus, the notion of design appears to embody an idea of combining functionality and aesthetics, affordance and teleology—and for that matter, of seduction and veneer. Talking about design in scientific research seems to be counterindicated at first sight—design has the appeal of a form of practice that is utterly uncharacteristic of research processes. The latter is to be seen as being endowed with a form of rationality thoroughly subjected to an entirely different set of characteristics. Research processes, insofar as they are assumed to generate unprecedented knowledge, seem to be characterized by non-teleology, bricolage, and an essential touch of tentativeness and precariousness, sometimes even clumsiness. We will see whether these basic features of research are compatible with an idea of design and, if so, with what kind of design.

My remarks proceed from a rather straightforward notion of design. The resulting woodcut-image with the distinctions and conclusions it allows us to draw is meant more as an incentive for discussion than as a conclusive argument.

Epistemic Things Cannot Be Designed

In characterizing scientific research processes, I have relied on a fundamental distinction inherent in the material constitution of experimental systems taken as units of research and at the same time as a concept facilitating their description. It is the distinction between epistemic things and technical objects. Since this distinction is essential for the clarification of the question of whether—and if so, in which sense—we can or cannot talk about design in scientific research, I shall begin with a brief recapitulative exposé of these two categories of objects.

In scientific experimentation we observe an oscillation between things with fuzzy boundaries on the one hand, and things with a relatively determined, stabilized structure on the other hand. Let us start with the fuzzy things, the epistemic things. They stay in the focus of interest because they are the part in need of further clarification. Experimental systems are arrangements for productively handling epistemic things at the borderline between what we know and what we don't know. Through their manipulation, one expects to produce bits and pieces of knowledge that do not yet exist. In a slightly different vein, but having the same situation in mind, the sociologist of science Robert Merton claimed that ignorance is a category central to the characterization of science as a process of knowledge acquisition. He spoke of "specified," or specifiable, ignorance in this context.[1] In this case, we can precisely point at what we do not yet know. We must, however, broaden this description by adding that, at the frontier of exploring the unknown, we are frequently confronted with ignorance at one remove—that is, a form of not knowing that can be characterized as "unanticipated" ignorance—a situation in which we are

1 Robert K. Merton, "Three fragments from a sociologist's notebooks: Establishing the phenomenon, specified ignorance, and strategic research materials," *Annual Review of Sociology* 13 (1987): 1–28.

unaware of imminent knowledge options, or at least in which it remains unclear what exactly one does not yet know. Accordingly, Robert Root-Bernstein has distinguished two ways of *overcoming* these two forms of ignorance. Encountering, in the course of research, serendipitous events can lead a scientist to formulate a way of seeing things that was impossible to anticipate; encountering pseudo-serendipitous events can lead to unexpected ways of solving a problem that was specifiable in advance but impossible to solve beforehand.[2]

About epistemic things, intrinsically, certain aspects remain in the dark, a situation that can be characterized as epistemic uncertainty. In order to prevent them from exhausting their capacity for knowledge generation, for knowledge-to-be-acquired, they must be handled in such a way that their potential for manifesting unprecedented aspects is not too tightly restricted by expectations that unavoidably accompany their handling. With respect to epistemic things, this means that design, in the usual sense of a deliberate shaping according to explicit goals, can definitely not be the guideline for an experimental research situation. At least, that would lead to unproductive time-wasting, or a dead end at worst. Things are epistemic things only as long as their potential of signification is not exhausted. The very essence of epistemicity consists in the fact that there is a promise of a very particular kind, an expectation that cannot be governed by rigid definitions. It is what animates researchers in their inability to tell what will show up around the next corner. It is the expectation of novelty

2 Robert Scott Root-Bernstein, *Discovering. Inventing and Solving Problems at the Frontiers of Scientific Knowledge* (Cambridge MA: Harvard University Press, 1989).

which by definition cannot be anticipated. This state of being-beyond-our-will and yet in the realm of our interaction with an epistemic thing is the reason why research is specifically and essentially oriented toward an open future. It is research only as long as it is able to uphold the precarious suspension between the known from which it tries to get away and the unknown, inaccessible for the time span of such an essential suspension.

We can describe the research situation in yet another way by looking at the individuals engaged in the process instead of the things involved in it. From the perspective of researchers, it amounts to an act of delegation. Setting up an experimental system that revolves around an epistemic thing and helps to explore some of the inexhaustible aspects of its thingness means subverting the subject-object constellation in the sense of a direct relation between an observer and the observed object. In an experiment, the act of observing is delegated to a technical device that one brings into interaction with the epistemic thing. But the interaction has to be crafted in such a way that the outcome — the traces it leaves behind — is not completely determined in advance. Were the latter the case, we would be concerned with an experimental demonstration rather than a research experiment.

A research experiment must have the potential to engender unintended effects—that is, to generate unexpected outcomes. Such outcomes cannot be intentionally designed; they can only be approached indirectly. Therefore, dealing with the unexpected and the unintended requires a particular kind of attention from the experimenter. A contemporary of Merton, Michael Polanyi, who trained in physical chemistry and moved on to philosophy of science later in his life, comes to our aid here with his distinction between two kinds of attention: focal, directed attention and subsidiary, undirected attention. These forms of attention correspond to two kinds of knowledge: explicit and tacit knowledge.[3] To direct focal attention toward something means to fix the thing before one's eyes from the viewpoint of one particular aspect to the exclusion of others. Focal attention can bring this particular aspect under sharp relief but it also tends to ossify the situation. Subsidiary attention, on the other hand, suspends the focus in favor of a hovering attentiveness that covers and allows scope for a range of possible events, none of which can be expected with certainty—in the sense that *any* event that deserves the name cannot be expected with certainty. What can be deduced from a present state of affairs is not an event; it is simply a consequence of that state. In all likelihood, events will escape the focused mind and senses that are based on explicit knowledge. Under subsidiary conditions, however, they can be traced and reveal the unexpected. Subsidiary awareness in its two forms—marginal and subliminal, which Polanyi distinguishes as directed outward and inward—helps to bring the unprecedented into the realm of the graspable.

Technical Objects Can Be Designed

In contrast to the nature of epistemic things, the technical objects that enter an experimental constellation are usually

3 Michael Polanyi, "The logic of tacit inference," in *Knowing and Being. Essays by Michael Polanyi*, ed. Marjorie Grene, (Chicago: The University of Chicago Press, 1969), 138–158.

characterized by mechanical precision of a certain degree, a precision that can, however, vary widely according to the development of the apparatus itself or to the research question at stake.[4] Generically, technical objects are subsumed under the notion of research technology. They are the pieces of instrumentation needed to create a situation in which an epistemic thing can be handled in a potentially knowledge-generating manner. In contrast to epistemic things, with technical objects it makes sense to consider design, in the common meaning of the word, as being purposefully conceived. Thus, although there is a core aspect of the research process that is difficult to recognize and consider adequately from the perspective of design, there are other aspects that offer perfect reasons to look out for design features. Let me briefly point to three of them.

Instrumentation

Perusing a phrase of Gaston Bachelard, we can claim that "*an instrument, in modern science, is veritably a reified theorem.*"[5] A research instrument that is supposed to function in accord with a theorem to which it gives body is a target for design. A design that hampers the realization of its physical principle can be qualified as suboptimal. Equally, the convenient handling of a research instrument is up for iterative optimization. In both respects, there are clear evaluation criteria available for the design of technical objects—research technologies are

4 Hans-Jörg Rheinberger, "Präzision und Unschärfe im Umgang mit Forschungsobjekten," in *Genau—leicht—konsequent: Ein dreifaches Rendezvous der Künste und Wissenschaften*, ed. Florian Dombois, Yeboaa Ofosu and Sarah Schmidt (Basel: Schwabe, 2009), 45–60.

5 Gaston Bachelard, *Les intuitions atomistiques. Essai de classification* (Paris: Boivin, 1933), 140. Italics in the original.

transparent in these respects. Think, for example, of the laws of optics, a microscope, and the corresponding equipment for its manipulation. Epistemic objects, in contrast, are opaque by nature.

Interfaces

Besides reifying a particular theorem, a research instrument must thus be designed, on the one hand, in view of its tuning and handling by an operator,[6] and on the other hand, in view of the specific function it is supposed to fulfill—that is, in view of its envisaged physical interaction with a certain range of epistemic things with which it has to share a common interface.[7] The interface, or intersection, between an epistemic thing and a technical object in an experimental setting is usually a tricky sphere of action. At stake is the question of whether a particular epistemic entity and a specific research technology can be brought together in such a way that suitable traces result from their interaction, and with that, potential knowledge effects.

Let me give an example. Relatively early in the development of the electron microscope, in the late 1930s, first attempts were made to use the new instrument in order to visualize biological structures—such as viruses—whose size was below the resolution power of a light microscope of the time. Their dimensions were such that they even challenged the new instrument's resolution capacities.[8] This borderline situation

6 See Rheinberger, *Epistemology of the Concrete*, Chapter 9.

7 Ibid., Chapter 11.

8 Nick Rasmussen, *Picture Control. The Electron Microscope and the Transformation of Biology in America, 1940–1960* (Stanford, CA: Stanford University Press, 1997); Falk Müller, *Jenseits des Lichts. AEG und die Anfänge der Elektronenmikroskopie in Deutschland* (Göttingen: Wallstein, 2021).

initiated a process of mutual calibration and reconfiguration of sample preparation on the biological side and sample reception on the technical side: samples and their preparation had to be designed in such a way that they reflected the technical conditions and requirements of the instrument, and the sample environment of the instrument had to be designed in such a way that it respected the biological conditions and requirements of the sample in a negotiation between the hard and the soft, the dry and the wet, the stable and the unstable.

Although such mutual design processes are particularly critical in the case of biological epistemic things, they reflect a general feature of experimentation. They are characteristic examples of the encounter between epistemic and technical things, and they can assume very different forms according to the research technologies involved and the specific epistemic objects at stake.[9] As a rule, however, the problems arising at this boundary can be stated explicitly and thus subjected to design procedures. The realm and range of design, however, is functionally determined in a rather strict manner in terms of 'affordances.'[10]

A research instrument, however, oscillates between two directions of affordance: one toward its sample, the other toward its user. The latter thus constitutes yet another interface. As far as research instruments are concerned, we can observe a general trend in their user-oriented design. At the beginning of the development of a new research technology, the device is usually clamped together and tinkered. It has to

9 Rheinberger, *Epistemology of the Concrete*, Chapter 11.

10 For the concept of affordance, see James J. Gibson, *The Ecological Approach to Visual Perception* (Boston: Houghton Mifflin, 1979), Chapter 8.

be operated by highly competent experimenters who are familiar with its intricacies. Sooner or later in the course of its development, however, the instrument becomes more and more black-boxed, and the interface with the user is reduced to a few crucial operations that are easy to learn and perform. The ultracentrifuge in biochemistry is a good example. In the 1920s only a handful of experts in the world were capable of operating the high-speed device, be it oil- or air-driven.[11] Researchers who wanted to use the oil-driven instrument had to bring their samples to Uppsala, were The Svedberg's machine was located in the basement of his laboratory. During the 1950s it assumed a form resembling a washing machine and accordingly soon populated biochemical laboratories all over the world.

Experimental Context

A third aspect of the experimental process in which design plays a role is in the overall arrangement of an experiment. Another notion is often used here as a synonym in laboratory shop talk: the so-called 'planning' of an experiment. Here, planning or design comes less with connotations of efficiency or effectiveness, but rather with a connotation of sophistication, care in the arrangement of parts, and placing of proper controls. What does that mean? To put it simply, it is impossible to hire an outsider to design an experiment within the context of a given experimental system in a given laboratory. Designing an experiment according to the state of the art and the local resources requires intimate contextual knowledge from within. Karl Popper, referring to Hermann Weyl,

11 Boelie Elzen, "Two ultracentrifuges: a comparative study of the social construction of artefacts," *Social Studies of Science* 16 (1986): 621–662.

famously depicted the experimenter as follows: "The theoretician puts certain definite questions to the experimenter, and the latter, by his experiments, tries to elicit a decisive answer to these questions, and to no others. All other questions he tries hard to exclude."[12] However, designing a good research experiment means more than that. It requires framing an experiment in such a way as to help answer a question that one is able to ask—Popper's focus—but at the same time with the potential to generate questions that cannot yet be asked. Clever design of an experiment tries to keep this possibility open. But here, design also comes up against its limits.

In *Toward a History of Epistemic Things,* I have tried to formulate a few rules of thumb or 'principles' that express such experimental awareness.[13] Among them are, first, a 'symmetry principle' which pertains to the arrangement of experimental controls to be built into the experiment. The second is a 'homogeneity principle' which states that the materials used need to be of a comparable quality in successive experiments. The third, an 'exhaustion principle,' postulates that the maximum possible number of options for combining things that an experiment allows should be tried. The basic reason for observing all these rules is the processuality of experimentation as an ongoing activity. Popper's fantasy of a single experiment as a test instance, ideally with a 'yes' or 'no' answer, the '*experimentum crucis,*' has been replaced by the notion of a stream of experimentation. It is an essential feature of research experi-

12 Karl Popper, *The Logic of Scientific Discovery* (New York: Harper and Row, 1968), 107; Hermann Weyl, *Philosophie der Mathematik und Naturwissenschaft* (Darmstadt: Wissenschaftliche Buchgesellschaft, 1976).
13 Rheinberger, *Toward a History of Epistemic Things*, 78.

mentation that it runs in temporal series of experimental acts—another expression for experimental systems.

Conclusion

Taken together, aspects of experimentation that lend themselves to design are biased toward the technical side of experimental systems: instrumentation, the interface between instruments and epistemic things, and the configuration of the experimental setup. At its core, however, lies an unruly thing, the epistemic thing, which defies design. The tension between these two poles, the designable and the undesignable, lends experimentation its peculiar rationality: a rationality that is not to be captured by a logic of anticipation.

This rich field for reflection has not been fully explored, neither for understanding the sciences nor for other areas of human knowledge production. In particular, it might provide space for discussing the problematic relations between the sciences and the arts. We have barely begun to explore the realm of an intersection between these two areas of cultural activity, both of which, in their similarities as well as their differences, in their congruences as well as their incongruities, coincide in that they aim at producing unprecedented things.

Experimental Performativity

There are two trivial images of the experiment, both of which need to be deconstructed in order to arrive at a more interesting, more productive and richer picture of experimentation. One of these trivial images has dominated traditional philosophy of science for a long time, insofar as the latter seriously dealt with experimentation at all. As a rule, it was treated as a marginal phenomenon. The story goes that an experiment is specifically oriented toward confirming or refuting a preconceived, precisely formulated hypothesis. This image also underlies the standard format of a scientific publication and has therefore become deeply engrained in teaching as well. A research paper starts with a hypothesis, then presents the materials and methods with which to approach it, followed by a presentation of the results. Ideally, the results confirm the hypothesis advanced at the outset, and from there, a conclusion proceeds to a question to be followed next or a gap left open.

The other trivial image is entrenched in the realm of the political and the social, and it looks at experimentation as a danger. It is seen as a kind of shortsighted, idle groping around in the dark, or else as the pursuit of a poorly thought-through idea with an uncertain outcome. This image has thoroughly negative connotations. The slogan 'No experiments' has acquired the status of something like a proverbial warning in conservative election campaigns against trying to alter the proven status quo.

What does it really mean, however, to experiment in a natural science laboratory? Both of the images just described may occasionally be observed when looking closer at research and the nitty-gritty of its daily practices. They are, however, ephemeral borderline cases that are by no means characteristic of a productive experimental research process. Rather, they are its degenerative versions. They conceal its delicate dynamics rather than illuminating it. Scientific experimentation lives from an interplay between precision and uncertainty that needs to be considered in its temporal extension, and that cannot be captured by equating it to mere testing or to blind poking in murky waters. Knowledge that is genuinely novel is knowledge that shows up only in that very process, and that would remain precluded without it. Opening up new avenues of knowing, exploring uncharted territory is at the core of an experimental research procedure. It displays a performativity of its own, one that is oriented toward fostering the instantiation of epistemic events. It is thus performative in its essence. If one restricts the conditions too narrowly, the process begins to turn in on itself. If one opens the bag too widely, one gets lost in the terrain of non-binding observations, in which, in any case, no epistemically significant surplus can show up anymore.

We have to do with a particular kind of performativity here. It can be described as a twofold process of delocalization and relocation, of decontextualization and recontextualization. On the one hand, phenomena of scientific interest are taken out of their natural surroundings and replaced in a laboratory context. It would not be possible to measure and to observe them in detail otherwise. On the other hand, transposition, that is, change of context, is an inherent characteristic of the research process itself,[1] which proceeds from traces of the phenomenon

1 Hans-Jörg Rheinberger, "Transpositions: From traces through data to models and simulations," in *Transpositions. Aesthetico-Epistemic Operators in*

in question to the data space, from there to models and other forms of temporary reifications of the epistemic object, and circles back into the space of the experiment.

I am talking about a delicate dynamic here. We are concerned with an activity that can be compared to a tightrope walk on which one cannot find any convenient steps to tread but on which for each move one has to search out the next stone that could carry one's weight. This, or similar images, are frequently to be found in the autobiographical literature written by scientists, for instance in the popular writings of the nineteenth-century physicist and physiologist Hermann von Helmholtz, to whom we owe pathbreaking contributions to thermodynamics and to the physiology of the senses.[2] Michel Meulders aptly summarized Helmholtz's position when claiming that "the experiment is first and foremost destined to find the causative conditions for the phenomena, not to test hypotheses, the latter being only of a secondary importance: it has to be an *ars inveniendi* rather than an *ars demonstrandi.*"[3]

However, to embark on such a path presupposes close acquaintance with the matter at hand. And one has to develop a constant watchfulness for the spiraling trajectory on which one has embarked and whose continuation needs be confirmed after each and every step. If one focuses one's gaze too narrowly, one loses sight of the surroundings. If one suspends one's gaze completely, one will fall out of step. The kind of performance that is required here, therefore, demands getting

Artistic Research, ed. Michael Schwab (Leuven: Leuven University Press, 2018), 215–224.

2 Compare also "On Seeing," in the present volume.

3 Michel Meulders, *Helmholtz. Des lumières aux neurosciences* (Paris: Editions Odile Jacob, 2001), 137.

closely involved and, at the same time, keeping a reflexive distance. This double action can be studied very well in countless variations on the example of scientific research processes for, as a rule, they leave behind a continuous paper trail, be it in the form of a series of published papers or, closer to the laboratory, in the form of notebooks and protocols that record the steps, at least to some extent.[4] Such continual redoubling appears to be characteristic of scientific processes of experimental exploration; at the same time it stresses the temporal and recursive dimension of these processes.

I would like, however, to go one step further and claim that explorative movements of this kind are inherent in all creative processes that underlie our cultural existence. They can, however, assume very different forms according to the various fields of activity. In this sense, *the experimental* reaches way beyond the realm of the sciences. To look at it more closely, whether in prose literature and poetry, in the fine arts or in music and in the performative arts in general, appears to me as both a rewarding and a crucial task, and one that has only begun to be tackled to date. It will be the starting point for an expanded epistemology that will be able to relate the sciences and the arts to each other with respect to their creative processes, their ways of making and doing, so that they can engage in mutually productive conversations instead of leaving it at inter-, trans- or post-disciplinary lip service.

4 Frederic L. Holmes, Jürgen Renn and Hans-Jörg Rheinberger (eds.), *Reworking the Bench. Research Notebooks in the History of Science* (Dordrecht–Boston–London: Kluwer Academic Publishers, 2003).

Acousmatic Experiences

In the first two sections of the following considerations, I address the tense nature of the acousmatic situation, both from the perspective of the person who speaks and is heard but cannot be seen, and from the perspective of the person who hears but cannot see the speaker. In both cases, the tension does not simply result from a deprivation of one of our senses, which leads to sharpening another sense and turning it back on itself. Rather, the tension is based on something being present and absent at the same time. Only from this doubling, from this being there and not-there at the same time, can the mobilization that triggers the acousmatic situation be understood, as well as the restlessness that accompanies this mobilization.

In the third and last section I describe a double Freudian Fort/Da game of the kind we often encounter in scientific experiments involving a researcher and their object of research. In this situation, the object of research is both present and absent at the same time, meaning that its existence can be assumed without being certain about it, and that we want to find out more about. The experimenter, too, is both present and absent at the same time in the experimental setup, insofar as they have installed it, but in such a way that they can withdraw from it. Understood in this sense, the 'acousmatic situation' reaches far beyond the acoustic realm to which it owes its name.

Acousmatic Reciting

At the invitation of Berlin-based conceptual artist and architect Mario Asef, I participated in his series of *Acousmatic Lectures* held in the space of the *Errant Sound—Sound Art Project* in Berlin in the fall of 2017 and sponsored by the Schering Foundation. Passing through a cool, narrow, dark hallway, I entered a back room where I was asked to take a seat on a stool in front of a small wooden table. I was sitting directly facing a dense beige curtain that separated me from the audience, which at that moment was gathering in the space beyond the curtain. I could hear them but was unable to make eye contact. In preparing for this evening, I had deliberately chosen not to worry about the situation I would be confronted with. As a result, I had prepared an ordinary lecture that included illustrations, since I wanted to speak about the work of the engraver Albert Flocon.[1] At that time I was working on a series of bibliophilic books that Flocon had created in Paris as a result of his encounters with the French philosopher of science Gaston Bachelard during the 1950s.[2] My subject for the lecture was chosen to appeal to the listeners' sense of sight but also, in relation to Flocon's work and his craft, copper engraving, to appeal to their sense of touch.

There I was, sitting behind the curtain, trying to cope with a very unfamiliar situation. I think two impressions are especially worth sharing here. The first is an experience that probably all speakers at microphones in broadcasting booths have

1 Compare "The Bottle, for Example: Gaston Bachelard Looks at Albert Flocon's 'Castles in Spain'," in the present volume.

2 Rheinberger, *Hand of the Engraver*.

had. The fact that the audience I was speaking to was somehow present in my imagination, but at the same time not there, made itself felt in the form of a strange inversion.[3] I had the impression that my voice was, as it were, reflected by the curtain, and in this way returned to me. I thus experienced myself as speaking not only to invisible others, but above all to myself. I became—vicariously, one could say—my own audience. Therefore, I heard myself speaking, which by no means happens in a normal lecture situation. In the latter case one ideally forgets oneself and one's voice while concentrating on the text and the audience. Here, on the other hand, a loop was set up by which I myself as the speaker simultaneously became the addressee. I had the feeling that I had to react directly to my own voice, through my voice. This feedback strangely duplicated my speech: Every word uttered became an echo of the preceding word. A resonance was created in the space of my speech as it was replicated to compensate for the lack of sense perceptions that normally accompany it, especially the sense of sight directed toward the listener.

My second impression concerns the description of an image accompanying my talk that the audience could not see while I tried to describe it. This is the archetypal situation of any *ekphrasis*: struggling with words to put a given, but absent, image before the listener's eyes. I tried with all the vocal means at my disposal, with modulations and accompanying epithets, with exclamations and finger-pointing—with verbal exclamations and proliferations—, to lend plasticity to the absent image.

3 There are pertinent reflections on this dialectic in Rainer Nägele, *fort/da. Topobiographien* (Innsbruck–Vienna–Munich–Bolzano: Edition Sturzflüge/ Studien Verlag, 2005).

I accompanied my descriptive efforts, which took on something grotesque, with gesticulations, although the listeners could not see them at all. I experienced the withholding of the image all the more strongly inasmuch as it was present in my mind, yet at the same time I had the feeling that what I had to offer verbally was only a weak substitute for the missing visual impression.

Acousmatic Listening

Let us now move for a moment to the other side of the curtain, the side of the audience. The fact that an acousmatic situation can lead to strong annoyance among the audience, especially if it occurs unexpectedly, may be briefly explained by means of an experiment. I witnessed it in a conference on the situation of European universities at the Catholic University of Leuven in February 2011. The education scientists around Jan Masschelein and Maarten Simons had organized the meeting and came up with a surprise to start it off—an experiment that they hoped would capture the participants' attention and sharpen their awareness. When the keynote speakers arrived on campus in the morning, they were told to go to an insulated sound box at the back of the auditorium from where, invisible to the audience, they were to deliver their talks by speaking into a microphone and that the assembled audience could only hear through the loudspeakers installed in the hall. The keynote speakers, including myself, were not exactly amused by this idea, but with a shrug we proceeded as instructed. The audience, too, were unprepared for this change. The organizers' idea was to confront them with this withholding of visuality and then to discuss their experience with them. However, things turned out differently to what the organizing committee had imagined.

By ten o'clock the auditorium was filled with several hundred participants. After the ceremonial opening, everyone sat in anticipation of the first plenary lecture by the—since deceased—French philosopher and media theorist Bernard Stiegler, with the rather long and somewhat cryptic title "Faced with the Proletarianizing of the Mind: Thinking and Practicing the Organology and Pharmacology of Knowledge." However, no one stepped up to the lectern. Instead, a voice began to speak through the loudspeakers in English with a French accent. At first, the audience was simply perplexed. But the longer the speech by the absent/present Bernard Stiegler lasted, the more uneasy people in the hall began to feel. In the end, the annoyance of the public increased to such an extent that resentment took over. The pressure on the organizers grew so strong that after the lunch break, they announced that the plenary lecture in the evening—my own—would take place as usual, not only with the vocal, but also with the physical presence of the speaker. This deprived me of the pleasure of my first acousmatic lecture. The bodily absence of a person who was actually present in the room had led to massive irritations among the listeners, some of whom may have come to Leuven especially to experience Stiegler lecturing in person. It finally forced the organizers to reunite the presence of the voice with the presence of its body again. The actual scandal here lay not in the mere absence of the speaker, but in the fact that his expected presence had been withheld from the audience. Had Bernard Stiegler been unable to come to Leuven for some reason, a recording of his speech would have surely been accepted without further ado.

What is all this about? Historically, the concept of acousmatics can be traced back to the teaching method of Pythagoras and,[4] later on, the orchestra pit in opera houses, but it only became virulent on a global social scale in the twentieth century when, with the development of telephone, radio technology, electric and finally electronic music the decoupling of voices from their bodies, and of instruments from their sounds, became more pronounced and experienceable in unheard-of new forms.[5] The resulting disconnection is accompanied by a twofold negation. In relation to the sound source, the sound can no longer be experienced directly together with the sounding body from which it originates. With respect to the listener, it is implicit in the situation that we are dealing with a reduction of the synergy of the senses, which contributes to a concentration on one sense alone, whereby hearing is turned back on itself and hypostatized into 'pure' hearing. Sound and voice are being reassigned to their own domain, respectively.

I hope that the two examples of an acousmatic hearing experience on either side of the curtain have shown that things are more complicated and much more multilayered than might be expected at first glance. And it might be that it is not least the acousmatic situation in which the precariousness of the voice makes itself felt to the extent that hearing fades away and leaves nothing behind except the imaginary trace of its own

4 Kurt von Fritz, *Mathematiker und Akusmatiker bei den alten Pythagoreern* (München: Bayerischen Akademie der Wissenschaften, 1960).

5 Imke Misch and Christoph von Blumröder (eds.), *François Bayle, l'image de son/Klangbilder* (Münster: LIT Verlag, 2003); Wolfgang Hagen, *Das Radio. Zur Geschichte und Theorie des Hörfunks – Deutschland/USA* (München: Fink, 2005); Brian Kane, *Sound Unseen: Acousmatic Sound in Theory and Practice* (Oxford: Oxford University Press, 2014).

authenticity. As is well known, Jacques Derrida has repeatedly referred to the result: its reversal into an inauthenticity of the voice[6]—a reversal that hat remained unthinkable without the cultural omnipresence of the new media.

Presence/Absence in the Experiment

The third part of these reflections deals with another form of the dialectic of presence and absence, namely the presence/absence of the experimenter in the experiment. I will offer a somewhat idiosyncratic reinterpretation of the title of the book in which a first version of this essay appeared,[7] *Akusmatik als Labor/Acousmatics as Laboratory*. Ultimately, I attempt to offer a generalization of what constitutes the core of the acousmatic experience: a game of presence and absence. When it comes to experimentation, language and hearing play a role here in a figurative sense. At the center lies what one might call experimental contingency. If we assume that scientific research processes are about generating new knowledge that cannot as such be derived from currently existing knowledge, then one can understand what Gaston Bachelard is essentially aiming at with his notion of "epistemological acts" which, according to him, ensure that "unexpected impulses are repeatedly brought into scientific development."[8] However, we must gain a more precise idea of such acts, for they are anything

6 Jacques Derrida, *La Voix et le phénomène* (Paris: Presses Universitaires de France, 1967); Derrida, *Grammatology*.

7 Sven Spieker and Mario Asef (eds.), *Akusmatik als Labor. Kultur – Kunst – Medien* (Würzburg: Königshausen & Neumann, 2023).

8 Bachelard, *Activité rationaliste*, 25.

but mere arbitrary positings of a free-floating subject. In an experimental process that is neither over-complex nor under-complex, it happens again and again that facets of the target phenomenon of which the experimenter was not aware when setting up the experiment become apparent. The art of experimentation consists in reacting to these things in the right way—in other words, by dealing appropriately with experimental contingency.

The subject who gets involved in dealing with things in an experimental manner has to satisfy a double prerequisite that may at first glance seem paradoxical.[9] One prerequisite is to be familiar with the material. There is a point at which experimenters come so close to their materials that they have the feeling as if they would, so to speak, act from within. At the same time, this results in conferring sovereignty on the matters themselves. To use a familiar topological image: in a Möbius strip there is, on the one hand, a seemingly obvious distinction between inside and outside, between front side and back side; on the other hand, no point can be indicated at which a boundary line could be drawn where inside and outside are separated from each other.

The outcome of this intimate bond between the experimenter and the material is the creation of a radical distance between them. The experiment hinges on the condition that experimenters set up the experiment with all their skill and ingenuity, but only in order to take themselves out of the game, leaving it on its own. What takes place here is an act of delegation. It is not the experimenters who interact with the

9 Compare on this and the following, Rheinberger, *Split and Slice*; and Rheinberger, "Vom Subjekt des Wissens."

epistemic thing, it is the instruments which they created and utilized for this purpose. In and through this interaction, the phenomenon shows itself—it becomes manifest. It is recalcitrant, petulant, evasive, immune to expectations; in short, the phenomenon responds in a way that is beyond the control of the experimenters precisely to the degree they have taken every conceivable care in setting up their experiment. Speaking of the sciences in his essay "Science and truth," Jacques Lacan put it this way: "The subject is, as it were, internally excluded from its object."[10]

We can also describe the situation as follows: in an experiment, agency is shifted. One does not organize an experiment in order to learn something about oneself—although that might of course happen, too. One learns what one did not know about the object that is brought into play. Despite the reciprocity just described, one must understand the experimental situation as fundamentally asymmetrical. The object of knowledge is ultimately the active partner in the experiment; it shows its own life. Here, also, lies the great weakness of constructivism: it attributes too much power to the subject. In an experiment, power is being displaced, and only because of such displacement does it have productive effects. Only in this way can an experiment become a generator of surprises. Constructivism is a philosophy of technology. What we need, however, is a philosophy of the epistemic situation, a philosophy of science that does justice to the *emergence* of knowledge through experiments.

10 Jacques Lacan, "Science and truth," *Newsletter of the Freudian Field* 3 (1/2) (1989): 4–29, on p. 10.

The 'distant proximity' that characterizes experiments includes a specific form of attention on the part of the experimenters. As already mentioned in a previous chapter,[11] philosopher of science Michael Polanyi has reflected on attention in a very instructive way.[12] Therefore, I will be brief here. Polanyi distinguishes explicit knowledge from tacit or mute knowledge, suggesting in addition that even knowledge which can be spelled out ultimately must remain embedded in tacit knowing. Categorically, he declares: "A completely explicit knowledge is unthinkable."[13] Tacit knowledge is embodied knowledge, which, according to Polanyi, is accompanied by two kinds of "subsidiary" attention.[14] When it concerns bodily perception, he calls subsidiary attention "subliminal"; with respect to object perception, "marginal." Liminality and marginality go together. Importantly, subsidiary attention in both guises is necessary for the experimenter to be open to the incidental noises of the experiment, to the epistemic object's recalcitrance and self-reporting. Under the exclusive rule of its counterpart, "focal" attention that corresponds to the design of the experiment, these signals would go unheard and unseen, and thus end up rendering the experiment circular.

Therefore, from the subject's perspective, in an experiment we are ultimately dealing with an action at a distance. As the German philosopher Hans Blumenberg pointed out in his *Theory of Non-Conceptuality* with a slant of anthropological exaggeration, such action at a distance is to be regarded as

11 See "Scientific research and design," in the present volume.

12 Polanyi, "Logic of tacit inference."

13 Ibid., 144.

14 Compare also Rheinberger, *Iterationen*, particularly "Augenmerk," 51–73.

the starting point of any human comprehension of what there is.[15] The technical device that served Blumenberg as an early example for such comprehension was the hunters' trap. A trap is an ingenious construct that must not only be carefully constructed and concealed, but also has to exhibit a certain degree of indeterminacy to capture animals whose size and properties cannot be clearly determined in advance. Blumenberg sees the trap as the first triumph of the concept—or of the non-conceptual dimension of the concept, one could say—in the history of mankind. The balance between precision and indeterminacy inherent in a trap also characterizes the instrumentally mediated access to objects of knowledge in an experiment. Experiments, especially experimental systems, are devices for making things happen that cannot be precisely anticipated. Ultimately, such systems are contingency-generating devices that operate on the same principle as the trap: they must be ingenious, and they must be constructed in such a way that they can catch the unanticipated.

Gaston Bachelard once described this situation as follows: "In order to *understand*, one must participate in an *emergence*."[16] In the context of the sciences, Bachelard spoke of the latter's essential nature as forming "cultures" that give "access to an emergence," not omitting to point out that these cultures are "effectively socially constituted."[17] Bachelard's remark may serve as a reminder that the subject of the sciences is ultimately a social one. The most trivial aspect of this constitutionality lies in the fact that scientific experimentation today

15 Blumenberg, *Theorie der Unbegrifflichkeit*.
16 Bachelard, *Rationalisme appliqué*, 11. Emphasis in the original.
17 Ibid., 133.

is mostly a matter of smaller or larger collectives. The second, less trivial aspect is that the instrumental mediation of the process of experimentation is itself eminently social. Instruments embody socially sedimented knowledge and keep it present in this wired form. In research technologies, the collectively produced state of knowledge of a certain period of time presents itself, and is—at least in principle—open to collective access. Third, and least obviously, sociality is present at the very heart of the experimental process: it is anchored in the act of delegation through which this process detaches itself from any single subject conceived as an individual, thus creating a discursive space whose essential characteristic is to be accessible to anyone who engages in an experiment on the same epistemic target.

As we can see, the disappearance of the body in an experiment is strangely mediated and entangled. But we can also see that the body is not simply made to disappear. Its voice persists, an acousmatic voice that can be heard even as detached from its origin. With this, however, another voice is being called forth at the same time, making itself felt as the event of a trace that can be, but need not be, an acoustic one. In order to make this voice speak to us, it has to be delegated back to the subject that had temporarily withdrawn from the event. The subject now has the task of articulating the traces as a voice that is not its own and that is nevertheless being provoked into existence by the experimental arrangement it has created.

THINGS

The Spiral and Its Aura

We encounter the geometry of the spiral as a form in nature, in particular in organic formations, but the aesthetic interest in the spiral has always already been shaped culturally and has found multiple and variegated figurations in history. This essay takes its starting point from two publications that appeared roughly a century ago, two remarkable books that focused on spiral tendencies in nature as well as in culture.[1] The first of them, *The Curves of Life*, was written by Theodore Andrea Cook, a well-known critic and writer of his time, and was published in the wake of World War I.[2] It refers back to another book, which Cook published about ten years earlier, at the height of *art nouveau*, with a somewhat narrower focus: *Spirals in Nature and Art*.[3] The other book, *On Growth and Form*, which appeared toward the end of World War I, was written by the Scottish biologist and biomathematician

1 A first outline of the essay was presented in the context of an exhibition (January 13 —April 15, 2018) at the art space of the Alfred Ehrhardt Foundation in Berlin. The exhibition had previously been shown in the Oldenburg Castle (May 20—August 27, 2017 and in the Art Gallery Erfurt (October 7—January 1st). See also Stefanie Odenthal and Christiane Stahl (eds.), *Nautilus: Schnecken, Muscheln und andere Mollusken in der Fotografie* (Petersberg: Michael Imhof Verlag, 2017).

2 Theodore Andrea Cook, *The Curves of Life, Being an Account of Spiral Formations and their Application to Growth in Nature, to Science and to Art* (New York: Dover Publications, 1979).

3 Theodore Andrea Cook, *Spirals in Nature and Art. A Study of Spiral Formations Based on the Manuscripts of Leonardo da Vinci, with Special Reference to the Architecture of the Open Staircase at Blois in Touraine. Now for the First Time Shown to Be from his Designs*, with a Preface by Professor E. Ray Lankester (London: John Murray, 1903).

D'Arcy Wentworth Thompson.[4] Cook was a cultural historian; Thompson a natural scientist. Both books were the result of their authors' longstanding preoccupation with spiral forms. Cook was a widely traveled writer, journalist, and authority on European architecture. In the context of his intensive focus on spirals he had devoted himself to studying the manuscripts of Leonardo da Vinci. Thompson, a passionate marine biologist, became professor of natural history at the University of St. Andrews. He won renown for pointing out the connection between the leaf position of plants and the Fibonacci numbers, the series named after the medieval Pisan mathematician Leonardo Fibonacci. We can rightly ask where the interest in spiral forms came from at the beginning of the twentieth century—an interest that spanned nature as well as culture and that these two books condensed and reflected in an exemplary fashion.

Beyond the general interest in spiral forms of *art nouveau* architecture, painting, and design, it can safely be assumed that one of the direct sources of inspiration was a volume of picture plates which caused a sensation around the turn of the century that reached way beyond Germany. Under the title of *Art Forms of Nature,* it was issued in folio and in several instalments by the gifted draftsman, pugnacious German evolutionary biologist and staunch Darwinian Ernst Haeckel. It contained one hundred lithographic plates filled with marine life forms, artistically organized in the manner of curiosity cab-

4 D'Arcy Wentworth Thompson, *On Growth and Form* (Cambridge: Cambridge University Press, 1917). Abridged edition by John Tylor Bonner (Cambridge: Cambridge University Press, 1961).

inets by the Bibliographical Institute in Leipzig and Vienna.[5] A glimpse through the plates is enough to convince the viewer of the omnipresence of spiral forms whose motifs were repeatedly adopted by the design language prevalent at the beginning of the twentieth century.

I will return below to this artistic and scientific conjuncture around 1900. First, however, to locate it historically let us take a brief staccato-like foray into the cultural history of mankind. As an ornament, the spiral has accompanied human cultures from very early on. We find it as a decoration on Neolithic pottery and as an element of Bronze Age body jewelry. It is an essential constituent of Ionic column capitals as well as of the winding ornaments on Greek vases. It is therefore not by chance that the first formal, mathematical framing of its simplest form—known today as the arithmetic spiral -, defined by its steadily increasing radius, goes back to the Hellenistic mathematician and technician Archimedes.[6]

One of the most striking features of the architecture of the Romanic and Gothic Middle Ages is the spiral staircase. To be precise, however, we are not dealing here with a spiral conically projected into three dimensions, but with what we may call a screw thread or helix. While its radius remains constant, its height increases in equal increments with every turn. Sometimes one can estimate the gradient of such spiral stairs from outside by the inclination of the window frames of a staircase tower.

5 Ernst Haeckel, *Kunstformen der Natur* (Leipzig and Vienna: Bibliographisches Institut, 1899–1904).

6 Archimedes, *On Spirals. The Works of Archimedes*, vol. 2, trans. Reviel Netz (Cambridge: Cambridge University Press, 2017).

Baroque Ornamentation

Spiral forms can, of course, also be found occasionally in Arabic and Persian as well as Chinese and Japanese ornamentation. But the genuine age of the spiral is the European and the Ibero-American, in particular Mexican baroque, the Churrigueresque.[7] The central motif of baroque ornamentation is, besides the shell of the scallop, the snail-like spiral in all possible shapes and forms. The basic shape of all of these spirals however, distinguishes itself significantly from the classical Archimedean spiral. It was René Descartes who first described its mathematical form. Its radius does not increase linearly in equal increments, but geometrically. Because of this form of progression, its mathematical representation is often called logarithmic. What remains constant here is the angle at which every section through its pole cuts the spiral. One generation after Descartes, the Swiss mathematician and physicist of the High Baroque, Jakob Bernoulli the Elder, called it *spira mirabilis* because of its "self-similar" proportions. The logarithmic spiral was one of his most-loved mathematical forms.

The Baroque Age was at the same time the age of curiosity cabinets.[8] The shells of snails, mollusks and other marine animals were among the most desirable, particularly exotic *naturalia* which reached the harbors of the Netherlands and of England on ships of the West Indian and the East Indian Company and their Dutch equivalents. They not only filled the cabi-

7 George Kubler and Martin Soria, *Art and Architecture in Spain and Portugal and their American Dominions, 1500 to 1800* (London: Penguin Books, 1959).

8 Horst Bredekamp, Jochen Brüning and Cornelia Weber, *Theater der Natur und Kunst. Wunderkammern des Wissens* (Berlin: Henschel, 2000).

net drawers of aristocrats, but also those of sufficiently wealthy patricians. Before long they had found a place on the shelves of painters who decorated their still lifes with them. Most often they remained a composition element in a rich assortment of objects, as seen in many still lifes with flowers and fruits from the first half of the seventeenth century, for instance those of Balthasar van der Ast from Middelburg in Zeeland. Another Dutch painter from the second half of the seventeenth century, Adriaen Coorte, also from Middelburg, took the principle of minimalism to extremes in his paintings.[9] Incidentally, he was rediscovered only at the beginning of the twentieth century; the first exhibition of his paintings was held half a century later. He painted still lifes consisting only of shells on a table plate with the unavoidable *memento mori*-crack. Here, we find flat and drawn-out spiral forms of *Prosobranchia* as well as those of sharply pointed *Terebridae*, among others. Coorte painted with oil on paper that was then mounted onto wooden plates. Brilliance is the mark of oil painting on canvas of that time. Wrested from the depths of the sea, the wet brightness has given way to the matte shimmer of Coorte's dried calcite shells whose rippled surfaces thus come into their own. His objects lie fully illuminated on the table and hardly cast shadows. They appear to be hovering horizontally rather than lying flat and still, as if they were on the verge of gliding off the plate. Coorte was a master of the game of spirals. He tried out everything between an Archimedean and a logarithmic spiral. The

9 Laurens J. Bol, *Adriaen Coorte: A Unique Seventeenth Century Dutch Still Life Painter* (Amsterdam: Van Gorcum, 1977); Quentin Buvelot, *The Still Lifes of Adriaen Coorte (active ca. 1683–1707)* (Den Haag and Zwolle: Koninklijk Cabinet van Schilderijen Mauritshuis en Waanders, 2008).

peculiar appeal of these shell ensembles derives from the back-and-forth movement between the two principles. They do not appear simply as a mass of similar objects, but rather, in all their plasticity, as the exposition of and the playground for a formal structure.

Polished shells showing their mother-of-pearl colors were also worked into splendid vessels held by gold or silver mounts, natural 'artificialia' of sorts. Above all, the spiral shells of the cephalopode *Nautilus pompilius* advanced to an emblem of baroque finery. As drinking cups set in jeweled holders, they formed part of aristocratic table settings and served as eye-catchers on countless seventeenth-century still lifes. And quite often, such paintings display yet another spiral reference: a partly peeled citrus fruit with its skin hanging over the table edge. This spiral-shaped object, half nature, half culture, belongs to the repertoire of the baroque table still life as well.

Grown and Wrapped

The logarithmic Nautilus curve suggests a dynamic that is not felt when looking at an Archimedean spiral. We might say that what one experiences here is the difference between something that has 'grown' and something that has been 'wrapped.' D'Arcy Thompson pointed out that the geometrically progressing spirals in living nature always contain, in one form or another, an "element of time," as he expressed it.[10] Whether we are considering shells of snails or the flower

10 Thompson, *On Growth and Form*, 175.

head of a sunflower, these organic structures do not grow as already existing structures by intussusception, which would simply make them expand, but rather by apposition, by the steady accretion of new segments, either from inside or at the periphery. In other words, either the older segments are pushed outward, which makes them expand as well, or the older segments remain in the apex and newer, bigger ones are added. Their growth is determined by a geometrical gnomon-principle, as Thompson calls it.[11] This means that each additional segment is formed in a similar fashion, proportionally enlarged and similarly situated in comparison with its predecessor; consequently, it is a gnomon of the whole preceding segment. It is this self-similarity, which is also connected to what is called the golden section that gives these structures their magical appearance by maintaining the dynamic of their growth. Their magic is even heightened by the fact that spirals produced by nature never represent pure and completely undistorted realizations of the mathematical relation used to describe them, a fact to which Theodore Cook pointed more than once. Beyond the temporal dimension of their construction, spirals owe their aesthetics and their liveliness, to quote Cook, "to those subtle changes" with which nature reacts to external and internal disturbances in the course of a growth process, and compensates them.[12] Our technical constructions stand in a double contrast to them: as a rule, if they employ the spiral motif they create Archimedean instead of logarithmic spirals or screws and perfect instead of slightly irregular ones. They display their own aesthetics, but it is not

11 Ibid., 181–187.
12 Cook, *Curves of Life*, 19.

the naturally evolved aesthetics of the golden section and the play around its proportions—it is the industrial aesthetics of perfection.

Parable of Life

After their climax in the baroque era and a temporary decline in Classicism, the spiral enjoyed a certain renaissance in the Romantic period—less as an ornament than as an ideal form. Johann Wolfgang von Goethe, for instance, saw the spiral as an allegory of life *tout court* and propagated it as the form principle of all of living nature. His reflections about the metamorphosis of plants are imbued with the idea that a spiral tendency spreading horizontally is kept under control by a straight vertical principle. As he wrote in a late, only posthumously published sketch: "Having grasped the concept of metamorphosis fully, we may go on to examine the development of the plant in more detail, and will begin by noting a *vertical* tendency. We can think of this as a spiritual staff supporting the plant's existence and maintaining it over long periods of time. [...] Thus, we must observe the spiral forms which wind about these plants. The system which rises vertically in the plant produces the enduring element, the solid, the lasting. [...] The spiral system is the element that develops, expands, nourishes; as such it is short-lived and different from the vertical. Where its effect predominates, it soon grows weak and begins to decay; where it joins the vertical system, the two grow together to from a lasting unity [...] Neither of the two systems can be considered as working alone; they are always and forever together. In complete balance they produce the most perfect development of vegetation."[13] In her book *Experiment Linie,* devoted to the arts and sciences around 1900, Sabine Mainberger gave an impressive description of the connection between line and spiral in Goethe's work.[14] And to recall another intellectually towering figure from the Romantic period: Georg Wilhelm Friedrich Hegel not only conceived the basic moving principle of philosophical thinking, that is, his dialectics, but also the emergence of the spirit in human history in the form of a spiral, although he appears not to have used the word itself explicitly either in his *Science of Logic*[15] or in his *Phenomenology of Spirit.*[16] In summary, we can state that Romantic natural historians as well as philosophers in the Romantic era tended to assign to the principle of the spiral a rather esoteric, neither mathematically nor empirically recoverable form. And as the nineteenth century progressed, empirically oriented natural scientists as well as archive-based historians definitely rejected such overarching figures of thought.

13 AnthroWiki.at Bibliothek:Goethe/Naturwissenschaft/Über die Spiraltendenz der Vegetation. Manuscript, ca. 1830, 1831. Last accessed: April 2025. Translation: "Excerpt from 'The Spiral Tendency in Vegetation (1829-31)'," in *The Essential Goethe,* ed. Matthew Bell (Princeton and Oxford: Princeton University Press, 2016), 995–998, on p. 996.

14 Sabine Mainberger, *Experiment Linie. Künste und ihre Wissenschaften um 1900* (Berlin: Kadmos, 2010), 41–58.

15 Georg Wilhelm Friedrich Hegel, *The Science of Logic,* trans. George Di Giovanni (Cambridge: Cambridge University Press, 2015).

16 Georg Wilhelm Friedrich Hegel, *The Phenomenology of Spirit,* trans. Peter Fuss and John Dobbins (Notre Dame, IN: University of Notre Dame Press, 2019).

Technologies of Research and Representation

What, then, under the conditions of another downswing, could have caused the renewed fascination with the spiral almost one hundred years later, at the turn of the twentieth century? My educated guess is that technology re-entered the game, although this time not as a structural principle of construction associated with architecture, but rather as technologies of research and of representation—in short, as cultural technologies of media. The nineteenth century brought a massive, unprecedented technological thrust in scientific research, in particular in relation to its media-technological visualization strategies and options for representation.

At least four dimensions can be distinguished here, each accompanied by its own form of visualization. The first dimension concerns the visualization of the macrocosm. Technological feats such as the giant telescope developed by Josef Fraunhofer, a parallactically mounted lens telescope with a big achromatic objective lens, opened up a new era in the observation of celestial bodies. The telescope built between 1818 and 1824 by Fraunhofer for the astronomer Friedrich Wilhelm Georg Struve in Dorpat was a milestone in this respect.[17] Not least, however, we have to consider the refinement and standardization of astronomical procedures of observation, which developed in parallel in the context of a nationwide establishment and interconnection of observatories throughout the major European countries.[18] This led astronomers such as

17 Myles W. Jackson, *Spectrum of Belief: Joseph von Fraunhofer and the Craft of Precision Optics* (Cambridge and London: MIT Press, 2000).
18 Compare, e.g., Hoffmann, *Unter Beobachtung.*

William Parsons, the third Earl of Rosse, to identify galactic spiral nebulae and represent them by drawings.[19] The far-flung cosmos began to unveil its physico-geometrical order, and it just happened to be of a spiral nature.

Second, new procedures for the fabrication of achromatic lenses helped to widen the gaze into the world of microscopically small living beings. Here again, however, it was the corollaries, in particular the microscopic techniques of preparing thin sections of specimens, their embedding, dyeing and contrasting that made it possible to exhaust the potential of the optical advancements.[20] The oceanic plankton in particular emerged as a treasure trove not only of bizarre life forms, but also of morphological regularities that had not been in focus so far. The second half of the nineteenth century saw a number of research expeditions spanning the oceans of the globe, such as, for instance, the British Challenger expedition (1872–1876) which, for the first time, inspected not only the coastal waters but also the depths of the sea.[21] Ernst Haeckel's lithographs of life under water in his *Art Forms of Nature* are, perhaps, the best-known expression of the fascination that this cosmos of minute entities hidden in the depths of the seas exerted on researchers and spectators alike. Exemplary in this respect are the unicellular *Foraminifera*, a group of marine inhabitants that comprises about ten thousand recent species from microscopically small up to twenty centimeters in size and about

19 Compare Omar S. Nasim, *Observing by Hand: Sketching the Nebulae in the Nineteenth Century* (Chicago: The University of Chicago Press, 2013).

20 Compare Jutta Schickore, *The Microscope and the Eye: A History of Reflections, 1740–1870* (Chicago: The University of Chicago Press, 2007).

21 Franziska Torma (ed.), *A Cultural History of the Sea in the Global Age* (London: Bloomsbury Academic, 2023).

four times as many species from which fossils have been identified.[22] These and many other 'natural art forms' are replete with indications of spirals as well as fully developed spirals, be it the casings of planktonic organisms, the bending movements of algae, the tentacles of medusae, the stems of glass sponges, brittle stars, or spiral worms.

Third, we have to consider the technologies for the representation of movement. In his book, Cook emphasizes the fascination evoked by cinematography at the turn of the twentieth century, with its time-lapse options, in particular the visualization of plant growth. Charles Darwin had already tried to record the more or less spiral-like movements of plants by drawing them, and he had described the orbiting of stipes and plant apices as "circummutation."[23] Well known are the time lapse films of the growth movements of plants by the German botanist Wilhelm Pfeffer, which he prepared in Leipzig between 1898 and 1900.[24] In this context Cook refers to the works of Henderina Dukinfield Scott, an early pioneer of scientific film and wife of the British paleobotanist Dukinfield Henry Scott.[25] Taking advantage of filmographic time-lapse options, the spiral movement of growth observed over long periods of time, which in its natural slowness remained

22 See, for example, Haeckel, *Kunstformen*, Plate 2.

23 Charles Darwin, *The Power of Movement in Plants* (London: John Murray, 1880).

24 Compare "Kinematographische Studien an Impatiens, Vicia, Tulipa, Mimosa und Desmodium von W. Pfeffer (1898-1900)," revised by Prof. Dr. F Bachmann from the Botanical Institute of the University of Leipzig for the Institute of Scientific Film. https://doi.org/10.3203/IWF/B-450. Last accessed April 20, 2025.

25 Cook, *Curves of Life*, 11–12.

invisible to an uncompressed gaze, could be visualized in an impressive manner.

Finally, fourth—but by no means least—the development of X-ray photography soon after the detection of X-rays in 1895 brought undreamed-of, previously unimaginable artistic light games into the foreclosed interior of organic structures.[26] One of the earliest X-ray photographs—showing the interior compartmentalization of a Triton shell—appeared in 1923 in the Dutch journal for art and architecture with the fitting title *Wendingen*.[27] That particular issue of the magazine, which appeared from 1918 to 1932 in Amsterdam and was close to the architectonic movement of the Amsterdam School, became known as the 'Shell Number.' In particular, two aspects of X-ray photography challenged its artistic usage. On the one hand, it offered the possibility of looking into the interior of organic structures without having to dismantle them mechanically. This made it possible to visualize construction principles without losing the contours of the outer covering. On the other hand, it was the game of light and shadow that could be orchestrated with the help of these short-wave rays in a previously unthinkable manner. Both options exerted their fascination on the German Bauhaus, for instance. Here, in particular, it was László Moholy-Nagy who tackled the potentials for light and shadow in technologies such as X-ray photography and photogrammetry. Francis Ponge, the poet of the

26 Compare Monika Dommann, *Durchsicht, Einsicht, Vorsicht. Eine Geschichte der Röntgenstrahlen, 1896–1963* (Zurich: Chronos Verlag, 2003).

27 X-ray photograph of a Triton shell by the physician Dr. J. B. Polak, in *Wendingen* (series 5, nr. 8/9, Amsterdam, 1923). Reproduced in *László Moholy-Nagy, Malerei, Photographie, Film* (Bauhausbücher, vol 8) (Munich: Albert Langen, 1925), 62.

little things of everyday life, must have had such images before his eyes when, in his *étude* on snails, he addressed these animals as living beings "beings whose existence is itself a work of art, rather than artists—makers of works of art"[28] To this day, photography of organic structures with X-ray light has not lost its attraction, as shown, for example, by the works of Nick Veasey.[29]

Precision and Aesthetics

The concentrated power of media and research technologies that was characteristic of the end of the nineteenth and the beginning of the twentieth centuries exhibited a peculiar distinction: it created a conjuncture between the sciences and the arts that, by making use of these techniques in their rich variations allowed for an interrelation of precision and aesthetics. Not least, it was expressed as a conjuncture of the spiral. A movement such as the Bauhaus was animated and inspired by this interpenetration. But—to mention in passing—a movement such as surrealism, which developed at the same time, while also being nurtured by this conjuncture, realized it in a distinctly different manner. And in the realm of the sciences, these technologies opened up new worlds as research instruments for the elucidation of morphogenesis—in the areas of the dynamics of matter as well as that of life processes. They

28 Francis Ponge, "Taking the side of things," in *The Voice of Things*, trans Beth Archer (New York: McGraw-Hill, 1972), 29–77, on p. 45.

29 Nick Veasey, *X-Ray: See Through the World Around You* (London: Goodman Books, 2008).

reached upward to cosmic dimensions and downward to the minute pelagic and terrestrial level, into the temporal order of nature as well as the depths of its organization. The two books by Theodore Cook and D'Arcy Thompson which were the starting point of my deliberations amply testify to this remarkable conjuncture around 1900.

These possibilities have been expanded once more in the course of the past one hundred years of potentiation of the technical means of micro-photography and the options of micrographic visualization. The world of the molecular is emblematic for this expansion. It is the diffraction of X-rays by crystallized substances that enabled the representation of a spiral that has had a deep transformative impact on the imagery of the living world: the DNA double helix, which became culturally omnipresent in the second half of the twentieth century. Its endless variations fill both scientific textbooks and medical advertisements, and it has become a motif for sculptural artwork and architectural design.[30] However, to be precise, the molecular double helix of deoxyribonucleic acid is not a spiral in the strict sense—it is, rather, a coil. In the chromosomes of the cellular nucleus it is once more wound up itself. Its early representations were reconstructions based on X-ray diffraction patterns.[31] It was only the development of the scanning tunneling microscope in the 1980s that offered the possibility of directly imaging the helix of a twin deoxyribonucleic acid thread.[32] Today, the molecular double helix has become a

30 Harmke Kamminga and Soraya de Chadarevian, *Representations of the Double Helix* (Cambridge: Whipple Museum of the History of Science, 2002).

31 James D. Watson and Francis Crick, "Molecular structure of nucleic acids," *Nature* 4356 (1953): 737–738.

32 Hennig, *Bildpraxis*.

synonym not only for the stability, but also for the variability, and with that, the manipulability of biological life.

Technology and Eye

I shall conclude this overview with an image that we owe to a technique dating back to the fifteenth century. It concerns a copper engraving to be found in an artist book, *Châteaux en Espagne*,[33] that grew out of the encounter between the engraver Albert Flocon and the philosopher Gaston Bachelard.[34] The book appeared in 1957 in Paris and contains a series of fifteen copper engravings by Flocon, which Bachelard accompanied with longer or shorter reflections. Albert Flocon—still known as Albert Mentzel at that time—studied at the Bauhaus in Dessau in the late 1920s and retained lasting impressions of Josef Albers and Oskar Schlemmer that deeply impacted his later work as an artist. Flocon's copper engravings live from the tension between forms of nature and geometrical abstraction, from perspective and counter-perspective. They create a space for surprises to happen, a space which opens up the possibility of multiple stories as soon as one begins to explore it.

The engraving, which occupies half a page and bears the simple title "Les Coquilles" is dated 1956. On a beach strewn with shells and lumps of rock covered with algae, an enormous Triton shell, mutilated by the breaking of the waves, juts out

33 Flocon/Bachelard, *Châteaux en Espagne.*

34 Compare Rheinberger, *The Hand of the Engraver*; see also "The Bottle for Example: Gaston Bachelard looks at Albert Flocon's Castles in Spain," in the present volume.

into the air. Beside it, its internal geometry is repeated in an abstracting duplication as a sectional cut through the casing. The mutilation of its screw has mutated into an opening. As if the shell were communicating its energy to the air into which it reaches, the sky above it is dominated by an enormous Nautilus spiral and appearing to suck up the surrounding clouds. Is it an exploding star, a flash of lightning, a vortex? The small, tower-like water castle in the background—Bachelard calls it a "Mont Saint-Michel"—is immersed in its glaring, shadowless light, as if singed by it. Bachelard comments: "Flocon throws himself body and soul into his spiralized destiny. The ladder of the snail is a living building. It ascends the sky. Filled with phantastic dreams, the casing forces the cloud into a spiral."[35] Just as the water castle becomes a mere island, the real Spanish castle in this copper engraving presents itself in a surrealistically honed apotheosis as the mutilated shell of a snail. The beach appears completely deserted, yet it is kept moving by the pelagic remnants left by the drift. The scene mutates into a cosmic-apocalyptic event to which, on the one hand, all of life has fallen victim—the bark as well, lying motionless in the water, is empty and the last little wave it makes is breaking on the shore and rolling up in itself. On the other hand, however, the scenery owes its shape completely to the left-overs of this life, and with that, it is an incarnation of a "dialectic of nature and counter-nature,"[36] of abstraction and concretion, of that "polemic of the figurative and the non-figurative,"[37] which

35 Flocon/Bachelard, *Châteaux en Espagne*, 53.
36 Ibid., 37.
37 Ibid., 13.

fascinated Bachelard so much in his encounters with Flocon's castles in Spain.

As we have seen, technology must be supplemented with the eye, whether we are dealing with the most modern physical electronics such as the scanning tunneling microscope or the traditional, age-old technique of copper engraving. Spiral dynamics in nature, whose microscopic variants derive from stereochemical principles, and whose macroscopic variants are due to differential growth processes, must be supplemented with cultural techniques that can provide options for encouraging ever new forms for representing them. In the course of the twentieth century, unprecedented research technologies and the procedures derived from them restored the aura of the spiral in a life-world increasingly dominated by straight lines.

Imag(in)ing the Wind Channel

Late nineteenth-century chronophotography — prominently represented by Eadweard Muybridge in Great Britain[1] and Etienne-Jules Marey in France[2]—amply demonstrated the analytical potential of photographs taken in rapid succession for the analysis of motion sequences of animals, such as horses, and of people. Around the same time, Ernst Mach and Peter Salcher managed to visualize bullets travelling through the air at high speed by making use of a sophisticated experimental setup. Both serial photographs and snapshots have complex technical preconditions, as shown in an exemplary fashion by historical accounts of Andreas Mayer[3] as well as Christoph Hoffmann and Peter Berz,[4] respectively.

The development of these techniques is not, however, the focus of the following considerations. Rather, the present

1 Jacob Davis Babcock Stillman, *The Horse in Motion as Shown by Instantaneous Photography. With a Study of Animal Mechanics Founded on the Anatomy and the Revelations of the Camera in which is Demonstrated the Theory of Quadrupedal Locomotion.* Photographs by Eadweard Muybridge (London: Trubner & Co., 1882); see, among a large amount of secondary literature, Philip Prodger, *Time Stands Still. Eadweard Muybridge and the Instantaneous Photography Movement* (Oxford: Oxford University Press, 2003).

2 Etienne-Jules Marey, *La Photographie du mouvement. Les méthodes chronophotographiques* (Paris: Hachette, 2022); see, among a large amount of secondary literature, François Dagognet, *Etienne-Jules Marey—La passion de la trace* (Paris: Hazan, 1987).

3 Compare, e.g., Andreas Mayer, *Science of Walking: Investigations into Locomotion in the Long Nineteenth Century*, trans. Robin Blanton and Tilman Skowroneck (Chicago: The University of Chicago Press, 2020.)

4 Christoph Hoffmann and Peter Berz (eds.), *Über Schall. Ernst Machs und Peter Salchers Geschossfotografien* (Göttingen: Wallstein, 2001).

review revolves around the scientific deployment of one of the follow-ups to serial photography, namely cinematography, in the earlier part of the twentieth century. In the context of the contemporary experimental sciences, cinematography was adapted as a phenomenological technique to analyze motion sequences in water channels and wind tunnels specifically constructed for this purpose. I shall limit myself to just a few brief remarks on this topic. They were prompted by a project of Florian Dombois and his students at the Zurich University of the Arts, now stretching over more than a decade and accompanied by a periodic publication, the *Wind Tunnel Bulletin*, published since 2013 in continuing issues, in irregular intervals, to this day.[5] The core of the project is a wind tunnel constructed by Dombois and his colleagues as an artistic research object, first located in a backyard of Zurich's Hafnerstraße, now on the roof of the main building of the new ZHdK campus on the Toni Areal in Zurich. I had the chance to visit the wind tunnel a number of times over these years and discuss topics connected to the project with the group, beginning in the spring of 2013 with an informal meeting, together with Bernd Mahr, on scaling and models.[6]

The film material that I was looking at when writing these lines was presented in *Wind Tunnel Bulletin No 09*.[7] The material stems from the former Kaiser Wilhelm Institute for Fluid Dynamics, founded in 1925 in Göttingen under its director

5 zhdk.ch/en/research/fspt/wind-tunnel-bulletin-2014. Last accessed: June 21, 2025.

6 Compare the posthumously compiled volume Bernd Mahr, *Schriften zur Modellforschung*, ed. Klaus Robering (Paderborn: Mentis, 2021).

7 Florian Dombois, Mario Schulze and Sarine Waltenspül (eds.), *Wind Tunnel Bulletin No 09*. Zurich: ZHdK, June 2019.

Ludwig Prandtl.[8] The films dating back to the 1920s and the 1930s have been preserved in the Archive of the Max Planck Society in Berlin.[9]

As far as research in fluid aero-mechanics is concerned, the film camera is basically regarded and used as a technical device that is inserted into an experimental setup designed to produce flow phenomena. The goal is to make these phenomena—or parts of them—visible and subsequently subject them to motion analysis in accelerated, decelerated, or immobilized, 'frozen' form. To achieve these goals, the motion phenomena at stake must be produced adequately in the first place. As mentioned, since the early twentieth century this was primarily done in spaces specially created for the purpose: in wind tunnels or water channels set up as laboratories in different shapes and sizes. When aerodynamic phenomena in particular were to be visualized, smoke or dust had to be added to the air to make the flow phenomena visible. In the case of hydrodynamic phenomena, streaks and swirls could be visualized in an enhanced form using a soluble dye.

In an ensuing, second step, the movement patterns have to be fixed by deploying another, technical medium. Here, chrono-photography enters the picture. It is only in this transposed form that the traces created in channels and tunnels can be further resolved and represented by taking advantage of the intrinsic possibilities of this technical medium of representation. In experimental practice, however, these two steps are not divorced from one another. Instead, they condition each

8 David Bloor, *The Enigma of the Aerofoil: Rival Theories in Aerodynamics, 1909–1930* (Chicago: The University of Chicago Press, 2011).

9 Editorial, *Wind Tunnel Bulletin No 09*, 263, and references therein.

other reciprocally and build each other up as an experimental ensemble. Thus, the phenomenon at stake in the space of the experiment and the medium of its fixation must be interconnected and compatible with each other, and yet in all their relatedness preserve their own, intrinsic characteristics and their respective potentials as well. Indeed, it is a key trait of the infrascopic core of experimentation that the fleeting and often invisible traces produced within an experimental setup are transformed into a permanent and visible stream of data. This is a precondition, in turn, for an appropriate, qualitative and quantitative analysis of these traces.[10]

We are not simply dealing here with technical reproducibility as a repeated evocation of the same natural phenomenon, a repetition that can be called up again and again at will. A good experimental setup does, of course, achieve reproducibility *grosso modo*, but in practice what is really interesting are always the nuances that emerge by repeatedly eliciting the phenomenon under slightly different conditions. It is the only way by which we can learn something new about the phenomena in question. This is the rather straightforward aspect of technical reproducibility concerning the experimental setup itself. By contrast, the less trivial aspect consists in making an event, once it has taken place, available in a technical medium that conserves it in a manipulable and reproducible form and thus enables the event to become an epistemic event in that medium to begin with. This also means that as a rule, epistemic events become analyzable in the very first place in the form of such a technical transposition, in the data space, through the duplication of the epistemic thing in a technically reified form. The

10 Compare Rheinberger, *Split and Splice*, Part One.

possibilities and options connected with this duplication decisively depend on the medium in and through which it occurs. I will now briefly discuss a few of the media-specific options and possibilities that chronophotography offers.

The focus of the images presented in the *Bulletin* lies on flow patterns, particularly on flow figures in the shape of more or less regular turbulences and swirls arising from various obstacles. Two different aspects of flows are named and addressed. In their filmic fixation, they are dependent on two different technical procedures: on the one hand, we are dealing with the representation of sequences of movements in time and the corresponding differential changes; on the other hand, the problem to be solved is the representation of flow patterns or flow figures in a metastable state of dynamic equilibrium.

First, let us briefly turn to the representation of motion courses. Here, film as a technical medium basically offers two possibilities of visualization, which can briefly be summarized as follows: What is too slow to be seen by the naked eye has to be technically accelerated; and what is too fast to be seen by the naked eye has to be technically decelerated. The procedures are known as fast-motion and slow-motion pictures. In scientific film, cinematic fast motion played a decisive role at the beginning of the twentieth century, e.g., for the visualization of plant movements that are too slow to be discerned by unaided observation.[11] Slow motion, on the other hand, is used to capture movements that are so fast that our sense of vision is unable to follow them. Many of the serial images shown in the *Bulletin* deal with one of these two phenomena. Here, the series has to stand in for a movement—it is, paradoxically, its

11 See, e.g., examples in "The Spiral and its Aura," in the present volume.

'frozen' form. The extreme form of slow motion is 'movement' that is reduced to a single image and thus completely immobilized: the still picture. Even a single picture, however, can convey the impression of a movement: it can suggest from where it comes and toward where it tends. Irregular phenomena of turbulence, on the other hand, resist immobilization — their representation requires moving pictures or whole series of stills.

This brings us to flow patterns. Flow figurations can be described as phenomena that remain constant at least for a given period of time. In film they are perceived as standing still. Since nothing changes over time, in principle even a single snapshot suffices to represent the phenomenon in its totality. Often, however, the dynamic of these phenomena appears to be inscribed in our perception. A textbook example of such a figure is the spiral,[12] which usually takes a shape in the phenomena of flow that approaches its logarithmic variant. Many of Prandtl's images shown in the *Bulletin* are spirals, among them particularly prominent ones, such as the impressive development of a logarithmic spiral in the form of a series of stills. In principle, however, each of the stills suffices to represent the whole developmental process; one gets the impression that the figure visualizes its own algorithm. While the phenomenon does not stand still here, the proportions in which it changes remain constant. Hence each image finally exposes the dynamic of which it is a part. In the end, we have to do, in an advanced technological environment, with one of the age-old problems of the fine arts: to convey

12 See also "The Spiral and its Aura," in the present volume.

the impression of movement in a non-moving object, be it a two-dimensional painting or a three-dimensional sculpture.[13]

13 The *locus classicus* is Gotthold Ephraim Lessing, *Laocoon: an Essay upon the Limits of Painting and Poetry*, trans. Ellen Frothingham (New York: Noonday Press, 1969); see also Ernst Gombrich, *Art and Illusion. A Study in the Psychology of Pictorial Representation* (New York: Pantheon, 1960); for a recent review, see Luca Marchetti, "Depicting motion in a static image: philosophy, psychology and the perception of pictures," in *British Journal of Aesthetics* 62 (2022): 353–371.

Approaching the Sponge

The following *aperçu* on the sponge is the result of a peculiar encounter. Invited to talk to students of the University of Applied Arts in Vienna about an object that would be sent to me by mail shortly before the event, one day I found myself confronted with an ordinary sponge.

What did I have to say about a sponge? Being a historian of science, I started by consulting the literature from the history and philosophy of science. I vaguely remembered having read a few remarks on the image of the sponge in one of Gaston Bachelard's books. No sooner said than done. There was not much time left anyway. But where should I begin?

The Epistemological Obstacle

It seemed natural to start with Bachelard's works on the poetic images of the elements. And indeed, his book, *Earth and Reveries of Will*, contains a few sentences about the material imagination of the earth as a sponge, but only briefly and in passing.[1] By contrast, in one of his epistemological volumes on *The Formation of the Scientific Mind*, which, as the subtitle suggests, he saw as a "contribution to a psychoanalysis of objective knowledge,"[2] Bachelard dedicated an entire chapter to the

1 Gaston Bachelard, *Earth and Reveries of Will. An Essay on the Imagination of Matter*, trans. Kenneth Haltman (Dallas: The Dallas Institute of Humanities & Culture, 2002), Chapter 4.

2 Hans-Jörg Rheinberger, "A remark on Gaston Bachelard's idea of a psychoanalysis of knowledge," *Bachelard Studies* 2 (2021): 173–184.

sponge in the context of what he called "the over-extension of familiar images." Here, he referred to the sponge as a "*Denkmittel* of naive empiricism," as a prime example of an "epistemological obstacle" of the kind found *en masse* in the history of the sciences.[3] The expression encapsulates the difficulties our everyday experience presents to scientific knowledge. According to Bachelard, scientific knowledge must break with everyday experience in order to constitute itself. Scientific knowledge can only be obtained against immediate appearances; it must get rid of them. The sponge as we know and use it in everyday activities such as washing, cleaning, and wiping, has something manifest and evidential to it, something immediately given in its appearance. It is obviously of a porous nature. The bits of organic matter that constitute it are connected like a meshed, three-dimensional network, but leave empty cavities between. For this reason, the sponge is well placed to absorb other matter—gases as well as fluids—and to saturate itself with them but without incorporating them. It is thus possible to squeeze them out again at any time. René Descartes, Bachelard wrote, saw the sponge as a typical example of what he called the "rarefaction of bodies," i.e., of bodies that have been rendered less dense and whose qualities are determined by this very reduction in density. In Bachelard's sardonic summary, "a sponge shows us sponginess. It shows us how one particular kind of matter 'is filled' with another. This lesson in heterogeneous fullness suffices to explain everything [...]. The metaphysics of space in Descartes is the metaphysics of the

3 Bachelard, *Formation of the Scientific Mind*, 81. German expression in the French original.

sponge."[4] This example clearly demonstrates why Bachelard describes the kind of epistemological obstacle that everyday knowledge puts in the way of scientific knowledge as a "verbal obstacle:"[5] it is ultimately nothing else than a linguistic tautology, the sponginess of the sponge. The medical history of the Early Modern period is full of explanations of this kind. All sorts of phenomena are identified with a peculiar principle that produces them. However, tautologies of this kind not only abound in medicine, they also pervade the history of physics, as Bachelard demonstrates in his chapter on the sponge. For instance, he cites the example of the early eighteenth-century French natural historian René Antoine Ferchault de Réaumur, who used the image of the sponge to explain the compressibility of air: the air is a sponge, but one that is even spongier than an ordinary sponge. It is certainly possible to compare the air with such a sponge, a comparison that also explains its elastic properties. But it does not lead to further questions. According to Bachelard, the example shows what it means to be "a generalized image, which is expressed by a single word, the *leitmotif* of a worthless intuition."[6]

Therefore, we must avoid this kind of "solely [...] linguistic manœuvre," Bachelard argues, "which, by associating an abstract word with a concrete one, believes that it has made thought progress,"[7] if we want to set out on the path toward scientific insight. Scientific knowledge, Bachelard continues, must begin by disposing of the images it has borrowed from

4 Ibid., 86.
5 Ibid., 81.
6 Ibid., 82. German expression in the French original.
7 Ibid., 83.

everyday empiricism so that it can replace them, ideally, with mathematical relations or with empirically substantial concepts. Such images can certainly come into play once again, albeit secondarily, when the aim is to restore "a little color" to relationships that have become too abstract, thereby providing derivative, additional fuel, as it were, to scientific thinking.[8] A contemporary textbook example of such secondary usage of imagery would be the illustration of energy potentials by reference to the lifting motions familiar to most people from everyday mechanical contrivances.

Consequently, in the history of science the sponge reveals itself as a telling example of a central concept in Bachelard's historical epistemology, the epistemological obstacle. As already stated, the starting point of Bachelard's historical epistemology is that scientific knowledge must manage to break with everyday experience and its concrete imagery, thereby escaping the "danger" of "immediate metaphors" in order to constitute itself.[9] Such epistemological ruptures, the complements to Bachelard's epistemological obstacles, are crucial. However, just as crucial in the further development of scientific knowledge is the fact that, once it is reached, each historical state of knowledge can sink back into everydayness, once again becoming an epistemological obstacle.

8 Ibid., 85.
9 Ibid., 88.

Wiping Out

A very different example, namely a literary and philosophical examination of the sponge, was provided by Jacques Derrida in his speech in praise of the twentieth-century French writer Francis Ponge that he gave at the 1975 colloquium "Ponge inventeur et classique," held at the Centre Culturel International de Cerisy-la-Salle.[10] The title of Derrida's talk, *Signéponge*, is a play on three words: Firstly, the name of the poet, "Ponge"; secondly, the notion of signature, which serves as the authorization of a text (*signé*, signed); and, finally, the word or image of the sponge (*éponge*). The author Francis Ponge—often quoted by Bachelard in his books on the material imagination of the elements—achieved fame by focusing his literary attention on the little things around us that usually escape attention. His 1942 text *Taking the Side of Things* is paradigmatic in this respect.[11] Although Ponge did not devote a separate text to the sponge, in an entry in *Taking the Side of Things* he compares it to an orange. Unlike the historical examples we encountered in Bachelard's work, which all take an empty and therefore absorptive sponge as their starting point, Ponge begins his meditation on the orange with its juicy flesh, which he compares to a saturated sponge, observing how it behaves when compressed. Both objects, when squeezed, try to "regain face" (*contenance*), their original form, but only the sponge is entirely capable of doing so, as its fibers remain intact when squashed,

10 Cerisy-la-Salle, August 2–12, 1975, under the direction of Philippe Bonnefis et Pierre Oster.

11 Ponge, "Taking the side of things."

whereas squeezing irreparably destroys the orange's cellular tissue even if its peel slowly recovers its form.[12]

By contrast, Derrida, who cites this passage but does not use it to develop his argument, sees the sponge as a metaphor for the ineluctable dialectics of enforcing and erasing the author who signs off the text and the matter he is dealing with, which is signed off in turn. Deeply skeptical toward the frequently heard slogan-like claim that things should be left to speak for themselves, Derrida attempts to find a different interpretation for Ponge's insistent efforts to give things a voice. Giving things a voice, Derrida contends, at the same time means silencing one's own voice. How are we to characterize an author who does not intend to use things to expose his own, innermost self, who does not aim to allow things to speak or bear witness for him, but instead wants to lend them a language that, on the one hand, expunges him as an author, as the subject of the text, but also, on the other hand, awards him sovereignty over the text?

"The thing is not just something conforming to laws that I would have to discuss objectively (adequately) or, on the contrary, subjectively (anthropomorphically). Beforehand, the thing is the other, the entirely other that dictates or writes the law, a law, which is not simply natural (*lex naturae rerum*), but an infinitely, insatiably imperious injunction to which I ought to subject myself, even when this involves trying to acquit myself afterwards, at the end of a duel, having offered it, with my life and desire, something akin to my signature."[13] And

12 Ponge, "Taking the side of things," 36.

13 Jacques Derrida, *Signéponge* (Paris: Seuil, 1988), 17. This and the following quotations are translated by the present author. Derrida's text has a

Derrida continues later in his text: "He [the author], therefore, is [i]ndebted. With respect to what he calls the thing. The thing dictates its conditions, silent though it is, and being silent, does not enter into the contract. It is irresponsible, he alone being responsible from the outset toward the thing, which remains entirely other, indifferent, never engaging itself."[14]

And the sponge? The sponge stands for this strange form of simultaneously extinguishing and empowering, as the emblem for this "state intermediate between all states—an analog in this respect to the written text, if it can put itself into every state, and serve as an intermediary, an intercessor, or a universal witness—the sponge not only constitutes the term of an analogy (allegory or metaphor), but also constitutes, in addition, the very medium of all figures, metaphoricity itself. As he [Ponge] himself says of somebody, by way of praising her, she has 'every quality and hence one quality more: that of having them all'."[15]

The sponge wipes out the signature "Ponge"—*éPonge*—and is it at the same time—*signéPonge*. It absorbs everything only to release it once more. It is simultaneously itself and its other, but without intermixing with its other. "On the one hand, the sponge expunges the proper name, puts it outside of itself, effaces and loses it, soils it as well as making it into a com-

convoluted history. Part of his presentation at the Colloque de Cerisy of 1975 was published in *Digraphe* 8 (May 1976); another part in *Francis Ponge, Colloque de Cerisy*, ed. Philippe Bonnefis and Pierre Oster (Paris, Union Générale d'Editions, 1977), 115–144, followeds by a discussion, 145–151. An English translation appeared in Jacques Derrida, *Signéponge/Signsponge*, trans. Richard Rand (New York: Columbia University Press, 1984). Derrida's own French book publication as of 1988 is a revised version of the 1984 bilingual edition.

14 Ibid., 42–43.

15 Ibid., 60.

mon noun; it contaminates the proper name on contact with the most pitiful, the most unqualifiable object, which is made to retain every sort of dirt. […] But simultaneously, the sponge can also retain the name, absorb it, shelter it, and keep it within itself. Then, too, it holds clean and proper water as well as dirty water, insatiably."[16]

As Ponge himself writes: "The sponge is only a muscle and fills up with air, clean or dirty water, whatever […]."[17] According to Derrida, the sponge as a thing has precisely those qualities that constitute Francis Ponge's literary relationship to the objects he describes. It expunges the proper noun (*le nom propre*), but only by absorbing it within itself. And it absorbs the proper noun without intermixing with it. Absorbed, the proper noun remains excluded within the sponge. And Derrida would not be Derrida if he did not apply 'the thing' that is the subject of this text to his own writing, to his own relationship to things, to his own phenomenology in the same breath. The reader will have noticed that the relation between subject and object that is at stake here is, in an implicit fashion, also the relation that, for Bachelard, is constitutive for the act of scientific knowledge acquisition, and which he characterizes, *ex negativo,* using the example of the everyday image of the sponge in the fourth chapter of *The Formation of the Scientific Mind.*

Let us attempt to access this dialectical figuration by going down the designated path in a more explicit fashion. As a writer, Francis Ponge behaves toward his literary objects like a scientist toward his or her epistemic objects of interest, that is, as an experimenter. Bachelard's considerations on the objects

16 Ibid., 54–55.

17 Ponge, "Taking the side of things," 36.

of scientific knowledge acquisition, on the necessity of getting rid of their immediacy of presence, seamlessly link up with Derrida's reflections on the relationship between the subject and the object in the writing process, particularly in Ponge's writing, and, of course, *ceteris paribus*, Derrida's own writing. The experimenter sets up her or his experiment in such a way that the object of epistemic interest can show itself from sides that it does not reveal of its own accord but that the experimenter cannot force on it either.[18] The views forced upon it regularly prove to be the epistemically uninteresting ones, a mere mirror of a will that remains foreign to them. Scientists thus do not enter into a forced relationship with the objects of their epistemological desire, a relationship of master and slave. Instead, they enter into a close, yet simultaneously detached relationship of a very different nature. They form this relationship with the greatest empathy but, at the same time, in such a way that, ultimately, they take themselves out of the game again. They create a "milieu," to use Derrida's wording, in which the object itself can become epistemic, that is, accessible to knowledge by entering into a productive interplay with the means of its configuration. The experimenter's undivided interest and entire finesse are directed at this interaction, these middle grounds of instruction. It is out of this finesse that epistemic effects emerge from epistemic things as events that are elicited by but at the same time elude the will of the experimenter. Epistemological obstacles cannot be removed frontally; they must be circumvented. It is this unique feature of the experimental method that allows us to compare it with the writing process, as Derrida understands it and sees

18 Rheinberger, "Vom Subjekt des Wissens."

it practiced, for instance, by Francis Ponge, and as he himself understands and practices it. In this way, the twofold historical as well as literary journey—by Bachelard and Derrida, respectively—toward things via one of these things, the sponge, has led us into the heart of my own considerations on the dynamics of scientific experimentation, to the 'epistemic things.'

A Brief Natural History of Zoophytes

These are ways of approaching the sponge from an epistemic and literary perspective. How else might we get at this object? From the perspective of biology what comes to mind is, of course, the natural history of sponges. How did these creatures from the seas and waters come into the focus of naturalists, and what place did they assign to this life form over the course of history? As far as I know, a comprehensive cultural history of "zoophytes," as the early modern British physician and zoologist, Edward Wotton, called them, has not yet been written. As early as the fourth century BC, Aristotle classified these creatures by locating them between plants and animals on the ladder of nature. Hence the later name zoophytes. He held that sponges were "virtually plants and nothing more. [...] For nature passes from lifeless objects to animals in such unbroken sequence, interposing between them beings which live and yet are not animals [...]."[19] In the eighteenth century, the medical doctor and naturalist Peter Simon Pallas was the first to devote an entire treatise to the zoophytes, the *Elenchus*

19 Aristotle, *On the Parts of Animals, Book IV*, trans. William Ogle (London: Kegan Paul, Trench & Co., 1882), para. 5.

zoophytorum.[20] And his somewhat elder contemporary Charles Bonnet, one of the most vocal proponents of a *scala naturae,* a classification of nature ascending from the most imperfect to the most perfect creatures, reserved a chapter for the "zoophyta, or plant animals without feet," in his *Contemplation de la nature.*[21] The English translation of Bonnet's book happened to be published in the same year as Pallas's *Elenchus.*

Briefly, from today's evolutionary perspective, sponges are a kind of predominantly marine living beings which have made the filtration of their surrounding waters the principle of their food intake, optimizing the resorption of plankton by internally enlarging their surface area. Present-day classifications consider them to be fully-fledged animals. But they are animals that do not have any special organs for food intake—they are, one could even say, a life form without organs. And it is precisely this life without organs that leaves behind the reticular, spongy skeletons that have served humans as sponges since time immemorial—among them the especially coveted skeletons of the *Demospongiae,* also known as bath sponges.

Finally, a cultural history of sponges would not be complete without the far more recent history of spongy materials made from synthetic polyurethane, which are a twentieth-century invention. It was the German chemist Otto Bayer who had a decisive impact on shaping our present lifeworld with the creation of foam rubber in 1937 and got a patent for his invention that same year. Its derivatives are used today in all kinds

20 Peter Simon Pallas, *Elenchus zoophytorum, sistens generum adumbrationes generaliores et specierum cognitarum succinctas descriptiones, cum selectis auctorum synonymis* (The Hague: Van Cleef, 1766).
21 Charles Bonnet, *The Contemplation of Nature,* trans. from the French (London: T. Longman in Pater-Noster-Row, 1766).

of applications, from mattresses to building insulation. The square sponge sent to me by mail to prepare for the teaching event that led to the present essay, which is much lighter than a natural bath sponge—and much less soft as well—, was made from crosslinked polyurethane, which brings us back to the starting point of this excursion.

Bibliography

Earlier versions of the texts in this book appeared in

Jens Hauser (ed.). *Paul Vanouse. Fingerprints ... Index—Abdruck—Spur/Index—Imprint—Trace.* Berlin: Argobooks, 2011, 87–104; Andreas Cremonini and Markus Klammer (eds.). Bildbeispiele. Zu einer pikturalen Logik des Exemplarischen. Paderborn: Wilhelm Fink, 2020, 75–84; Sandra Boeschenstein, *Die Grazie der Erkenntnisgrenze/Grace at the Boundary of Knowledge.* Bielefeld: Bielefeld University Press, 2019; Philipp Fischer, Gabriele Gramelsberger, Christoph Hoffmann, Hans Hofmann, Hans-Jörg Rheinberger and Hannes Rickli. *Natures of Data. A Discussion Between Biology, History and Philosophy of Science and Art.* Zurich and Berlin: Diaphanes, 2020, 141–144; Hanni Schierscher, *Innen und Aussen.* Edited by Axel Jablonski. Hohenems-Vaduz-München-Zürich: Bucher, 2020, 197–203; Katrin von Lehmann, *Textura performativa 5.* Berlin: Distanz Verlag, 2021, 109–111; Andreas Greiner, *Anatomy of a Fairy Tale.* Edited by Stefan Vicedom. Wien: Verlag für moderne Kunst, 2016, 124–149; Susanne Witzgall and Kerstin Stakemeier (eds.). *The Present of the Future.* Zurich and Berlin: Diaphanes, 2016, 109–117; *Performance Research* 25/3 (2020): 65–71; Alex Arteaga and Nikolaus Gansterer (eds.). *Contingent Agencies. Inquiries into the Emergence of Atmospheres.* Berlin: Hatje & Cantz, 2025, 238–247; Jens Badura, Selma Dubach, Anke Haarmann (eds.), *Künstlerische Forschung. Ein Handbuch.* Zurich und Berlin: Diaphanes, 2015, 311–314; *Modern Language Notes (MLN)* 139/5 (2024): 937–946; *Das Magazin* (Beilage zum *Tagesanzeiger*), No. 34 (August 24, 2019), 13–14; *Unternehmen Region* (BMBF) 2021/1: 38–39; Jan Silberberger (ed.), *Against* and for *Method. Revisiting Architectural Design as Research.* Zürich: gta Verlag ETH, 2021, 132–141; Katrin Dod and Patrick Wildermann (eds.), *Producing Performing Arts. Aus dem Maschinenraum der freien darstellenden Künste.* Berlin: Alexander Verlag, 2023, 37–38; Sven Spieker and Mario Asef (eds.), *Akusmatik als Labor. Kultur—Kunst—Medien.* Würzburg: Königshausen & Neumann, 2023, 161–168; *Lettre International* 122

(Fall 2018): 129–133; Florian Dombois, Mario Schulze and Sarine Waltenspül (eds.), *Wind Tunnel Bulletin No. 9*. Zurich: ZHdK, 2019, 272–273; Ruth Mateus-Berr (ed.), *Edu: Transversal No. 1*. Berlin/Boston: De Gruyter/Edition Angewandte, 2022, 104–115.

Works quoted

Ammann, Katharina and Priska Gisler (eds., vol. 1); Dombois, Florian, Priska Gisler, Schirin Kretschmann and Markus Schwander (eds., vol. 2). *Präparat Bergsturz*. Lucerne: Periferia, 2012 and 2013.

Archimedes. *On Spirals. The Works of Archimedes*. Vol. 2. Translated and commented by Reviel Netz. Cambridge: Cambridge University Press, 2017.

Aristotle. *On the Parts of Animals, Book IV*. Translated by William Ogle. London: Kegan Paul, Trench & Co., 1882.

Arteaga, Alex and Nikolaus Gansterer (eds.). *Contingent Agencies. Inquiring into the Emergence of Atmospheres*. Berlin: Hatje Cantz, 2025.

Bachelard, Gaston. *Les Intuitions atomistiques. Essai de classification*. Paris: Boivin, 1933.

Bachelard, Gaston. "Le surrationalisme." *Inquisitions. Organe du groupe d'études sur la phénoménologie humaine* 1 (1936): 1–6.

Bachelard, Gaston. "Surrationalism." Translated by Julien Levy. In *Surrealism*. Edited by Julien Levy, 186–189. New York: Black Sun Press, 1936. Originally published as "Le surrationalisme" (*Inquisitions* 1 (1936): 1–6).

Bachelard, Gaston. *Lautréamont*. Paris: Librairie José Corti, 1939.

Bachelard, Gaston. *L'Eau et les rêves. Essai sur l'imagination de la matière*. Paris: Librairie José Corti, 1942.

Bachelard, Gaston. *L'Air et les songes. Essai sur l'imagination du movement*. Paris: Librairie José Corti, 1943.

Bachelard, Gaston. "Une rêverie de la matière." In: José Corti, *Rêves d'encre*. Vingt-cinq images présentées par Paul Eluard, René Char, Julien Gracq et Gaston Bachelard. Paris: Librairie José Corti, 1945, n.p.

Bachelard, Gaston. *Le Rationalisme appliqué*. Paris: Presses Universitaires de France, 1949.

Bachelard, Gaston. *L'Activité rationaliste de la physique contemporaine*. Paris: Presses Universitaires de France, 1951.

Bachelard, Gaston. *The Poetics of Space*. Translated by Maria Jolas. New York: Orion Press, 1964. Originally published as *La Poétique de l'espace* (Paris: Presses Universitaires de France, 1957).

Bachelard, Gaston. *The Psychoanalysis of Fire*. Translated by Alan C. M. Ross. Boston: Beacon Press, 1964. Originally published as *La Psychanalyse du feu* (Paris: Gallimard, 1938).

Bachelard, Gaston. *The Poetics of Reverie. Childhood, Language, and the Cosmos*. Translated by Daniel Russell. Boston: Beacon Press, 1969. Originally published as *La Poétique de la rêverie* (Paris: Presses Universitaires de France, 1960).

Bachelard, Gaston. "Noumène et microphysique". In *Etudes*. Edited by Georges Canguilhem. Paris: Librairie philosophique J. Vrin, 1970, 11–24. First published in 1932/33.

Bachelard, Gaston. *Water and Dreams. An Essay on the Imagination of Matter*. Translated by Edith R. Farrell. Dallas: Dallas Institute of Humanities and Culture, 1983. Originally published as *L'Eau et les rêves. Essai sur l'imagination de la matière* (Paris: José Corti, 1942).

Bachelard, Gaston. *Air and Dreams. An Essay on the Imagination of Movement*. Translated by Edith R. Farrell and Fredrick Farrell. Dallas: The Dallas Institute of Humanities and Culture, 1983. Originally published as *L'Air et les songes. Essai sur l'imagination du movement* (Paris: Librairie José Corti, 1943).

Bachelard, Gaston. *The New Scientific Spirit*. Translated by Arthur Goldhammer (Boston: Beacon Press, 1984). Originally published as *Le Nouvel esprit scientifique* (Paris: Alcan, 1934).

Bachelard, Gaston. *The Formation of the Scientific Mind. A Contribution to a Psychoanalysis of Objective Knowledge*. Translated by Mary McAllester Jones. Manchester: Clinamen, 2002. Originally published as *La Formation de l'esprit scientifique. Contribution à une psychanalyse de la connaissance objective* (Paris: Librairie philosophique J. Vrin, 1938).

Bachelard, Gaston. *Earth and Reveries of Will. An Essay on the Imagination of Matter*. Translated by Kenneth Haltman. Dallas: The Dallas Institute of Humanities & Culture, 2002. Originally published as *La Terre et les rêveries de la volonté* (Paris: Librairie José Corti, 1948).

Bachelard, Gaston. *Imaginationen der Materie. Surrealismus und Nachkriegskunst*. Eingeleitet, herausgegeben und übersetzt von Hans-Jörg Rheinberger. Berlin: Matthes & Seitz, 2026.

Badura, Jens, Selma Dubach and Anke Haarmann (eds.). *Künstlerische Forschung. Ein Handbuch*. Zurich and Berlin: Diaphanes, 2015.

Barad, Karen. *Meeting the Universe Halfway*. Durham and London: Duke University Press, 2007.

Bernard, Claude. *Introduction to the Study of Experimental Medicine* (1865). Translated by Henry Copley Greene. New York: Dover Publications, 1957. Originally published as *Introduction à l'étude de la médecine expérimentale* (Paris: Baillière, 1865).

Barany, Michael and Donald MacKenzie, "Chalk: Materials and concepts in mathematics research." In *Representation in Scientific Practice Revisited*. Edited by Catelijne Coopmans, Janet Vertesi, Michael Lynch and Steve Woolgar, 107–130. Cambridge MA: MIT Press, 2014.

Beckmann, Johann. *Beyträge zur Geschichte der Erfindungen*. Band 5, erstes Stück. Leipzig: Kummer, 1800.

Bello, Mónica and José-Carlos Mariátegui (eds.). *Quantum. In Search of the Invisible*. Barcelona: Centre de Cultura Contemporània de Barcelona, 2019.

Bernard, Claude. *Lectures on the Phenomena of Life Common to Animals and Plants*. Translated by Hebbel E. Hoff, Roger Guillemin and Lucienne Guillemin. Springfield, IL: Charles C. Thomas, 1974. Originally published as *Leçons sur les phénomènes de la vie communs aux animaux et aux végétaux* (Paris: Baillière, 1878/79).

Bloor, David. *The Enigma of the Aerofoil: Rival Theories in Aerodynamics, 1909–1930*. Chicago: The University of Chicago Press, 2011.

Blumenberg, Hans. *Theorie der Unbegrifflichkeit*. Edited by Anselm Haverkamp. Frankfurt am Main: Suhrkamp, 2007.

Boeschenstein, Sandra. *Die Grazie der Erkenntnisgrenze/Grace at the Boundary of Knowledge*. Bielefeld: Bielefeld University Press/Transcript Verlag, 2019.

Bol, Laurens J. *Adriaen Coorte: A Unique Seventeenth Century Dutch Still Life Painter*. Amsterdam: Van Gorcum, 1977.

Bonnet, Charles. *The Contemplation of Nature*. Translated from the French. London: T. Longman in Pater-Noster-Row, 1766. Originally published as *Contemplation de la nature* (Amsterdam: Marc-Michel Rey, 1764).

Borgdorff, Henk A., Peter Peters and Trevor Pinch (eds.). *Dialogues between Artistic Research and Science and Technology Studies*. New York: Routledge, 2019.

Bourdieu, Pierre. *The Logic of Practice*. Translated by Richard Nice. Cambridge: Cambridge University Press, 1990. Originally published as *Le Sens pratique* (Paris: Les Editions de Minuit, 1980).

Bourdieu, Pierre and Loïc Wacquant. *An Invitation to Reflexive Sociology*. Chicago: The University of Chicago Press, 1992.

Brecht, Bertolt. *Leben des Galilei. Schauspiel*. Werkausgabe Edition Suhrkamp, Band 3. Frankfurt am Main: Suhrkamp, 1967. Originally written 1938/1939.

Bredekamp, Horst, Jochen Brüning and Cornelia Weber. *Theater der Natur und Kunst. Wunderkammern des Wissens*. Berlin: Henschel, 2000.

Bücking, Heribert. *Kupferstiche und Zeichnungen 1994–1996*. Berlin: Studio Bildende Kunst Lichtenberg/Werkstattgalerie Bücking, 1996.

Bücking, Heribert. *Der lange Augenblick. Zeichnungen und Kupferstiche*. Berlin: Selbstverlag, 2011.

Bücking, Heribert. *Auf Bildsuche. Zeichnungen, Kupferstiche, Collagen, 1980–2020*. Berlin: Katalogdruck Berlin, 2020.

Buvelot, Quentin. *The Still Lifes of Adriaen Coorte (active ca. 1683–1707)*. Den Haag and Zwolle: Koninklijk Cabinet van Schilderijen Mauritshuis en Waanders, 2008.

Cave, Roderick. *Impressions of Nature: A History of Nature Printing*. London: British Library Publishing, 2009.

Chargaff, Erwin. "Chemical specificity of nucleic acids and mechanism of their enzymatic degradation." *Experientia* 6(6) (1950): 201–209.

Collins, Harry and Robert Evans. *Rethinking Expertise*. Chicago: The University of Chicago Press, 2007.

Conquergood, Dwight. "Performance studies: Interventions and radical research." In *The Performance Study Reader*. Edited by Henry Bial, 311–322. London: Routledge, 2002.

Cook, Theodore Andrea. *The Curves of Life, Being an Account of Spiral Formations and their Application to Growth in Nature, to Science and to Art*. New York: Dover Publications, 1979. First published 1914.

Cook, Theodore Andrea. *Spirals in Nature and Art. A Study of Spiral Formations Based on the Manuscripts of Leonardo da Vinci, with Special Reference to the Architecture of the Open Staircase at Blois in Touraine. Now for the First Time Shown to Be from his Designs*. With a Preface by Professor E. Ray Lankester. London: John Murray, 1903.

Cuvier, Georges. *Essay on the Theory of the Earth*. Translated by Robert Kerr. New York: Kirk & Mercein, 1818. Originally published as *Discours préliminaire, Recherches sur les ossemens fossiles* (Paris: Deterville, 1812).

Dagognet, François. *Etienne-Jules Marey—La passion de la trace*. Paris: Hazan, 1987.

Damerow, Peter, Hans J. Nissen and Robert K. Eglund. *Archaic Bookkeeping. Early Writing and Techniques of Economic Administration in the Ancient Near East*. Translated by Paul Larsen. Chicago: The University of Chicago Press, 1993.

Dante (Alighieri). *Divine Comedy. Inferno, Purgatorio, Paradiso.* Translated by Allen Mandelbaum, illustrated by Barry Moser. Berkeley: University of California Press, 1980.

Darwin, Charles. *The Power of Movement in Plants.* London: John Murray, 1880.

Deleuze, Gilles. *The Logic of Sense.* Translated by Mark Lester and Charles Stivale. New York: Columbia University Press, 1990. Originally published as *La Logique du sens* (Paris: Les Editions de Minuit, 1969).

Derrida, Jacques. *La Voix et le phénomène.* Paris: Presses Universitaires de France, 1967.

Derrida, Jacques. *Grammatologie.* Translated by Hanns Zischler and Hans-Jörg Rheinberger. Frankfurt am Main: Suhrkamp, 1974. Originally published as *De la grammatologie* (Paris: Les Editions de Minuit, 1967).

Derrida, Jacques. *Of Grammatology.* Translated by Gayatri Chakravorty Spivak. Baltimore: Johns Hopkins University Press, 1976, revised edition 1997. Originally published as *De la grammatologie* (Paris: Les Editions de Minuit, 1967).

Derrida, Jacques. "Plato's pharmacy." In *Dissemination.* Translated by Barbara Johnson, 63–171. Chicago: The University of Chicago Press, 1981. Originally published in *La Dissémination* (Paris: Editions du Seuil, 1972).

Derrida, Jacques. "Dissemination." In *Dissemination.* Translated by Barbara Johnson, 287–398. Chicago: The University of Chicago Press, 1981. Originally published in *La Dissémination* (Paris: Editions du Seuil, 1972).

Derrida, Jacques. "Signéponge." In *Ponge, Colloque de Cerisy.* Edited by Philippe Bonnefis and Pierre Oster, 115–144. Paris: Union Générale d'Editions, 1977.

Derrida, Jacques. *Writing and Difference.* Translated by Allan Bass. Chicago: The University of Chicago Press, 1978. Originally published as *Ecriture et Différence* (Paris: Editions du Seuil, 1967).

Derrida, Jacques. *Signéponge / Signsponge.* Translated by Richard Rand. New York: Columbia University Press, 1984.

Derrida, Jacques. *Signéponge.* Paris: Seuil, 1988.

Dombois, Florian, Mario Schulze and Sarine Waltenspül (eds.). *Wind Tunnel Bulletin No 09*. Zurich: ZHdK, June 2019.

Dombois, Florian. https://floriandombois.net

Dommann, Monika. *Durchsicht, Einsicht, Vorsicht. Eine Geschichte der Röntgenstrahlen*, 1896–1963. Zurich: Chronos Verlag, 2003.

Domnitch, Evelina and Dmitry Gelfand. *Opening Coccyx*, Milano: Die Schachtel Editions, 2005.

"Du mot à la vie: un dialogue entre Jacques Derrida et Hélène Cixous." Propos recueillis par Aliette Armel. *Magazine litéraire*, no 430, April 2004, 22–29.

Elzen, Boelie. "Two ultracentrifuges: a comparative study of the social construction of artefacts." *Social Studies of Science* 16 (1986): 621–662.

Feyerabend, Paul K. "Art as a product of nature as a product of art." *World Futures* 40/1 (1994): 87–100.

Feyerabend, Paul K. *The Conquest of Abundance: A Tale of Abstraction versus the Richness of Being*. Edited by Bert Terpstra. Chicago: The University of Chicago Press, 1999.

Fischer, Philipp, Gabriele Gramelsberger, Christoph Hoffmann, Hans Hofmann, Hans-Jörg Rheinberger and Hannes Rickli. *Datennaturen. Ein Gespräch zwischen Biologie, Kunst, Wissenschaftstheorie und –geschichte/ Natures of Data. A Discussion between Biology, History and Philosophy of Science and Art*. Zurich and Berlin: Diaphanes, 2020.

Fischer-Lichte, Erika. *The Transformative Power of Performance. A New Aesthetics*. London and New York: Routledge, 2008.

Fischer-Lichte, Erika. *The Routledge Introduction to Theatre and Performance Studies*. London and New York: Routledge, 2014.

Fisher, Mark. *Ghosts of My Life. Writing on Depression, Hauntology and Lost Futures*. Winchester, VA: Zero Books, 2014.

Fleck, Ludwik. *Genesis and Development of a Scientific Fact*. Translated by Fred Bradley and Thaddeus J. Trenn. Chicago and London: The University of Chicago Press, 1979. Originally published as *Entstehung und Entwicklung einer wissenschaftlichen Tatsache* (Basel: Benno Schwabe, 1935).

Fleck, Ludwik. “Die Krise der ’Wirklichkeit’.” In *Ludwik Fleck: Erfahrung und Tatsache*. Edited by Lothar Schäfer and Thomas Schnelle, 46–58. Frankfurt am Main: Suhrkamp, 1983.

Flocon, Albert. “Le philosophe et le graveur.” In *Bachelard*, 271–278. Paris: Colloque de Cerisy, 1974.

Flocon, Albet. *Suites expérimentales, 1943–1983*. Vienna: Medusa/Bauhaus Archiv, 1983.

Flocon, Albert. “Main ouvrière et main rêveuse. Entretien avec Gil Jouanard.” *Solaire* 10 (1983), special issue *Bachelard ou le droit de rêver*: 57–65.

Flocon, Albert. *Une Poétique de la vision. Du Bauhaus à la perspective curviligne/ Eine Poetik des Sehens. Vom Bauhaus zur kurvenlinearen Perspektive*. Metz: Ecole des Beaux Arts, 1992.

Flocon, Albert and Gaston Bachelard. *Paysages*. Rolle (VD): Eynard, 1950.

Flocon, Albert and Gaston Bachelard. *Châteaux en Espagne*. Paris: Le Cercle Grolier, 1957.

Foerster, Heinz von. *Sicht und Einsicht. Versuche zu einer operativen Erkenntnistheorie*. Wiesbaden: Springer, 1985.

“‘Forming and being informed.’ Hans-Jörg Rheinberger in conversation with Michael Schwab.” In *Experimental Systems. Future Knowledge in Artistic Research*. Edited by Michael Schwab, 198–219. Leuven: Leuven University Press, 2013.

Friedmann, Herbert C. “From Friedrich Wöhler’s urine to Eduard Buchner’s alcohol.” In *New Beer in an Old Bottle. Eduard Buchner and the Growth of Biochemical Knowledge*, ed. Athel Cornish-Bowden, 67–122. València: Universitat de València, 1997.

Fritz, Kurt von. *Mathematiker und Akusmatiker bei den alten Pythagoreern*. München: Bayerische Akademie der Wissenschaften, 1960.

Geus, Armin (ed.). *Natur im Druck. Eine Ausstellung zur Geschichte und Technik des Naturselbstdrucks*. With contributions by Armin Geus, Peter N. Heilmann and Stephan Oettermann. Marburg an der Lahn: Basilisken-Presse, 1995.

Gibson, James J. *The Ecological Approach to Visual Perception*. Boston: Houghton Mifflin, 1979.

Gilbert, Walter. “A vision of the grail.” In *The Code of Codes*. Edited by Daniel J. Kevles and Leroy Hood, 83–97. Cambridge: Cambridge University Press, 1992.

Gisler, Priska, Guelfo Carbone and Philippe Sormani (eds.). *Practicing Art/Science: Experiments in an Emerging Field*. London: Routledge, 2020.

Goethe, Johann Wolfgang von. „Über die Spiraltendenz der Vegetation.“ Manuscript, ca. 1830–1831. AnthroWiki.at Bibliothek:Goethe/Naturwissenschaft/Über die Spiraltendenz der Vegetation.

Goethe, Johann Wolfgang von. “The Spiral Tendency in Vegetation (1829-31).” In *The Essential Goethe*. Edited by Matthew Bell, 995–998. Princeton, NJ and Oxford: Princeton University Press, 2016.

Gombrich, Ernst. *Art and Illusion. A Study in the Psychology of Pictorial Representation*. New York: Pantheon, 1960.

Gould, Steven Jay Gould. *Time's Arrow, Time's Cycle*. Cambridge MA: Harvard University Press, 1987.

Gracq, Julien. “Eclosion de la pierre.” In: José Corti, *Rêves d'encre*. Vingt-cinq images présentées par Paul Eluard, René Char, Julien Gracq et Gaston Bachelard. Paris: Litrairie José Corti, 1945.

Gramelsberger, Gabriele. *From Science to Computational Sciences. Studies in the History of Computing and its Influence on Today's Sciences*. Chicago: The University of Chicago Press, 2015.

Greiner, Andreas. *Anatomy of a Fairy Tale*. Edited by Stefan Vicedom. Vienna: Verlag für Moderne Kunst, 2016.

Grene, Marjorie. *The Knower and the Known*. Washington DC: Center for Advanced Research in Phenomenology & University Press of America, 1984.

Groß, Matthias, Holger Hoffmann-Riem and Wolfgang Krohn. *Realexperimente. Ökologische Gestaltungsprozesse in der Wissensgesellschaft*. Bielefeld: Transcript, 2015.

Günther, Gotthard. *Das Bewusstsein der Maschinen. Eine Metaphysik der Kybernetik.* Krefeld and Baden-Baden: Agis-Verlag, 1963.

Guerrini, Anita. "The ghastly kitchen." *History of Science* 54 (2016): 71–97.

Hacking, Ian. *The Taming of Chance.* Cambridge: Cambridge University Press, 1975.

Hacking, Ian. *Representing and Intervening. Introductory Topics in the Philosophy of Natural Science.* Cambridge: Cambridge University Press, 1983.

Haeckel, Ernst. *Kunstformen der Natur.* Leipzig and Vienna: Bibliographisches Institut, 1899-1904.

Hagen, Wolfgang. *Das Radio. Zur Geschichte und Theorie des Hörfunks—Deutschland/USA.* München: Fink, 2005.

Hauser, Jens (ed.). *Paul Vanouse, Fingerprints ... Index—Abdruck—Spur/ Index—Imprint—Trace.* Berlin: Argobooks, 2011.

Hegel, Georg Wilhelm Friedrich. *The Science of Logic.* Translated by George Di Giovanni. Cambridge: Cambridge University Press, 2015. Originally published as *Die Wissenschaft der Logik* (Nürnberg: Johann Leonhard Schrag, 1812–1816).

Hegel, Georg Wilhelm Friedrich. *The Phenomenology of Spirit.* Translated by Peter Fuss and John Dobbins. Notre Dame, IN: University of Notre Dame Press, 2019. Originally published as *System der Wissenschaft. Erster Theil, die Phänomenologie des Geistes* (Bamberg and Würzburg: Joseph Anton Goebhardt, 1807).

Heidelberger, Michael. "Force, law, and experiment: the evolution of Helmholtz's philosophy of science." In *Hermann von Helmholtz and the Foundations of Nineteenth-Century Science.* Edited by David Cahan, 461–497. The University of California Press, Berkeley CA, 1993.

Helmholtz, Hermann von. *On the Sensations of Tone as a Physiological Basis for the Theory of Music.* Translated by Alexander John Ellis. London: Longmans, Green & Co., 1895. Originally published as *Die Lehre von den Tonempfindungen als physiologische Grundlage für die Theorie der Musik* (Braunschweig: Friedrich Vieweg & Sohn, 1863).

Helmholtz, Hermann von. *Treatise on Physiological Optics*, 3 vols. Translated from the 3rd German edition by Optical Society of America and edited by James P. C. Southall. Menasha, WI: Banta Corporation, 1924–1925. Originally published as *Handbuch der physiologischen Optik* (Leipzig: Voss, 1867).

Helmholtz, Hermann von. „The facts of perception," in *Selected Writings*. Translated by Russell Kahl, 366–408. Middletown: Wesleyan University Press, 1971. Originally published as "Die Thatsachen in der Wahrnehmung" (1878).

Henning, Jochen. *Bildpraxis. Visuelle Strategien in der frühen Nanotechnologie*. Bielefeld: Transcript, 2011.

Heynen, Julian (ed.). *La Biennale di Venezia: Deutscher Pavillon/German Pavillon* (Thomas Scheibitz—Tino Sehgal). Köln: Snoeck, 2005.

Hoffmann, Christoph. *Unter Beobachtung. Naturforschung in der Zeit der Sinnesapparate*. Göttingen: Wallstein, 2006.

Hoffmann, Christoph. *Schreiben im Forschen. Verfahren, Szenen, Effekte*. Tübingen: Mohr Siebeck, 2018.

Hoffmann, Christoph and Peter Berz (eds.). *Über Schall. Ernst Machs und Peter Salchers Geschossfotografien*. Göttingen: Wallstein, 2001.

Holmes, Frederic L., Jürgen Renn and Hans-Jörg Rheinberger (eds.). *Reworking the Bench. Research Notebooks in the History of Science*. Dordrecht—Boston—London: Kluwer Academic Publishers, 2003.

Holmes, Frederic L. *Investigative Pathways: Patterns and Stages in the Careers of Experimental Scientists*. New Haven: Yale University Press, 2004.

Husserl, Edmund. *Ideas Pertaining to a Pure Phenomenology and to a Phenomenological Philosophy. Second Book: Studies in the Phenomenology of Constitution*. Translated by Richard Rojcewicz and André Schuwer. Dordrecht: Kluwer, 1989. Originally published as *Ideen zu einer reinen Phänomenologie und phänomenologischen Philosophie. Allgemeine Einführung in die Reine Philosophie. 2. Buch. Phänomenologische Untersuchungen zur Konstitution* (Den Haag: Martinus Nijhoff, 1950).

Husserl, Edmund. *Formal and Transcendental Logic*. Translated by Dorion Cairns. The Hague: Martinus Nijhoff, 1969. Originally published as *Formale und transzendentale Logik. Versuch einer Kritik der logischen Vernunft* (Halle: Niemeyer, 1929).

Husserl, Edmund. *Cartesian Meditations: An Introduction to Phenomenology*. Translated by Dorion Cairns. The Hague: Martinus Nijhoff, 1960. Originally published as *Cartesianische Meditationen, und Pariser Vorträge* (Den Haag: Martinus Nijhoff, 1950).

Hyder, David. "Foucault, Cavaillès and Husserl on the historical epistemology of the sciences." *Perspectives on Science* 10 (2003): 107–129.

Ingrisch, Doris, Marion Mangelsdorf and Gerd Dressel (eds.). *Wissenskulturen im Dialog. Experimentalräume zwischen Wissenschaft und Kunst*. Bielefeld: Transcript, 2017.

Jackson, Myles W. *Spectrum of Belief: Joseph von Fraunhofer and the Craft of Precision Optics*. Cambridge and London: MIT Press, 2000.

Jackson, Myles W. *Harmonious Triads: Physicists, Musicians, and Instrument Markers in Nineteenth-Century Germany*. Cambridge MA: MIT Press, 2006.

Jacob, François, Roman Jakobson, Claude Lévi-Strauss, Philippe l'Héritier (réalisation: Michel Treguer). "Vivre et parler." *Les Lettres françaises* 1221 & 1222 (1968): 1–7 & 4–5

Jacob, François. *The Possible and the Actual*. Translated by Betty E. Spillmann. Seattle: Washington University Press, 1982. Originally published as *Le Jeu des possibles* (Paris: Fayard, 1981).

Jacob, François. *The Statue Within. An Autobiography*. New York: Basic Books, 1988. Originally published as *La Statue intérieure* (Paris: Editions Odile Jacob, 1987).

Jacob, François. *Of Flies, Mice, and Men*. Translated by Giselle Weiss. Cambridge (MA) and London: Harvard University Press, 1998. Originally published as *La Souris, la mouche et l'homme* (Paris: Editions Odile Jacob, 1997).

Journal for Artistic Research (JAR, since 2011).

Judson, Horace F. *The Eighth Day of Creation. The Makers of the Revolution in Biology*. New York: Simon & Schuster, 1979.

Kamminga, Harmke, and Soraya de Chadarevian. *Representations of the Double Helix*. Cambridge: Whipple Museum of the History of Science, 2002.

Kane, Brian. *Sound Unseen: Acousmatic Sound in Theory and Practice*. Oxford: Oxford University Press, 2014.

Karafyllis, Nicole C. "Das Wesen der Biofakte." In *Biofakte. Versuch über den Menschen zwischen Artefakt und Lebewesen*. Edited by Nicole C. Karafyllis, 11–16. Paderborn: Mentis Verlag, 2004.

Kittler, Friedrich. *Gramophone, Film, Typewriter*. Translated by Geoffrey Wintrop-Young and Michael Wutz. Stanford: Stanford University Press, 1999. Originally published as *Grammophon Film Typewriter*. Berlin: Brinkmann & Bose, 1986.

Kleist, Heinrich von. "On the gradual construction of thoughts during speech" (1805/1806). Translated by Michael Hamburger. *German Life and Letters* 5 (1951): 42–46. Originally (posthumously) published as „Über die allmähliche Verfertigung der Gedanken beim Reden," *Nord und Süd* 4 (1878): 3–7.

Knorr Cetina, Karin. *Epistemic Cultures. How the Sciences Make Knowledge*. Cambridge MA: Harvard University Press, 1999.

Kölreuter, Joseph Gottlieb. *Vorläufige Nachricht von einigen das Geschlecht der Pflanzen betreffenden Versuchen und Beobachtungen nebst Fortsetzungen 1, 2 und 3 (1761–1766)*. Edited by Wilhelm Pfeffer. Leipzig: Engelmann, 1893.

Kragh, Helge. *Quantum Generations. A History of Physics in the Twentieth Century*. Princeton: Princeton University Press, 1999.

Kubler, George. *The Shape of Time. Remarks on the History of Things*. New Haven, CT and London: Yale University Press, 1962.

Kubler, George, and Martin Soria. *Art and Architecture in Spain and Portugal and their American Dominions, 1500 to 1800*. London: Penguin Books, 1959.

Lacan, Jacques. "Science and truth." *Newsletter of the Freudian Field* 3 (1/2) (1989): 4–29. Originally published as "La science et la verité." In *Ecrits*. Paris: Le Seuil, 1966, 855–877."

La Logique du vivant: François Jacob rencontre Claude Lévi-Strauss." *Office national de radiodiffusion television française*. Documentaire, Sciences et techniques, Arts et culture (réalisation: Roger Kahane), 1972.

Latour, Bruno. "Do Scientific Objects Have a History? Pasteur and Whitehead in a Bath of Lactic Acid." *Common Knowledge* 5/1 (1996): 76–91.

Latour, Bruno. *An Inquiry into Modes of Existence. An Anthropology of the Moderns*. Translated by Catherine Porter. Cambridge MA: Harvard University Press, 2013. Originally published as *Enquête sur les modes d'existence. Une anthropologie des modernes* (Paris: La Découverte, 2012).

Latour, Bruno and Peter Weibel (eds.). *Iconoclash—Beyond the Image Wars in Science, Religion, and Art*. Cambridge: MIT Press, 2002).

Latour, Bruno and Steve Woolgar. *Laboratory Life. The Construction of Scientific Facts*. Princeton: Princeton University Press, 21985.

Lehmann, Katrin von. *Textura performativa* 5. Berlin: Distanz Verlag, 2021.

Lehner, Christoph, Jürgen Renn and Matthias Schemmel. *Einstein and the Changing Worldviews of Physics*. Basel: Birkhäuser, 2011.

Leonelli, Sabina. *Data-Centric Biology. A Philosophical Study*. Chicago: The University of Chicago Press, 2016.

Lessing, Gotthold Ephraim. *Laocoon: an Essay upon the Limits of Painting and Poetry*. Translated by Ellen Frothingham. New York: Noonday Press, 1969. Originally published as *Laokoon oder über die Grenzen der Mahlerey und Poesie* (1766).

Lévi-Strauss, Claude. *Introduction to a Science of Mythology I: The Raw and the Cooked*. Translated by John and Doreen Weightman. New York: Harper & Row, 1969. Originally published as *Mythologiques I. Le Cru et le cuit* (Paris: Plon, 1964).

Lévi Strauss, Claude. *Wild Thought*. Translated by Jeffrey Mehlman and John Leavitt. Chicago: The University of Chicago Press, 2021. Originally published as *La Pensée sauvage* (Paris: Plon, 1962).

Luhmann, Niklas. *Art as a Social System*. Translated by Eva M. Knodt. Stanford: Stanford University Press, 2000. Originally Published as *Die Kunst der Gesellschaft* (Frankfurt am Main: Suhrkamp, 1995).

Lynch, Michael. *Art and Artifact in Laboratory Science: A Study of Shop Work and Shop Talk in a Research Laboratory*. London: Routledge Kegan & Paul, 1985

Mach, Ernst. *The Science of Mechanics. A critical and Historical Account of its Development*. Translated by Thomas J. McCormack. Chicago: The Open Court Publishing Company, 1902. Originally published as *Die Mechanik in ihrer Entwicklung, historisch-kritisch dargestellt* (Leipzig: Brockhaus, 1883).

Mahr, Bernd. *Schriften zur Modellforschung*. Edited by Klaus Robering. Paderborn: Mentis, 2021.

Mainberger, Sabine. *Experiment Linie. Künste und ihre Wissenschaften um 1900*. Berlin: Kadmos, 2010.

Marchetti, Luca. "Depicting motion in a static image: philosophy, psychology and the perception of pictures." In *British Journal of Aesthetics* 62 (2022): 353–371.

Marey, Etienne-Jules. *La Photographie du movement. Les méthodes chronophotographiques*. Paris: Hachette, 2022. First published 1892.

Mateus-Berr, Ruth and Richard Jochum. *Teaching Artistic Research: Conversations Across Cultures*. Berlin and Boston: DeGruyter, 2020.

Maupertuis, Pierre Louis Moreau de. *Vénus physique. Œuvres Vol. II*. Reprint of the Lyon 1768 edition. Paderborn: Georg Olms Verlagsbuchhandlung, 1965.

Mayer, Andreas. *Science of Walking: Investigations into Locomotion in the Long Nineteenth Century*. Translated by Robin Blanton and Tilman Skowroneck. Chicago: The University of Chicago Press, 2020.

Merleau-Ponty, Maurice. "The philosopher and his shadow." In *Signs*. Translated by Richard C. McCleary. Evanston ILL: Northwestern University Press, 1964.

Merleau-Ponty, Maurice. *Phenomenology of Perception*. Translated by Donald A. Landes. New York: Routledge, 2012.

Merton, Robert K. *Social Theory and Social Structure.* New York: Free Press, 1957.

Merton, Robert K. "Three fragments from a sociologist's notebooks: Establishing the phenomenon, specified ignorance, and strategic research materials." *Annual Review of Sociology* 13 (1987): 1–28.

Merton, Robert K. and Elinor Barber. *The Travels and Adventures of Serendipity: A Study in Sociological Semantics and the Sociology of Science.* Princeton: Princeton University Press, 2006.

Meulders, Michel. *Helmholtz. Des lumières aux neurosciences.* Paris: Editions Odile Jacob, 2001.

Misch, Imke and Christoph von Blumröder (eds.). *François Bayle, L'Image de son/Klangbilder.* Münster: LIT Verlag, 2003.

Moholy-Nagy, László. *Malerei, Photographie, Film* (Bauhausbücher, vol 8). Munich: Albert Langen, 1925.

Müller, Falk. *Jenseits des Lichts. AEG und die Anfänge der Elektronenmikroskopie in Deutschland.* Göttingen: Wallstein, 2021.

Müller, Johannes. *Zur vergleichenden Physiologie des Gesichtssinnes des Menschen und der Thiere nebst einem Versuch über die Bewegungen der Augen und über den menschlichen Blick.* Leipzig: C. Cnobloch, 1826.

Müller, Olaf. *Zu schön, um falsch zu sein. Über die Ästhetik in der Naturwissenschaft.* Frankfurt am Main: Fischer, 2019.

Musil, Robert. *The Man without Qualities.* Vols. 1 & 2. Translated by Sophie Wilkins. New York: Vintage, 1996. Originally published as *Der Mann ohne Eigenschaften* (Berlin: Ernst Rowohlt Verlag, 1930–1933).

Nägele, Rainer. *fort/da. Topobiographien.* Innsbruck-Vienna-Munich-Bolzano: Edition Sturzflüge/Studien Verlag, 2005.

Nasim, Omar S. *Observing by Hand: Sketching the Nebulae in the Nineteenth Century.* Chicago: The University of Chicago Press, 2013.

Odenthal, Stefanie and Christiane Stahl (eds.). *Nautilus: Schnecken, Muscheln und andere Mollusken in der Fotografie.* Petersberg: Michael Imhof Verlag, 2017.

Pallas, Peter Simon. *Elenchus zoophytorum, sistens generum adumbrationes generaliores et specierum cognitarum succinctas descriptiones, cum selectis auctorum synonymis*. The Hague: Van Cleef, 1766.

Patton, Lydia. "Helmholtz's physiological psychology." In *Philosophy of Mind in the Nineteenth Century*. Edited by Sandra Lapointe, 96–116. London: Routledge, 2018.

Peirce, Charles Sanders. "Logic as semiotic: The theory of signs." In *Charles Sanders Peirce, Philosophical Writings*. Edited by Justus Buchler, 98–119. New York: Dover Publication, 1955.

Pfeffer, Wilhelm. "Kinematographische Studien an Impatiens, Vicia, Tulipa, Mimosa und Desmodium von W. Pfeffer (1898-1900)." Revised by Prof. Dr. F. Bachmann from the Botanical Institute of the University of Leipzig for the Institute of Scientific Film. https://doi.org/10.3203/IWF/B-450

Pickering, Andrew. *The Mangle of Practice. Time, Agency, and Science*. Chicago: The University of Chicago Press, 1995.

Polanyi, Michael. The Tacit Dimension. London: Routledge & Kegan Paul, 1966.

Polanyi, Michael. "The unaccountable element in science." In *Knowing and Being: Essays by Michael Polanyi*. Edited by Marjorie Grene. Chicago: University of Chicago Press, 1969, 108–120. First published in *Philosophy* 37, no. 139 (1962).

Polanyi, Michael. "The logic of tacit inference." In *Knowing and Being. Essays by Michael Polanyi*. Edited by Marjorie Grene, 138–158. Chicago: The University of Chicago Press, 1969. First published in *Philosophy* 41, no. 155 (1964).

Ponge, Francis. *Le Parti pris des choses*. Précédé de Douze petits écrits et suivi de Proêmes. Paris: Gallimard, 1967. First published 1942.

Ponge, Francis. "Taking the side of things." In *The Voice of Things*. Translated by Beth Archer. New York: McGraw-Hill, 1972, pp. 29–77. Originally published as *Le Parti pris des choses* (Paris: Editions Gallimard, 1942).

Popper, Karl. *The Logic of Scientific Discovery*. New York: Harper and Row, 1968. Originally published as *Logik der Forschung* (Tübingen: J. C. B. Mohr, 1935).

Pravica, Sandra. *Bachelards tentative Wissenschaftsphilosophie*. Vienna: Passagen Verlag, 2015.

Prodger, Philip. *Time Stands Still. Eadweard Muybridge and the Instantaneous Photography Movement*. Oxford: Oxford University Press, 2003.

Purkinje, Johann. *Beiträge zur Kenntnis des Sehens in subjectiver Hinsicht*. Prag: Franz Vetterl Edler von Wildenbrunn, 1819.

Rasmussen, Nick. *Picture Control. The Electron Microscope and the Transformation of Biology in America, 1940–1960*. Stanford, CA: Stanford University Press, 1997.

Research Catalogue (RC).

Rheinberger, Hans-Jörg. *Experiment, Differenz, Schrift. Anmerkungen zur Geschichte epistemischer Dinge*. Marburg: Basilisken Presse, 1992.

Rheinberger, Hans-Jörg. *Iterationen*. Berlin: Merve Verlag, 2005.

Rheinberger, Hans-Jörg. "Präzision und Unschärfe im Umgang mit Forschungsobjekten." In *Genau—leicht—konsequent: Ein dreifaches Rendezvous der Künste und Wissenschaften*. Edited by Florian Dombois, Yeboaa Ofosu and Sarah Schmidt, 45–60. Basel: Schwabe, 2009.

Rheinberger, Hans-Jörg. *An Epistemology of the Concrete. Twentieth Century Histories of Life*. Durham: Duke University Press, 2010.

Rheinberger, Hans-Jörg. "Making visible." In *The Exhibition as Product and Generator of Scholarship*, 9–23. Berlin: Max Planck Institute for the History of Science, Preprint No. 399, 2010.

Rheinberger, Hans-Jörg. "Zeit zu schreiben." In: *Vademecum der Inspirationsmittel*. Edited by Christoph Markschies and Ernst Osterkamp, 126–127. Göttingen: Wallstein, 2012.

Rheinberger, Hans-Jörg. "Episteme zwischen Wissenschaft und Kunst." In Milena Cairo, Moritz Hannemann, Ulrike Haß and Judith Schäfer (eds.), *Episteme des Theaters. Aktuelle Kontexte von Wissenschaft, Kunst und Öffentlichkeit*, 17–27. Bielefeld: Transcript, 2016.

Rheinberger, Hans-Jörg. *The Hand of the Engraver. Albert Flocon Meets Gaston Bachelard.* Translated by Kate Sturge. Albany: SUNY Press, 2018.

Rheinberger, Hans-Jörg. "Transpositions: From traces through data to models and simulations." In *Transpositions. Aesthetico-Epistemic Operators in Artistic Research.* Edited by Michael Schwab, 215–224. Leuven: Leuven University Press, 2018.

Rheinberger, Hans-Jörg. "Vom Subjekt des Wissens aus der Perspektive der Historischen Epistemologie." In *Selbstsein als Sich-Wissen? Zur Bedeutung der Wissensgeschichte für die Historisierbarkeit des Subjekts.* Edited by Sandra Janßen and Thomas Alkemeyer, 25–36. Tübingen: Mohr Siebeck, 2021.

Rheinberger, Hans-Jörg. "A remark on Gaston Bachelard's idea of a psychoanalysis of knowledge." *Bachelard Studies* 2 (2021): 173–184.

Rheinberger, Hans-Jörg. *Split and Splice. A Phenomenology of Experimentation.* Chicago: The University of Chicago Press, 2023.

Rickli, Hannes. *Spurenkugel, ein Schreibspiel.* Berlin: Hochschule der Künste, 1996.

Rickli, Hannes (ed.). *Videogramme. Die Bildwelten biologischer Experimentalsysteme als Kunst- und Theorieobjekt/Videograms. The Pictorial Worlds of Biological Experimentation as an Object of Art and Theory.* Schriftenreihe des Instituts für Gegenwartskünste, vol. 6. Zürich: Scheidegger & Spiess, 2011.

Root-Bernstein, Robert Scott. *Discovering. Inventing and Solving Problems at the Frontiers of Scientific Knowledge.* Cambridge MA: Harvard University Press, 1989.

Rotman, Brian. *Signifying Nothing: The Semiotics of Zero.* New York: St Martin's Press, 1987.

Runge, Friedlieb Ferdinand. *Zur Farben-Chemie: Musterbilder für Freunde des Schönen und zum Gebrauch für Zeichner, Maler, Verzierer und Zeugdrucker.* Berlin: Mittler, 1850.

Runge, Friedlieb Ferdinand. *Der Bildungstrieb der Stoffe.* Berlin: Matthes & Seitz, 2014. First published in 1855.

Schickore, Jutta. *The Microscope and the Eye: A History of Reflections, 1740–1870*. Chicago: The University of Chicago Press, 2007.

Schierscher, Hanni. *Without Title*—Hans-Jörg Rheinberger, *One Does Not Exactly Know What One Does Not Know. On the Art of Exploring the Unknown.* Publication Series "Positions & Discourses." Schaan: Schichtwechsel/Liechtensteiner Kunstverein, 2012.

Schierscher, Hanni. *Innen und Außen*. Edited by Axel Jablonski. Hohenems-Vaduz-München-Zürich: Bucher, 2020.

Schmidt, Gunnar. *Weiche Displays. Projektionen auf Rauch, Wolken und Nebel.* Berlin: Wagenbach, 2011.

Schwab, Michael (ed.). *Experimental Systems. Future Knowledge in Artistic Research.* Leuven: Orpheus Institute and Leuven University Press, 2013.

Schwaiger, Josef. Runge *Revisited.* Texts by Josef Schwaiger and Friedrich Weltzien. Artist's book. Self-produced in 63 copies, 2018–2020.

Seitter, Walter. *Physik der Medien: Materialien – Apparate –Präsentierungen.* Weimar: VDG, 2002.

Serres, Michel. *The Natural Contract.* Translated by Elizabeth MacArthur and William Paulson. Ann Arbor: University of Michigan Press, 1995. Originally published as *Le Contrat naturel* (Paris: François Bourin, 1990).

Shapin, Steven. *The Scientific Revolution.* Chicago: The University of Chicago Press, 1996.

Siegert, Bernhard. „Kulturtechnik." In *Einführung in die Kulturwissenschaft.* Edited by Harun Maye and Leander Scholz, 95–118. München: W. Fink (UTB), 2011.

Smith, John Maynard and Eörs Szathmáry. *The Major Transitions in Evolution.* San Francisco: W. H. Freeman, 1995.

Snow, Charles Percy. *The Two Cultures and the Scientific Revolution.* Cambridge: Cambridge University Press, 1959.

Spieker, Sven and Mario Asef (eds.). *Akusmatik als Labor. Kultur – Kunst – Medien.* Würzburg: Königshausen & Neumann, 2023.

Stillman, Jacob Davis Babcock. *The Horse in Motion as Shown by Instantaneous Photography. With a Study of Animal Mechanics Founded on the Anatomy and the Revelations of the Camera in which is Demonstrated the Theory of Quadrupedal Locomotion.* Photographs by Eadweard Muybridge. London: Trubner & Co., 1882.

Struth, Thomas. *Nature & Politics.* Texts by Tobia Bezzola, D. Graham Burnett and Dirk Baecker. London: Mack Books, 2016.

St. Werner, Jan. *Transcendental Animal Numbers* (https://vimeo.com/80817468. Last accessed: April 9, 2025.

St. Werner, Jan. *Mouse on Mars* (https://www.youtube.com/watch?v=cRMRbC51Bfo. Last accessed: April 9, 2025).

Te Heesen, Anke. *The Newspaper Clipping. A Modern Paper Object.* Translated by Lori Lanz. Manchester: Manchester University Press, 2014. Originally published as *Der Zeitungsausschnitt. Ein Papierobjekt der Moderne* (Frankfurt am Main: Fischer, 2006).

Thompson, D'Arcy Wentworth. *On Growth and Form.* Abridged edition by John Tylor Bonner. Cambridge: Cambridge University Press, 1961. First published 1914.

Torma, Franziska (ed.). *A Cultural History of the Sea in the Global Age.* London: Bloomsbury Academic, 2023.

Trummer, Thomas. *Artistic Research.* Köln: Walther König, 2014.

Tzara, Tristan. *Grains et issues.* Edited by Henri Béhar. Paris: Garnier-Flammarion, 1981. First published 1935.

Varenne, Frank. *From Models to Simulations.* London: Routledge, 2019.

Veasey, Nick. *X-Ray: See Through the World Around You.* London: Goodman Books, 2008.

Vogl, Joseph. *Über das Zaudern.* Zürich and Berlin: Diaphanes, 2007.

Vydra, Anton. "Gaston Bachelard and his reactions to phenomenology." *Continental Philosophy Review* 47 (2014): 45–58.

Wacquant, Loïc and Aksu Akçaoglu. “Pratique et pouvoir symbolique chez Bourdieu vu de Berkeley.” *Revue de l’Institut de Sociologie (ULB)* 86 (2016): 35–60.

Watson, James D., and Francis Crick. “Molecular structure of nucleic acids.” *Nature* 4356 (1953): 737–738.

Wendingen (series 5, nr. 8/9). Amsterdam: 1923.

Weyl, Hermann. *Philosophy of Mathematics and Natural Science.* Translated by Olaf Helmer. Princeton: Princeton University Press, 1949. Originally published as *Philosophie der Mathematik und Naturwissenschaft* (München: Leibniz Verlag, 1927).

Wind, Edgar. *The Experiment and Metaphysics. Towards a Resolution of the Cosmological Antinomies.* Translated by Cyril Edwards. Oxford: European Humanities Research Center, University of Oxford, 2001. Originally published as *Das Experiment und die Metaphyisik* (Tübingen: J. C. B. Mohr, 1934).

Wind, Edgar. “Some points of contact between history and the natural sciences.” In *Philosophy and History: Essays Presented to Ernst Cassirer.* Edited by Raymond Klibansky and Herbert James, 255–264. Oxford: Clarendon Press, 1936.

Zilsel, Edgar. *Die Geniereligion. Ein kritischer Versuch über das moderne Persönlichkeitsideal mit einer historischen Begründung.* Frankfurt am Main: Suhrkamp, 1990. First published 1918.

Zimmermann, Michael F. „Cézanne und die Zeit des Stilllebens. Die Entfaltung des Œuvres als Allegorie der Gattungsgeschichte.“ In *Allegorie. DFG-Symposion 2014.* Edited by Ulla Haselstein, 303–332, 748–756. Berlin: DeGruyter, 2016.

Figures

Fig. 1: ©Paul Vanouse, LFP.pET-11A.6.08.09, commonly referred to as *Chicken and Egg*.

Fig. 2: © Thomas Struth, *The Seven Brothers' Hills*, Seorak Mountains, Gangwon-do 2007. Chromogenic print, 173,5 x 214,0 cm.

Fig. 3: Albert Flocon, *La bouteille*. From Albert Flocon, Gaston Bachelard, *Châteaux en Espagne*, Paris 1957. 28 x 18,5 cm. With friendly permission of Catherine Ballestero.

Fig. 4: © Sandra Boeschenstein, *Ein Wort und sein Double auf dem Weg zum Souffleur/ a word and its double on the way to the prompter*, pencil on paper; 50 x 35 cm; from the 36-part series of drawings *Grace at the Boundary of Knowledge* 2018.

Fig. 5: © Hannes Rickli, Spurenkugel Phase II 14. Zustand, 1994–1996, color photography, digitally reworked. From the Project "Spurenkugel—Ein Schreibspiel."

Fig. 6: ©Hanni Schierscher, *3C3A0905 Kopie*, 2009, 70 x 140 cm, Foto: ©Roland Korner.

Fig. 7: ©Katrin von Lehmann, *Proxy 8-07*, 2018, Buntstifte auf Papier, gelocht, versetzt, 51 x 51 cm, Foto: ©Bernd Hiepe.

Printed with support of the
Kulturstiftung Liechtenstein

First Printing
ISBN 978-3-0358-0841-4

Layout: 2edit, Zürich
Cover image: Hannes Rickli, *Spurenkugel Phase II 14. Zustand, 1994–1996*. © Hannes Rickli
Printed in Germany

DIAPHANES AG – Schöneggstrasse 5 – 8004 Zürich – kontakt@diaphanes.net
DIAPHANES Berlin – Dresdener Strasse 118 – 10999 Berlin – berlin@diaphanes.net